DREAM CHILD

Hilary Hemingway
and Jeffry P. Lindsay

TOR®

A TOM DOHERTY ASSOCIATES BOOK
NEW YORK

This is a work of fiction. All the characters and events portrayed in this book are either products of the author's imagination or are used fictitiously.

DREAMCHILD

Copyright © 1998 by Hilary Hemingway and Jeffry P. Lindsay

A Tor Book
Published by Tom Doherty Associates, LLC
175 Fifth Avenue
New York, NY 10010

Tor Books on the World Wide Web:
http://www.tor.com

Tor® is a registered trademark of Tom Doherty Associates, LLC

ISBN: 0-812-57119-3
Library of Congress Catalog Card Number: 98-12682

First edition: June 1998
First mass market edition: July 1999

Printed in the United States of America

0 9 8 7 6 5 4 3 2 1

For Hannah and Lindsay

Acknowledgments

Sincere thanks to those who generously gave assistance and guidance during the writing of this novel: Susan Crawford, Doris Hemingway, Natalia Aponte, Dr. August Freundlich, Tommie Freundlich, Dr. Mary Held, Anne Hemingway Feuer, Chris Freundlich, and the continuing studies by NASA Goddard Institute for Space Studies, Geophysical Fluid Dynamic Laboratory, National Oceanic and Atmospheric Administration, advance analysis from the Global Climate Coalition, National Institute of Health, Centers for Disease Control, British Museum of Natural History; also, this novel was inspired by the work of Edgar Cayce and continuing research by Erich Von Daniken, Bob Lazar, Glenn Campbell, Dr. David Jacobs, Dr. John Mack, and Budd Hopkins.

The cosmic religious experience is the strongest and the noblest driving force behind scientific research.

> Albert Einstein, quoted in his obituary, 1955

Of course God told Noah he would never flood the world again, He knew mankind would do the job for him.

> Dr. Eva Yi, on Global Warming Study, 1998

The old grandfather clock down the hall chimed midnight and the sound was startling as it broke through the steady pounding of the rain on the roof. Max woke up, his dark eyes wet. He'd had that dream again. *An odd pool of liquid blue, like bath water, but not water. He remembered floating in it, breathing it, healing in it. The calm, warm sensation filled him with every breath. There was nothing scary about it. It seemed natural, comforting. It was almost like—like being home.*

Max Carol Katz shoved back his *Men in Black* comforter and sat up in his race car–style bed. He was shorter and thinner than most five-year-olds and his hair was still baby fine and almost white. His room was filled with books and toys, a regular boy's room, except that each item looked as new as the day it had been bought. Even the HO Gauge train set in the corner. Max never played with it. In fact, he never played with anything in his room. His father, Stan, had bought these things, things Max did not care about.

How Max wished he could talk, communicate.

The rain got louder. Max wondered if Stan had come home yet. His mother would worry. Though she never said anything,

Max sensed it. He sensed a lot of things, although they never showed on his face.

A flash of lightning cut the darkness outside, followed by a loud clap of thunder. Most children would have bolted under the covers, but Max did not react. Instead he sat oddly still, staring at a point on the wall where his eyes had first focused and in his mind he called out.

Father, where are you?

LYMAN HALL, SYRACUSE UNIVERSITY, SYRACUSE, NEW YORK. 12:10 P.M.

"Damn." A bony fist pounded on the desk top and Dr. Stan Katz, a rail-thin, fiercely gawky, forty-two-year-old professor, sat up straighter in front of his computer. He had fed in the latest figures on chlorofluorocarbons, methane, nitrous oxide and carbon dioxide. The graph that now came up on his screen showed NOAA's projected global air temperature rise within a hundred-year period from 8 degrees to 24.2 degrees Fahrenheit. This was a critical jump that had been adjusted from the rise a year earlier of 4 to 16 degrees because they had not considered the additional ocean water vapor, and because CO_2 was the most prominent greenhouse gas. If the global temperature did indeed rise by 24.2 degrees, it would make the earth uninhabitable.

"Jesus!" he swore again. Even an 8-degree rise would give New York City the average temperature of Daytona Beach, Florida. Stan shook his head. "No more hot pretzels on a cold morning, no skating at Rockefeller Center—" He was not a poetic man, but as a native New Yorker he would prefer to preserve his culture. And if these figures were correct . . .

Stan stood and looked out the window of his office in the Lyman Hall science building. The patter of rain did not ease up. It was February and instead of the normal four feet of snow, the whole Northeast was drowning in its eleventh day of warm wet drizzle. The low-lying areas were flooded under El Niño's thirty-two inches of rain. The rest of the country baked in unheard-of 90-degree summerlike heat.

They called it the heat wave of the century, except there had already been one a couple of years earlier that had killed eighty-four people in the Midwest. Since then, there had been a winter of fierce blizzards as the earth's weather tried to stabilize itself. It failed, and the news headlines read BLIZZARD OF THE CENTURY, FLOOD OF THE CENTURY, HURRICANE OF THE CENTURY, as unusual weather became routine. So far, all the data indicated that global warming was having a greater impact on weather than any change recorded by man or by geology in the past ten thousand years. That was not what Stan had hoped to find.

The fan in the office kept a steady hum while Stan waited for his boss to join him. He had checked his watch twice before the heavy door opened and Dr. Alexis Campbell, a stylish redhead in her thirties, strolled in. She was soaked to the skin and her wet clothing clung to her. Her eyes were dark, her lips moist, and her skin reflected the light so that her body seemed perfectly balanced, slender and full-bosomed.

"I bloody well had to swim it, love," Alexis said in her soft English accent, closing and locking the door.

Stan moved quickly to her side and embraced her. "I was starting to get worried."

"Dear boy," she whispered. "Hold me, so I don't catch my death of cold."

Stan held Alexis, his hands gently massaging her back as he inhaled her sweet fragrance and nuzzled her neck.

"I finished inputting the latest stats."

"Oh, sweet nothings," she said, rubbing her cheek against his. "And?"

"I think Noah was onto something," Stan sighed and brushed the fiery red hair from Alexis's cheek. She smiled at him and he kissed her.

"Forget the rain," Alexis laughed. "This business can get so depressing."

Stan forced a smile. There was truth in what she said. Still holding their embrace he looked beyond her, out the window, to where he could see the reflections of the campus streetlights dancing in small lakes that were once the school parking lots. The last three days of classes had been canceled. Though the Weather Channel reported that a high was expected to move through in a week and that it would push the storm away, the general mood on campus remained gloomy.

"Lover," Alexis said.

Stan looked startled. Alexis had meant this in an affectionate way, but Stan's guilt made it an accusation.

"What?"

They had been lovers for only two short months. Everything about their relationship was new, exciting and, of course, forbidden. So while their work included a full-time teaching load—Alexis geophysics, and Stan quantum mechanics—they made time for each other. Time they were supposed to be working on the global warming study.

"Help me off with these wet things."

She dropped her skirt to the floor while Stan eagerly unbuttoned her blouse. It hung loose at her sides and he unsnapped her bra to free her breasts. His hands caressed her, until her nipples grew hard under his touch. His whole body ached with passion. He buried his face in her bosom.

"Missed me, did you?" Alexis laughed as she ran her fingers through his hair.

Stan smiled. "Let's say it's been a long day."

Stan lifted Alexis onto the smooth mahogany desk. His tongue moved from her mouth and neck to between her breasts, and down. She smiled at him, then gasped. He felt the softness of her thighs wrapped around him as he made love to her.

Stan's lust was equaled only by his guilt. Having the affair with Alexis bothered him a great deal, although not enough to stop. Being Stan, he had logically figured out all the alternatives, and finally placed the fault for the whole affair on his wife, Annie.

Shortly after the birth of their son, Annie had said she was simply too tired for sex, and Stan had accepted that without complaint. But months passed. Stan pretended it was okay, but it was not okay and it got less okay with each passing week. After a year, things began to change—mean little sexual in-jokes led to arguments and finally to complete lack of communication. The only time they got together was to fight.

If the office had become Stan's escape, Alexis had become his lifeboat. She had gradually, subtly, shown an increasing interest in him, his work and his life. And before he knew what was happening, he found himself telling her everything, even the most personal details. Then it was only one step, a surprisingly short step, to their becoming lovers.

Stan and Alexis moved from the desktop to the floor. She straddled him while he caressed her firm round buttocks. Her breasts bounced and bobbled against his lips. Why was it so easy with her? Why couldn't it be Annie? It was a damn shame that he could have a perfectly wonderful affair and still be thinking about his wife. But Stan did think about his wife. And his son.

His troubled little boy. Stan's dreams of Little League, science projects and college had all but vanished.

He found comfort in believing it was the aliens' fault, but still he wondered. Was he just hiding from his own fears? Were Max's troubles really some genetic disorder of his own? His mother had a retarded brother. Anything was possible. Stan tried to turn off these thoughts, to leave his home troubles as far away from his work escape as possible.

"I brought some oil, love." Alexis said, rubbing her hands with clear fluid that smelled like cinnamon. Stan closed his eyes and felt the warm sensations working with every stroke of Alexis's hand.

"Yes," he whispered and pulled her down hard on him. Their bodies moved in natural, joyful rhythm. It had never occurred to him that Alexis might have a secret motivation for making love. He had just accepted her line, "It's easier with married men," as a way of saying she was on the career track and did not want to get bogged down with a relationship.

Everything seemed just fine. But then—things changed.

Dr. Alexis Campbell, head of the Syracuse Geophysics Department, whispered softly above the sound of pattering rain, whispered her true intentions.

"Stanley, I want to have your baby."

"What?"

"I want to have your baby."

"Oh, no." Stan collapsed, then weakly sat up and pushed away from Alexis. "This isn't happening."

"What's wrong with you?"

Stan toppled her off of him and reached for his pants. He jumped to his feet to pull them on. "Alexis, you don't understand. I mean—I have a *son*."

"I know. That's why I chose you. High intelligence and a proven breeder. I didn't want to waste my—"

"No, no, no. You're making a terrible mistake."

Alexis looked astonished. When she had mentally worked out this scenario, she had never considered that Stan might have such a reaction. And reactions that deviated from her plans troubled her. "Take it easy, Stanley. I don't want any money or support. I just want your baby. My biological clock is ticking. You know, most lovers have this reaction to HIV, not to babies."

Stan had already tucked his shirt into his pants and was reaching for the door when he paused. "Alexis, you're a beautiful woman, a brilliant woman, but trust me, *you don't want to have my child.*" And with that, Stan left.

Alexis stood puzzled. "What's so bloody wrong with your son?" she asked. But there was no answer, only the sound of rain.

CHAPTER 2

U.S. SPACE COMMAND, CHEYENNE MOUNTAINS, COLORADO. 10:15 P.M.

"I want exact coordinates—now!" Commander John McKay demanded, pacing between the six orbital analysts seated in front of their green radar screens. The one on his far right answered.

"Bearing one eleven degrees by—I'm sorry, sir. This pattern is just too erratic."

McKay stood looking over the airman's shoulder at the screen showing the southeastern United States. The blip bounced like a Ping-Pong ball across the screen.

"Well, it's inside the Fence. Stay with it."

"The Fence" is what Commander McKay called the Naval Space Surveillance System, a man-made energy field of radio waves that stretched in a fan shape three thousand miles across the United States and extended fifteen thousand miles into space. When an object passed through this beam, the Fence was tripped. If the unidentified body had certain characteristics—apparently under intelligent control, able to make right-angle turns at Mach 10 speeds—it was given a Code Blue status and the name Fallen Angel.

"Commander McKay, if these readings are correct, that last

jump took it across South Florida at nearly fourteen thousand miles an hour."

"Affirmative. We have a Fallen Angel, gentlemen. Now follow that bouncing ball and get a lock on it."

This was not the first time the U.S. Space Command under the Cheyenne Mountains had tracked a Fallen Angel. McKay had seen dozens of them since the system went on line ten years earlier. Though there had a been a lull of three years when none were sighted, they had recently returned, and in even greater numbers. But most were spotted in the southwest desert of New Mexico, and this one—

The airman looked up from his scope. "Sir, it's moving out of our range. Do you want a hookup with HAARP?" He held his finger on the blip.

"Affirmative, I'll make the call." Commander McKay picked up a direct line to the remote secret facility in the black spruce forest of central Alaska. HAARP was the High-Frequency Active Auroral Research Program. It worked on the same principle of injecting high-frequency radio energy for tracking, only on a much larger scale. HAARP was a full global shield that worked by saturating the ionosphere. The effect was a huge blanket of radio waves bouncing to and from earth. Anything passing through this blanket would create holes and thus could be tracked. Only it had to be used sparingly because of the enormous amounts of energy it consumed.

"Base Commander McKay, we need a linkup 227. Code Tango, Alpha Ten clearance. Tracking on my mark—now."

The airman watched as the screen overlay changed from the southeast United States to South America. But there was no sign of a Fallen Angel blip.

"Nothing, sir."

"Give it a minute."

The screen stayed clear for two minutes. In the room's deathly silence McKay reached for his cigarettes and lit up. There was no smoking in the underground bunker, but that didn't stop the Commander. Hell, it was his watch—and goddammit, he *needed* the damned thing.

"I've got it," the airman said, breaking the deafening quiet.

Commander McKay snuffed his smoke and moved to the airman's shoulder. They watched as the blip on the screen bounced its way south. As it passed over the southern tip of Chile, a new overlay came up, this one of the Antarctic.

Suddenly the object slowed, then stopped.

"Sir, we have a lock-on, confirmed. Fallen Angel is holding steady over the Ross Ice Shelf."

"Good work, stay on it," McKay said and reached for his phone. He had been briefed by a Colonel Michael Andros that the Fallen Angels were a squadron of top secret aerospace planes designed to replace the space shuttle as low-earth-orbit transatmospheric vehicles. And while it was common to track them over the American Northwest, he was to report any bogey that left the continental airspace. In such an event, it meant America's security had been breached and a plane had been stolen.

"Colonel Andros," McKay said. "Commander McKay, U.S. Space Command. We have a confirmed Fallen Angel. Yes sir, it left our air space at twenty-three hundred hours and we tracked it to the Antarctic . . . Thank you, sir."

McKay rolled his shoulders back to attention. "I'll download tracking, stat. And may I also add, good hunting, sir."

DREAMLAND BASE, GROOM LAKE, NEVADA. 9:20 P.M.

Out in the remote Nevada desert known as Area 51:S4 there were several large hangars, rebuilt offices and a few living quarters. In one such suite, Colonel Michael Andros hung up the phone.

"Ahhhh, damn," he whispered as he pushed the big leather chair back from the desk. He stood and stretched. The desert sun had tanned his skin to a freckled sunburn, but he was still classically handsome.

He walked through his living room, glancing at his few possessions. Three moon rocks from the fourth Apollo mission, an antique copper telescope, a rose entombed in a glass pyramid, and a huge CD selection. He picked one out. It was not jazz, pop or classical but a disc called *Earth Sounds*, something he had found on a trip to the Bodhi Tree in Los Angeles. It was a recording of nature, from waterfalls to whales. He dimmed the lights and lay back on his couch. While the stress melted away, he ran his fingers across his bristly blond hair.

There had been enormous changes in his life. To be the new head of MJ-12, filling the shoes of his old nemesis, Colonel Wesley, had been more than challenging. In the past five years, he had worked hard to release information to the brightest of the world's scientists about the aliens' advanced technology. The action did not win him many friends among the highly placed military members of the top secret group. It did, however, make things more efficient for the small group of scientists of MJ-12. The advances in genetics alone—Andros's field—were outstanding. Reports came in daily of new discoveries, from obesity genes, to genes predisposed to cancer, to the controversial identification of violence genes. And of course these discoveries would be followed by gene therapy.

For a brief period, Andros successfully "leaked" information to the general public about the government's relationship with the aliens; from a flood of hard news TV shows about the Roswell crash, MJ-12 documents, even the release of a documentary film of an alien autopsy. But this was to be a short-lived era of honesty. Something occurred that even he had not expected.

The aliens had returned.

Just three years after they left, a new group arrived—not in one ship, but in dozens. It was just as Wesley had predicted, an invasion. Only there had been no sign of war, no bloodshed. It was simply global conquest and it took less than eleven seconds.

The ships did not enter the earth's atmosphere. Instead they remained in a high orbit, like so many tiny stars, twinkling high above every power plant on the planet.

The Russians were the first to react, launching a single 500-kiloton nuclear warhead from an SS-25 mobile launch pad. The alien response came as the missile broke the upper atmosphere. In a small town just north of Kiev, the land around an aging power plant suddenly shook. A cloud of radiation escaped and all life in the area fell sick.

Andros never called the town by its Russian name, but its English translation was Wormwood. Just like the Revelation quote:

"A great star shot from the sky, flaming like a torch; and it fell on a third of the land, rivers and springs. The name of the star was Wormwood; and men in great numbers died of the poisoned water and land."

NORAD was well aware of the Russian situation and went to DEPTHCON 4, ready to launch a full nuclear strike. But the war was already over. Power grids across the upper Midwest went dark and the entire United States ICBM power base sat dead in its silos. The President stood down and ordered contact made.

The meeting took place at a military base and Andros was chosen to negotiate. To his surprise, the aliens were the same short gray race as those at Roswell and seemed to have the same intense interest in human genetics. They agreed not to interfere with world governments, and were given a large underground base in Dulce, New Mexico.

Sadly, MJ-12 was not to communicate with this group. In fact, there was to be no official human contact, except for a small military presence that served as security at the Dulce facility. These aliens came and went as they wished, and did whatever they chose to whomever they wished. One provision in the agreement was that they were to stay in the continental United States. Andros had told them it was for their own protection, but of course it was clearly an attempt to learn more from the aliens. Even if it meant cleaning up after cattle mutilations and chasing down human abductions. Whatever it took to find the answer.

Why had they returned? It had become the directive of MJ-12 to find out.

Ross Ice Shelf, Antarctica. 5:57 a.m.

In the continuous daylight of the Antarctic summer, Lieutenant Scott Neister, a tall, stocky man of thirty-seven, looked more like a polar bear than a human as he stepped into his lab wearing a heavy white parka. He stomped his feet on the metal grid and knocked off some of the thick snow from his boots.

"Three more days," he muttered to himself. Just three more and his "tour of the Antarctic," as he called this science expedition, would be over. Not because they had finished, but because they were running out of provisions.

The U.S. Navy had sent him around the world to study the rising sea levels. They had a personal stake in the study—79 percent of all U.S. military bases were located along coastal shorelines. And while the Navy takes everything personally, Neister clearly saw the larger picture—99 percent of all nuclear power plants and 95 percent of the world's population also were along coastal shorelines.

Neister did not have any grand plan to save the world. He had been chosen for this job for a typical military reason: he knew how to work the equipment—a sonar-base seismograph probe. Designed to read the amount of water in an ocean basin, including sea ice in glaciers. This was what had brought him to Byrd Glacier near the Ross Ice Shelf.

He checked over the graphs. Nothing yet. In theory his hardware worked much like the probes used by oil companies, which detonate a small charge and read returning sound waves bouncing off buried objects. But because of the size of the area he was covering, this probe worked using seismic waves. And in the weeks he had been there, seismic activity had been zero. That should have served as a warning since the area was known to have continual earthquakes—one of several reasons why field teams, regardless of nationality, were ordered to report in to Palmer Station each morning. He flipped on the shortwave radio.

"Palmer Station, Palmer Station. This is U.S. Naval Science team Alpha, over."

There was a crackle of static, followed by a cheerful woman's voice. "Good morning, Lieutenant. How goes it?"

He lifted the mike. "Six weeks, four days, thirteen hours on the world's biggest stinking ice cube. It's great. If that's what you like."

"No, sir," the voice answered. "I've got two weeks of R and R calling my name in Brazil."

"Oh baby." Neister smiled. "You know how to warm a man's heart."

"Thank you, sir."

Neister laughed, "Okay, Naval Science team Alpha, standing clear on sixteen."

"Palmer Station out," the voice answered.

He looked around his mobile military trailer, which served as lab and housing. A couple of bunk beds, chairs, tables, heaters and equipment. It was home for him and two Navy personnel assigned to him. He had sent them out earlier to check the probes laid in expanding circle patterns with the trailer being ground zero.

"Damn." He looked out the snow-glazed window. Nothing but white mountains. Three and half miles thick, they contained 90 percent of the earth's water. They were the single strongest influence on the world's climate, and a humbling moment for himself. Here he had been bitching about the cold, but without it, the sun's heat would raise the ocean temperature to a boil.

"Coffee," he muttered, trying to put things in perspective. This was his little ritual that defined morning. In the continuous daylight of February, he had found that his internal clock did not know whether it was morning, noon or night. But regardless of his drowsiness, Neister suffered through his day with a ritual four-sugar espresso.

He had just turned on the coffee maker when the first big jolt hit. He remembered turning to the wall clock and seeing it read 6:01 as everything in the room was thrown crashing to the floor.

The heavily insulated walls wobbled like Jell-O. There was a shrill whine of metal twisting, then suddenly the trailer's roof caved in.

Neister ducked as debris fell. His knees buckled and he found himself under a lab table. The floor began to roll like waves in a shallow bay. He reached out and grabbed the table leg. As curiosity overcame fear, he found himself turning his attention toward his equipment.

He could see that the probes' recording light had blinked on; the equipment had been activated. Thank God it had been bolted to the floor.

He watched as the building continued its shaking. Neister found that the padding from his parka and pants helped to soften the beating from the waves in the floor. When the quake finally stopped, one minute twenty-eight seconds later, Lieutenant Neister was curled in a fetal position under the table.

He thought about the Los Angeles quake and the destruction of Kobe, Japan—neither compared to what he had just felt. After fifteen years in the Navy the closest thing to that kind of terror had been his advanced survival training in twenty-five-foot seas in only a life jacket.

He took a deep breath and tried to relax. He saw that his left hand was still gripping the table leg. His knuckles were white. It took him a good minute to flex his fingers out into something other than a claw. The outside Antarctic air now filled the trailer.

Neister's breath froze with every exhalation. He pulled on his gloves and wrapped his scarf around his face.

The reading—how big had that been?

A wall of fallen insulation blocked his way to the equipment. It took him ten minutes to make his way eight feet to the suitcase-like container housing the seismograph.

That can't be right, he thought. He tapped the side of the case automatically, a reflex from his early days with old equipment. But it was right, and he knew it.

The recorder showed a magnitude of 9.3. The only larger quake ever recorded was a 9.5 in southern Chile in 1960.

Okay, he thought. The numbers had left him nearly as

breathless as the quake, but he was beginning to think again. The same fault line comes down from South America and runs into the Antarctic Peninsula, so a 9.3 was theoretically possible. With this kind of jolt he should be able to register all the submerged glacier ice this side of the continent.

The door to his lab burst open.

"Lieutenant! Are you okay?" Two men in Navy-issue cold weather gear pushed their way in. Lieutenant Neister turned to his aides, Thomson and Hancock.

"It was nine point three—a nine point three!" he shouted with the excitement of a small boy.

"Sir, we got a much bigger problem," said Hancock, a thin black man sporting an ice-covered goatee under his heavy white parka.

"What?" Neister asked, wondering what could possibly be bigger than a mega quake.

"You've got to see *this!*" said Thomson.

"What?"

"Sir, I'd rather not say," Hancock said.

Neister stared at them and they stiffened slightly. "The Lieutenant better look for himself, sir," said Thomson.

Puzzled at their suddenly formal behavior—you can't spend time on the icecap with two men and not relax a little—Neister shook his head. "What in the world—?"

"No, sir, not at all," Hancock said. "Not in *this* world, anyway."

CHAPTER 3

211 DEMONG DRIVE, SYRACUSE, NEW YORK. 1:16 A.M.

The Katz home sat in a charming suburb comprised mostly of re-stored Victorian houses, on a hillside lined by huge oak trees. Annie had painted the two-story house a cheery yellow with white trim. It had four bedrooms, three baths, two fireplaces, a living room, formal dining room, and a remodeled kitchen. But what she enjoyed most about the house was the great view from the wraparound porch. She could sit there in her rocker and look down at the dark beauty of the pine woods that overflowed into their backyard.

But Annie was not thinking about the woods now. She lay awake upstairs and pulled the thick paisley comforter higher around her shoulders. She felt small in the huge four-poster bed. Small and alone. This was the time of night most people lie awake and think about the problems of their lives.

With Annie, she could pinpoint the minute that everything had gone wrong. The night she found the signal. An alien beacon. It had happened five years earlier in Los Alamos.

Working at her radio observatory, she had been looking into a Vegan anomaly when the speakers from the antenna changed from sounds of deep space—a white-noise roar of random hisses and crackles—to a symphonic twirl of sound, as though somebody had taken the bleeps and chirps of telemetry and composed an eight-bar fugue. It formed a strange kind of music that rose to a soaring ethereal climax, then died away, and repeated from the beginning. A signal, very clear and very real.

Annie knew this was not a solar flare or shortwave skip. Max Berger, her friend and co-worker, phoned NORAD, but of course it was not one of their dark bird satellites. It was an alien signal and she had caught it.

But the thrill of the signal ended when bad things began to happen. Her beloved observatory had burned, not in the way that happens when wires melt, but completely incinerated. All that was left was a crater and a few small heaps of blackened building blocks.

Annie had been targeted. The group whose job it was to keep the aliens top secret killed her partner and burned the observatory—all because of the signal and what it meant to the aliens held here.

Had that been the end of it, she would have counted herself lucky. But it wasn't. A copy had been made. The Black Berets came after her, and executed her best friend, Carol.

Was the signal an omen? Nothing good had come from it—and nothing would ever be the same after it.

She and Stan had left Los Alamos for Syracuse. Stan had a good university job, but she had nothing. Radio astronomers in Syracuse were simply unemployable. The closest job in her field was part-time work at the local planetarium. And while it was beneath her qualifications, it was at least something. Even now, she found herself occasionally missing it.

Max's birth and subsequent problems had forced her to give up working. She was a housewife. A housewife with a Ph.D. in astrophysics and an overwhelming need to help her son.

"Damn them," Annie whispered and punched her pillow. By the time she finally drifted off, her dreams took her back aboard an alien ship. She twisted her body and her face grimaced as she relived the worst of her abductions.

She could feel their cold fingers touching her skin, their jerky, buglike movements as they pulled off her jeans and underpants. She willed her legs to stay closed, but they were forced apart. Her feet were raised and something very cold inserted below her waist. And while she tried with every fiber of her being to scream, run, escape, she could not move. When the pain began, the deep burning inside built to a sharp cutting sensation, Annie knew *they were taking her baby.*

Covered with sweat and awake again, she rolled over and wept. Why won't they leave me alone? They're gone, she told herself. They're gone. But part of her didn't believe.

Ross Ice Shelf, Antarctica

"You guys going to let me in on this?" Neister asked.

"It should be just over the next ridge," Hancock answered.

Neister, Hancock and Thomson had walked a quarter of a mile in the thick snow. Their dark polarized goggles protected them from the blinding white of Antarctica. The only differences in the white were the shades of brightness. Because of rolling mounds from a long ago frozen sea, the gleaming, shining white grew dull between wave crest and hollow. And so it was that the orange-glowing craft seemed surreally painted on the white canvas of snow.

The alien ship hovered a hundred feet in the air and still a mile away. Neister and his men dove behind a snowbank and watched.

"What the hell is that!" Neister demanded.

"We don't know, sir."

"I didn't see it until after the quake hit," Thomson added. "It was moving real slow, like it was looking for something."

The craft dipped left, right, then jumped up a hundred feet like a leaf caught in a breeze. It dipped slowly to the left again.

"If I didn't know better," Neister said, "I'd guess it was running some kind of probe of its own."

Lieutenant Neister wiped the frost from his goggles and took a second look, unable to believe the size of the thing. He measured it off against his hand and the horizon. It had to be more than four hundred feet in length, yet it was as silent as a Macy's parade balloon. It was not at all like the pictures of flying saucers he had seen in an old *Life* magazine. But there was no question in his mind—*this craft is not of this world.*

It was beautiful, a smooth delta-winged boomerang in shape with the grace of an ocean-going manta ray. The snowbanks reflected the glow of the alien light, the way a calm sea picks up the pinks and golds of an evening sunset.

"What do we do, sir?" Hancock asked.

"Shoot it," Thomson countered and lifted his Special Forces 9mm Heckler & Koch submachine gun.

"No, Thomson," Neister hissed. "This is a once in a lifetime thing."

"Sir?"

Neister straightened to his full height and pushed up his goggles. "We're going to make contact."

"Sir, this isn't a friendly little ET. We don't know if they're hostile or what." Thomson's protests went unheard as Neister left the safety of the bank, followed hesitantly by Hancock. They moved slowly toward the hovering craft.

"How do we signal them, sir?" Hancock asked.

"Don't know." Neister grinned nervously. He pulled off a glove. "This works in New York," he said, and put two fingers in his mouth and gave a loud shrieking whistle.

Nothing—the ship did not change its pattern.

Hancock gave a loud yell, "Yo, homey!"

Still no change in the alien craft.

Hancock shrugged nervously. "The brothers must be deaf."

Thomson's fear was rising. He couldn't believe his superior officer would be so crazy as to invite his own death. He glanced over the top of the snowbank and watched. Neister and Hancock looked like two cowboys walking over to a grazing bull.

Didn't they know the danger they were in? The bull would

charge. Thomson felt he had to do something to protect them, to protect the mission. The sweat on his forehead was icing. He wiped it off with a glove and then mumbled two short words.

"Screw it."

Thomson did not remember pulling the trigger. There had only been a few seconds for a short burst before the alien ship turned toward them.

Neister shoved Hancock down as they took cover from the gunfire, though he knew they were not the targets.

"You stupid son-of-a-bitch!" Neister yelled, waving Thomson off.

"Oh shit," Hancock said, seeing that they now had the attention of the alien craft. He pointed this out to Neister and screamed, "Run for it!"

A bright focused blue light came from the center of the craft's underbelly and hit the frozen land. While the beam was still a mile away, the men could feel a vibration in the ground. Only slight at first, then building, until finally they could neither run nor stand. They fell together and watched Thomson, still ahead of them, finally slip midstride.

Huge cracks formed in the glacier ice pack—deep rips that went from thirty to a thousand feet down. The ice color ran the gamut from bright white to ocean blue.

As the shaking continued, Neister saw the ice under Thomson suddenly open up. He and Hancock began crawling toward their buddy but the twenty feet between them seemed like twenty miles.

"Hold on!" Hancock yelled.

"Hurry!" Thomson screamed, slipping deeper into the rift. When they finally reached Thomson, his body was over the edge, his feet swept out from under him by the shifting ice.

Hancock gripped Thomson's gloves while Neister held on to the back of Hancock's legs, anchoring him. But the shaking got worse. All three men were being slowly pulled over.

"I can't hold you, man," Hancock cried. He could see it was a drop of several hundred feet.

"Then let go," Thomson said and gave a hard kick to break free of Hancock's grip.

"*No!*" Hancock yelled, but it was too late.

Thomson sailed backward as his hands flailed and his legs kicked in a bizarre midair backstroke. He turned half over, then back, growing smaller and smaller . . .

It was over in seconds. A loud thump echoed up the ice walls, and Thomson was dead. Neister pulled Hancock back and glanced over. He could see Thomson's white parka blushing red.

Just then, the alien light flickered off and the ground stopped shaking. Slowly, unsteadily, the two men climbed to their feet. Neister scanned the sky.

The craft was gone.

He turned to Hancock staring down at the lifeless body. "We got to get to him," he said. "We've got to—"

"He's dead, Hancock. There's nothing we can do."

"No—we can't just leave him!"

"Yes we can. We've got no climbing gear. Anything we do will leave us just as dead. Palmer Station can send help."

"But, sir—"

"We'll come back," Neister added. Hancock did not look happy, but he knew an order when he heard one. "Yes, sir," he said. The lab was a ten-minute walk, but with the adrenaline pumping, Neister and Hancock made it in two.

While Hancock struggled to find the VHF radio in the rubble, Neister pushed his way through to the probe monitor. The fact that it had failed to register an image did not surprise him. It was, after all, not a real earthquake. The waves radiated horizontally instead of vertically. But the sonar-seismogram analysis did surprise him. "My God," he whispered.

"What is it?" Hancock asked, looking up from the radio.

"We're on a free-floating megaberg, about six hundred feet thick, twenty-three miles wide and forty-eight miles long."

"What?"

"Did you get Palmer Station?"

"Yes, sir. A plane will be here in ninety minutes."

"Ninety minutes? Jesus fucking Christ, we don't even know if we'll be alive in ninety minutes."

"Sir?"

Just then, a soft beeping sound came from the floor. Both men were on the edge of panic. Hancock kicked at the floor debris. Neister found the source—the alarm on a hand-held Magellan Global Positioning System unit.

"What's wrong with it?" Hancock asked.

Neister held the unit and looked at the changing latitude and longitude. He shook his head, "It doesn't make sense—we're moving."

"Impossible."

"Apparently not. North northeast at half a mile an hour!" He double-checked to make sure the unit was working right. It was. The GPS had acquired its satellites and figured the course and speed. The beeps were the position alarm setting.

"This can't get worse," Hancock said. But a second later, it did. All the equipment in the lab went dead, from the GPS to the half-million-dollar sonar-seismogram probe.

"Now what?"

An intense blue light suddenly glared through the rip in the roof. Neister shielded his eyes and saw the alien ship hovering above. "Sweet Mother of God. The bastards are back."

There was a low humming sound coming from the alien craft outside. Neister glanced at Hancock. They had no place to run, no place to hide.

"Sir?" Hancock yelled.

"Pray!" Neister answered.

Then, as abruptly as it had begun, the intense blue light cut off. Neister pushed his way through the rubble and looked out the door at the bright glowing craft. It hovered fifty feet above. The light appeared to be coming from luminous scales on the craft's underbelly.

"What's it doing?" Hancock asked.

"Just hovering. Getting brighter. I—" Neister shook his head. "There's something—not quite right."

"What do you mean?"

"I don't know . . ."

Neister watched as the light turned from a warm orange to white hot and the ship's fine edges blurred, as if it were vibrating at a high rate. Then without a sound, it vanished.

"It's gone."

"No way." Hancock pushed his way out to take a look. Both men stepped out of what was left of the trailer and scanned the sky.

"Over there," Hancock said pointing to a white ball of light as it reappeared several miles away. "How'd it do that?"

"I'm not sure," Neister answered.

As they watched, the craft streaked to the horizon, then vanished for good.

"Should we report it?" Neister asked.

"How? We don't even know what *it* is."

"The hell we don't," Neister said and turned back to the trailer. "Look at this mess. Six weeks of freezing hell and all we have is one dead co-worker to show for it."

He kicked his way back into the trailer as the electricity came back on. The overhead lights dangled from the collapsed ceiling, the computer booted up, the rhythmical beeps of machinery filled the room. Hancock looked at the screen on the computer and shook his head.

"Well, the main frame is whacked."

"Why's that?" Neister asked and stepped closer.

"Look at it."

The screen showed only a series of numbers that filled the page. "Odd, it's some sort of a pattern," Neister said, staring at the screen.

16 6 69 11, 16 6 69 11, 16 6 69 11, 16 6 69 11, 16 6
69 11, 16 6 69 11, 16 6 69 11, 16 6 69 11, 16 6 69 11,
16 6 69 11, 16 6 69 11, 16 6 69 11, 16 6 69 11, 16 6

69 11, 16 6 69 11, 16 6 69 11, 16 6 69 11, 16 6 69 11,
16 6 69 11, 16 6 69 11, 16 6 69 11, 16 6

"What's it mean?"

"I don't know, but I want a printout," Neister said. Hancock typed in the command to print screen. Neister grabbed the page and stared at it.

"Same four numbers repeated."

"It's gotta mean something."

"Yeah," Neister agreed. He picked up a chair and turned it over to sit down. Just then he caught sight of the GPS on the floor. Its small green screen was flashing. Neister picked it up. "Same numbers."

"What?" Hancock asked.

"I got it." Neister laughed. He turned the GPS around in his hand and showed him. "It's longitude and latitude. Sixteen degrees six minutes south by sixty-nine degrees eleven minutes west."

"Where is that?" Hancock asked.

Neister began searching the mess on the floor. Lifting some roof debris, he found his charts.

"Get a table up."

Hancock righted a lab table while Neister rolled out the chart. His finger raced down the longitude edge while Hancock searched the latitude. When their fingers met, both had the same puzzled look.

"Peru?"

"What the hell is in Peru?"

CHAPTER 4

211 DEMONG DRIVE, SYRACUSE, NEW YORK

Stan had returned home, and in the hours that had passed since he left Alexis he had not slept. He did not have a clue how he would cope with life at the office now. There was no place to run. Having another child was not an option. He did not want to hear about her biological clock, nor about her surplus of financial support.

He knew Alexis had family money. And while most men might be flattered to donate sperm to such a beautiful woman, Stan was not. He still did not know the answer to some very important questions.

He had spent five years turning these questions over in his mind and now, as he pulled the bed covers up, he was no closer to the answers than he had been when he first noticed something different about Max.

Different . . . Were Max's troubles his fault? Or Annie's DNA? Or were they the result of—the *visitors*?

Stan had no answers, and thinking about it kept him awake. He finally drifted off only minutes before Annie came in and woke him.

"It's past time you were up," she said, shaking him. "Get out of bed."

"No. Good morning. How are you?" he asked and blinked his eyes open, feeling stupid, dull and still yearning for Annie, even as she stood there, looking down at him with disapproval. So distant, so cold.

"What time is it?"

"Eight o'clock," she answered.

"Shit." He lurched up out of bed and past her to the bathroom. The MRI appointment had been made months earlier, and he did not want to be late. This was the one thing they had not tried and as a man of science, someone who believed in the tools and toys of technology, Stan had been waiting anxiously for this day, this test. He tried not to hope, there had been too many disappointments already, but even so—

He washed his face and dressed quickly, pausing only long enough to grab a bagel in the kitchen and swig from the orange juice container.

Within an hour of waking, Stan stood in the magnetic resonance imaging control room looking at video monitors showing his son, Max Carol Katz.

Max was not your average five-year-old. Besides his wispy white hair, he had large peaceful dark eyes, high cheekbones accentuated by a pointed chin, and very thin lips. Stan told himself the boy was not ugly, just a little different. He had kind of a baby-faced mad professor look.

What did bother Stan was his son's shuffling walk and inability to talk. Doctors had diagnosed him as emotionally and mentally retarded. But the cause of these problems was still a mystery. If the MRI could show the cause, it might point toward a cure.

"Don't worry about him, Dr. Katz. We'll have a visual on him the entire time," the thin, dark-haired MRI technician continued. "I haven't lost anyone yet."

Stan watched as Annie lifted Max up onto the smooth white table. She placed his yellow Bananas in Pajamas doll under his arm and kissed his cheek while the technician slid the table into the white cylinder of the powerful rotating magnet. Soft music played through speakers built into the unit.

From what Stan could see, his son did not react to the music, nor to his mother. He just stared without emotion at the ceiling.

The door opened and a tall, blond woman walked in. "Dr. Katz," the neurologist said, holding out her hand, "I'm Dr. Sarah Feuer." She held her hand there for a moment while Stan stared at it, then refocused his eyes on her face and reached for her hand, flushing.

"Ah, sorry. I, um, was awake most of the night."

"Well, you can stop your worrying," the doctor smiled. "The MRI is the most sophisticated equipment we have. We'll find out what's wrong with your son."

Dr. Feuer bent a microphone down and called for the room to be cleared. Stan watched as Annie and the lab tech left Max. A minute later, the hum of the powerful high-speed magnet began.

Stan had read up on how the MRI was different from an X-ray or CAT scan. The MRI functioned on the principle that a magnetic field forces the axis of the hydrogen nuclei in the patient's water molecules—70 percent of the body—to line up in parallel. A radio pulse briefly tips the magnetic axis to one side, and when the pulse stops the axis relaxes back into line, emitting a weak but detectable radio signal. From that signal a clear image appears, cleaner and sharper than any X-ray.

There was a steady hum, a series of clicks, and the first of seventy-two images began to fill the banks of the video monitors in the control room.

"In an hour, we'll be done with the scan. Then our computer assembles the images to create a three-D picture of Max's brain. That's when the fun begins. We visually explore the brain in ways that before were only possible through exploratory surgery. If there is anything unusual—it'll stand out."

"Unusual?" Stan asked, his mind racing with images of the

small aliens gathered around his pregnant wife. *Just what did they do?*

"Yes. You know, tumor or chemical changes or synaptic disorders, whatever. It all shows up clearly." Dr. Feuer smiled reassuringly.

"Right." Stan smiled nervously. "Well, it's in your capable hands." He flushed again, thinking how awkward that had sounded. But his palms were sweating. He felt his heart racing. There was no telling what they might find. It made no sense, but he was sure it would be bad. Everything had been turning bad lately. On the other hand, the anxiety of not knowing was exhausting.

"This is the time-consuming part. Why don't you and your wife go get something to eat," Dr. Feuer said, punching up the first of the MRI images to fill the video banks.

Stan rubbed his eyes. "Yeah, I could use some coffee." He left the room and joined Annie out in the waiting room. Aside from the coffee, he had to talk to her. The need had been building for months, and the emotional strain of his scene with Alexis followed by the MRI—their last chance, as far as Stan was concerned—had pushed him to the limit. He had to talk.

Annie was sitting pretending to read a magazine. Stan sat miserably next to her, hands clasped between his knees, waiting for her to say something, look at him, clear her throat—anything to give him an opening, to let out some of the hard things he needed to say.

But the article she pretended to read was fascinating, apparently, and she stared at the page for five minutes before Stan gave up.

"How about a cup of coffee? Something?" he finally asked.

"If you can think about food while your son is in there, in that machine, more power to you, Stanley," she said. "I'll wait here. Thanks."

It was a low blow, and Stan felt it in the pit of his stomach. He stared at her as she turned her gaze back to the magazine, still smiling with that poisonous sweetness that had come out of nowhere and taken her over during the past year.

Several things occurred to him that he might say, but too much time had passed to say anything, so he simply got up and slumped halfway toward the door.

"Really, Stan," she said, glancing up. "I just think I should stay. Maybe you could bring me back a muffin or something."

"Oh," the technician interrupted from the small window set in the wall behind her. "Mrs. Katz, your son will be fine. Go grab a bite, this can take forever."

"I really think—" Annie said.

"I'll look after him, don't worry. Go on."

Stan came back, absurd hope blooming in him again like a weed that wouldn't die. "Come on, Annie. Please, we need to talk."

Annie clearly did not want to leave, but now, with the unanticipated outside help, he would not give up. His guilt about his affair, exhaustion, and worry about his son had pushed him to the edge. If she didn't need to talk—too bad. He did.

"Come on." He grabbed her hand.

The cafeteria was not the setting where Stan had expected to bring this up, but he had no choice. In the past five years, Max had undergone eleven tests to determine what was wrong with him. Six of the tests were physiological, five were psychological, and one—well, a psychic in the mall gave the boy a reading. All failed to find answers, though the psychic gave them the most hope.

Oddly, Stan only remembered the part about a "butterfly being freed from its cocoon," a line which could have been taken a thousand ways, but his wife chose to make it mean a literal metamorphosis. And while there was no medical rationale for it, she had scarcely left his side since that prediction.

Stan did not believe in such nonsense. It was hard for him to believe in anything anymore. All that he had held dear—family, love, trust—had been violated. Worse, he had done the violating. Maybe it was a thought he'd picked up from TV talk shows, but he had the idea that talking about their problems would help. He just had no idea where to begin.

So he waited. They both picked at their food, until he felt he had to begin somewhere, say something, or he would burst.

"Annie," Stan began, trying to meet her stare without turning away. "Honey, even if we do find out what is wrong, it may not be something that can be helped. I want you to be ready for that."

"Is this about money again?" Annie asked.

Stan shook his head hopelessly. Damn. This was about a lot of things. Money? Well, now that she mentioned it, sure, money could be a part of it. Lately Annie had managed to pull every "discussion" they had onto the wrong level, focusing on one small aspect until Stan couldn't see the whole picture anymore. To be truthful he would have to admit that money was a factor and deal with the shame she would make him feel. After all, who can put a price on a child's health?

"Did I say anything about money?" he retaliated.

"It's always about money, Stanley. You don't want any more tests! The truth is—you've given up on our son."

"Given up?" Stan stared across the Formica table.

"That's right, you've quit," she said. "You fought harder to get grant funding than you're willing to fight for your son."

"That's not fair—"

"But giving up on your son *is* fair?"

Stan looked at her, feeling all the tension, frustration and rage of the past year build to a boil—and then overflow. He slammed his hand down on the table.

"Okay, you want me to say it? I'll say it. I've given up! I quit! We have spent all of our savings, my Aerocorp pension, everything. We have nothing left, Annie, and when it comes right down to it, maybe I am selfish, or maybe reality has finally hit. But I'll tell you one small difference between you and me: I accept my son for *what he is. I love Max!* Not some ideal picture of him. I love *him*. Faults and all. He doesn't have to change for me—and if that is giving up, so be it."

And he pounded his fist on the table again. The shock knocked his plate onto the floor. And as he bent to pick up the pieces, his face flaming red, Stan saw that Annie looked just as shocked as he felt.

"Stanley, I—" For the first time, Annie looked away. "Goddammit," she whispered. "I do believe Max is okay. I don't expect you to understand this."

"You're right. I don't. But since I can't change you, I just want to know—how long, Annie? Just how long before you accept the fact that our son is retarded? I'm sorry. I don't like it, but there is not a damn thing I can do about it. I want—no, I *need*—to put *our* lives back together. *You and me, Annie.*"

"Stanley," Annie said slowly, with gathering force. "This isn't about you and me. It's about Max. You say you love him, but when you lose hope—you've lost love. I think you're the one with the problem." She stood up. "I'm going back to our son now."

Annie headed out to the yellow-tiled hallway. She paused and glanced back only once. Stanley hadn't followed. He just watched her go. There was nothing left to say. He let out a breath and wished tension were that easy to release.

He sat at the table for what seemed a very long time. His coffee was cold, the broken plate with Annie's muffin sat beside him. Annie's words rang true. *Lost hope, giving up*—maybe she was right, this was *his* problem. But knowing right from wrong and having the drive to fix it were two separate things. How could he regain his moral compass?

Where was hope in his miserable life?

CHAPTER 5

"Is that one yours?" an older woman with an oxygen tube dangling from her nose asked. She had walked slowly over to stand next to Annie.

"What?" Annie looked up, startled, seeing the woman for the first time.

"That baby, is it yours?" the woman asked again.

"Oh, ah, I'm just a friend." Annie smiled uncomfortably.

"Well, that's my Hannah, over there. Born about midnight, eight and a half pounds. My third granddaughter. She's—"

"She's very beautiful," Annie managed to work in while the woman continued on about the active baby in the second row wrapped in a pink blanket.

Annie found herself inching away from the proud grandmother, surprised to see where she had come. She remembered leaving Stanley and walking. She must have made a wrong turn and her subconscious saw the maternity window and just stopped. Now, as if for the first time, she really looked at the babies. They were so beautiful, so healthy, so perfect. Like rows of little dolls for sale.

How much for that robust little boy over there? Did he come with a guarantee? Would they take a trade-in? Did any of these mothers realize how lucky they were?—Did her pain of a less than perfect baby show?

Annie bolted down the hall, wiping a solitary tear from her cheek. Had she betrayed her son thinking such things? As she rounded the corner to the next hall, she remembered the great smile Stan wore when he first saw Max. What a happy time. Their dreams and hopes had seemed so real. He had been such a beautiful baby.

While there had been no fanfare at Max's birth, no bright star in the east, Annie had expected her baby to be different. Of course, how different she could not know. All she had been promised was, "The baby will be all right. Maybe even better than all right."

She turned a corner and there, in the corridor, was a large machine on wheels—a respirator, she guessed. But something about the arrangement of the row of lights— Her heart lurched and she did not know why for a moment.

Then she recognized the pattern the lights made. It was not the same, but similar—Annie's subconscious mind had taken her back on board the alien ship.

Now she was standing in the operating room where they had taken her baby. She looked at the table with its strange ob-gyn stirrups. Next to the table was a blue liquid-filled tank with a large fetus floating in it. Human? It was supposed to be human. It was supposed to be her baby.

Better than all right?

There was a small gray alien hand at her side. She looked down into the creature's dark eyes; the warmth, depth, strangeness seemed to overpower her. He reached his hand up to touch the side of her face and almost against her will, Annie relaxed. *My baby,* she thought and smiled.

She envisioned an idyllic image of a sunlit field, a Labrador retriever playing with a small child while she and Stan watched fondly.

Annie had been so sure this was to be real, that she talked Stan into buying a Labrador, despite all his allergies. But Max never played with Buddy. There was no rolling in the fields. He barely reacted to anything . . . the dog . . . Stan . . . her. A few months passed and finally Stan convinced her he had found a good home for Buddy. A dairy farm upstate. A place they could visit any time they wanted. But of course, they never did. Stan got more involved with his work and she spent her time with Max.

Better than all right? It was a lie.

Max was not all right. She had known this ever since he came into the world—a second time.

Max had shown no physical signs that he had been taken by aliens or that he had been genetically altered. He had two arms, two legs, ten fingers and ten toes. Annie remembered that Stan had counted twice. In fact the only thing odd at first was that her baby never cried and his head was slightly larger than normal.

While Max should have had the genetic makeup to be a genius, all medical tests showed him to be borderline retarded.

Impossible!

Call it denial, call it whatever you want, Annie thought, and started walking faster toward the MRI room. Her son was not stupid. And no matter how hard Stanley wanted her to just accept him *as is,* she'd refused. Tests and more tests—and more, whatever it took. She would not rest until she found the answers.

It was cold and quiet inside the MRI tube. The MRI's loud thumps and bangs had stopped, followed by a whole lot of nothing. The only sound Max heard was his own breathing and the rain outside.

Rain, beautiful rain. Max's face did not show emotion, but inside, he was bursting with sensations. Like the cold he felt from the table. He knew his body should shiver the way his mother's did, but it did not. Max wanted to shout for his mother or Stan, or even the nice lady who had helped him into this strange place. But while he commanded his voice to speak, there was only silence.

If others talk, why can't I?

He filled his lungs and thought hard about a strong full yell he should produce, but all that came out was his breath. Max tried several times before getting dizzy and stopped. In frustration he cried, but there were no real tears. Like his voice, tears, laughter and all that was inherently human would not work for him.

In a way he was going through a self-realization, an awakening. Max closed his eyes and forced himself to clear his mind. The frustrations he held inside seemed to melt away. Instead of thoughts, he created a calm static, white noise. There was a cooling sensation behind his eyes. A sudden calmness filled him. Now, with direct focus and from deep inside his mind, he yelled. It was loud, and clear.

Help—I need help—now!

While Max had no idea who might actually hear him, he felt as though the message had been successfully sent. A feeling of accomplishment came over him. He lay very still for another moment, then suddenly his legs and arms started to flail. He thrashed about without any fine motor control. As awkward as this was, his squirming began to work. He moved down the tube. When Max finally emerged from the MRI he looked more like a half-beaten fish flopping on a dock than a five-year-old child.

The room was empty. Max caught his breath. The rain seemed louder now that he was out of the tube. Max focused his attention on the window behind the equipment. He could see the rain moving in drenching sheets, like waves washing up on a beach. He slid off the table and walked toward the window. There was something about it; not just the sound—something . . .

The light. The blue light of the window.

The way the sun filtered through rain clouds gave the window a blue tint. Max held out his finger and touched the glass. A bead of water formed, then slowly snaked down the glass.

His dream. Everything seemed to remind him of his dream. The rich blue liquid. Max stared at the window for what seemed a very long time. He did not know why his dream affected him so. But somehow there was a strange sense of self attached to it, beyond anything he had ever felt. This was more than *my toy, my house*. It was more like *I belong*.

"Oh, there you are," the MRI technician said as she spotted him. "You weren't supposed to get out by yourself."

Max turned silently toward her. He wanted to tell her about the window, the rain, his dream. But nothing came when he opened his mouth. How he wished he could talk.

The woman reached out and touched his silky smooth cheek. "You're quite a little boy. It'll be just a couple more minutes. The doctors and your parents are talking now. Just relax. There's nothing to be afraid of."

Afraid? Max thought. He had never been afraid of anything.

Not yet.

"Pull up image sixty-one-A," Dr. Feuer said to the radiologist. Annie and Stan stood behind the two doctors who were seated at the MRI control table. The video monitor flickered with a new black and white image.

"Dr. and Mrs. Katz, as you can see, this slice is looking at your son's brain at eye level. There are many extra folds and creases here in his cerebral cortex. It's almost as if nature intended it to grow even more. But Max already has a twenty-three percent larger brain than most children his age."

"So what are you saying, Doctor?" Stan asked.

"Well, we don't really know. It doesn't appear to be life threatening, but it is something very different and I want to keep track of it. Don't want to risk a chance of hemorrhage."

"Have you found anything that explains Max's problems?" Annie asked.

"Well, yes—"

Annie smiled and glanced at Stan.

Dr. Feuer continued. "There are two things going on here. First"—the doctor pointed to the highlights within the MRI—"there is clear evidence of a serious lack of cyneurotonin. Without that, the brain cannot activate its neural synapses. We believe it is similar to serotonin, but we can't add it, have not been able to synthesize it, and we're not even sure exactly how it regulates these electrical impulses. We do know the imbalance throws the whole biochemical makeup of the brain out of whack. But—"

Dr. Feuer paused and took a breath. She could see Annie's level of hope had risen in contrast to the father's unexpected resentment. She continued, "That's not to say Max is untreatable. With time and effort the brain can be tricked into producing more cyneurotonin on its own. We call it proactive sensory input, or programming. Repeated actions may find new neural pathways to the cerebral or higher thought part of the brain from the body's senses."

"Programming is old news, Doctor. It's what they use to help stroke victims relearn basic physical movements. We all know that. We've had our hopes up before. Just tell us truthfully, how is this going to help our son?" Stan asked.

"Dr. Katz, the human brain contains somewhere between ten billion and one hundred billion neurons. They form as many as a hundred trillion connections."

"Doctor," Stan interrupted impatiently.

She raised a hand. "Bear with me, Dr. Katz. The background is important. You see, it's the electrical signal between the connections that's the core of any mental or physical process— voluntary or involuntary. Every thought, reflex or sensation triggers an electric pulse. In Max, these signals aren't getting through properly, or in the right order. What we want is for Max to work on trying to pick out one useful signal and work on it until the connection is good. Even if it's an action he already knows, doing it over and over again may stimulate the brain to produce more cyneurotonin."

"And that will cure this problem?" Stan asked.

Dr. Feuer gave him a sad, tired smile, the smile of a kind person who gave nice people bad news for a living. "Let's not talk about a cure, Dr. Katz. Let's take this one step at a time and call this a starting point."

Dr. Feuer pulled out a card and handed it to Annie. "Dr. Natalia Aponte works out of the Sensory Perception Lab up on University Drive. She started this program, and I think she'll be able to help Max."

"Thank you, Doctor."

"Wait a minute . . . wait a minute. How much is this going to cost?" Stan asked impatiently.

"I can't believe you." Annie glared at her husband.

Dr. Feuer smiled. "That's a legitimate concern, Mrs. Katz. Give him a break. But you can both relax. The Sensory Perception Lab is funded by federal grants. It's not going to cost anything. They only take unusual cases. Which brings me to the second problem. Pull up the last MRI slide." Dr. Feuer leaned back toward the radiologist. "Seventy-two-A," she said, looking down at her notes.

The monitor flickered again with a new image. This one, instead of showing deep into the brain, was of Max's outer skull.

"Can either of you tell us what this is?" Dr. Feuer asked, pointing to the screen. "It's about the size of a BB and positioned just behind the left nasal cavity in the outer lining of the brain."

Stan bent closer to look at the odd object. "What *is* that?"

"We've never seen anything like it," the radiologist answered. "But sometimes you get a kid who's shoved something up his nose, like a cherry pit, and everybody knows about it but the doctor."

"No." Stan looked at his wife and shrugged. "I don't think so."

Annie looked back at him with a small shake of her head, and then answered the doctor. "No. Is he in any danger?"

"Not that we can tell. But we don't really know. If it becomes irritated, fluid could build up and cause pressure on the brain."

"If that happened, what would we look for?"

"Eccentric behavior," Dr. Feuer answered. "Irrational rage, mood swings, maybe unusual sleep patterns. Anything unusual."

Stan shook his head and wondered how much more eccentric his son could be.

"So what can we do?" Annie asked.

"Safest thing is to leave it alone. If we did exploratory surgery to remove it, it might exacerbate the region and do serious damage."

"Well, what the— I mean, there's no way we'll ever know what it is?" Stan shook his head.

The radiologist answered. "If it was organic it would have come up a different hue. If it was common plastic, like most toys, there would have been infection or decay. And, well, we know it's not metal." She gave Stanley such a strained smile as she spoke that he leaned forward intensely.

"Why's that?" Stan asked.

"The MRI's magnet would have ripped it out."

"Oh." Stan looked at Annie. Neither had realized how close to losing their son they had just been.

"So it stays a mystery," Dr. Feuer said.

Annie and Stan looked at each other. What passed between them in their glance was certain, shared, and better left unsaid. It was not a mystery to them. And it was not a mystery to the mysterious beings who had, very likely, put the thing, whatever it was, into their son's head.

Stan held his hand out and Annie accepted it. Dr. Feuer relaxed a little. This was a more normal reaction, the test results— good or bad—bringing the parents together. "We will get in touch if there's anything else," she assured them.

"Thank you, Doctor," Stan said. He took his hand gently from Annie's and stood up.

Annie seemed dazed. The doctor's voice seemed a million miles away and all Annie could clearly focus on was the BB-like dot on the MRI. From the moment she saw it, Annie knew what it was.

And she knew, even more than Stan, what it meant.

The old Volvo splashed its way through flooded streets as Stan and Annie made their way home. Max sat stiffly in the back seat with all the energy and movement of a store mannequin.

"Annie?" Stan broke the silence that had weighed heavily between them since they left the hospital.

"Mm?"

"That little thing. That, you know, the MRI showed."

"Uh-huh."

"Is it—uh, you know . . . ?"

"I . . . I'm not sure," Annie said, knowing that confirming what he already knew was the truth might escalate into another of their fights.

"Listen," he said. "We both know damned well where it came from and there's nothing we can do about it. But if you know *what* it is, I have the right to know, too."

Annie frowned, lost in her memories. She had been only a child when she had last seen something like that. She remembered staring at a long black wire with something like a BB on the tip, then the thing plunging deep into her ear. The pain, the sharp pain working its way in. She thought her head would explode, until the dark reptilian eyes calmed her. She was lost in his stare and the pain was no more. She knew what the device was—it was so they could always find her.

Annie looked back at Stan. In some way she saw the change in him for the first time; the new worry lines on his face, the sprout of gray at the temples. *Max is his child,* she thought. *He needs to know.* Annie braced herself. "It, ah—it could be some kind of . . . tracking device."

"Tracking device?" Stan made the left turn as the words sank in. "Tracking—Annie, do you know what you are saying?"

Annie nodded. "Yes, Stan, I do. I have one in my left ear."

"Damn them. They've done nothing but cause us misery."

Annie shook her head. "That's just it. Why would the aliens do it? They left, remember? They went home." The thought that had been troubling Annie was now clear and terrifying. "Stanley, what if it wasn't the aliens? That major who worked for Wesley— what was his name?"

"Andros," Stan said, surprised that he remembered. "But they haven't been in contact since we left Los Alamos."

"Stanley," Annie interrupted, "with that device, they've never stopped being in contact."

At the traffic light, only blocks from their warm, dry home, both Annie and Stan boiled all the confusion and all the questions down to the same thought.

Was Max safe?

CHAPTER 6

DREAMLAND BASE, GROOM LAKE, NEVADA

While a spectacular desert sunset unfolded, running through the entire spectrum of reds and cooling into purples, the unmarked military base known as Area 51:S4 got a second phone call from the Deep Space Command.

Colonel Andros listened intently to McKay on a secure line.

"Sir, Fallen Angel has left the Antarctic and is headed north along the South American coast."

"Good. Stay with it."

"Sir, I'm sorry to report a second Fallen Angel has left the Southwest and is heading east toward Florida. It appears to be on a similar flight path."

"I see," Andros said, trying not to show his surprise. Just what were the aliens up to?

"If I may suggest, sir, Eglin Air Force Base in Florida is best located for an intercept."

"Of course." Andros paused. Never in a thousand years had he thought he would ever order an intercept mission on the visitors. Still, if he did nothing, MJ-12 would see his inaction as a lack of leadership, especially the military members. Besides, what were the chances a plane could really catch one of these craft?

Andros raced through this thought process with only the slightest of pauses, and continued, "I'll call Elgin. Keep me advised, Commander."

"Will do, sir."

Andros hung up, tapped his fingers lightly on the desktop for a moment, and made his decision. He would assemble the MJ-12 team. And while he had always resented the paranoia of Colonel Wesley, it had become clear now that the aliens were up to something. Without dialogue, the situation could escalate. *He needed to find a way to communicate with the aliens.*

Andros hesitated. He knew he held the trump card and that was something the aliens did not realize. But could he use it? Could he do that, exactly the way Wesley would have? Play that card without measuring the human consequences?

He decided that he could. Everything he had ever worked for was at stake—and more, so very much more. He had something that could swing the balance his way. Something they would need.

An alien hybrid living among humans.

Max Katz.

Yes, he could do it.

The question was how best to use the boy.

GULF OF MEXICO, OFF FLORIDA

Stars filled the night sky above the calm sea and the lights of the small town of Gulf Breeze danced on the distant horizon. The twenty-one-foot Whaler dipped gently while two retired brothers, Edward and Brendan Hall, fished. Brendan took a sip of his drink before leaning back and sending his spinner thirty yards out into the black water.

"No, it's not beer, Ed. I told you I gave it up. Doc said I had to."

"Course you had to. The Lord teaches us to change our wicked ways, brother."

Brendan looked at Ed's worn leathery face. He thought

about how different they had become over the years. Not just physically. While both were tall, over six feet, he had become a real estate success, added sixty pounds of spare tire and maybe a touch of attitude. Ed, on the other hand, just seemed to get skinnier and meaner, and he had become increasingly and obnoxiously religious.

"Get off the soapbox. I'm already at peace with the Almighty."

"Better be. The Second Coming is at hand."

"It's been at hand your entire life. I think you were spouting Bible before you could walk."

"Go ahead, blaspheme. You'll land in Hell, brother."

"And you're already there. God's truly faithful. You lose the family farm and raise a daughter who hates you— Damn." Brendan regretted his words right away. But God Almighty, his brother got under his skin.

Edward turned away. He put his rod down against the side of the boat and looked out over the water. The salt air burned in his nostrils. Brendan was right, he'd had his share of sorrow. Why? He had done nothing to deserve his troubles. He had been a good Christian. Was God testing him?

"The Bible tells us of Job," he said slowly.

Brendan snapped, right in the middle of regaining his self-control. "For God's sake, Ed, you're not Job. Don't go blaming this on God. You've just always worried more about the next world than the one you're living in."

"You'd do well to think about the next world yourself, Brendan, at your age."

"What's my age got to do with it? Damn it, Edward, you've thrown away a good life for your Bible thumping. I bet you haven't even heard from your sweet Annie in ten years."

"What do you care?" Edward asked.

"She's my niece. I care," Brendan said, though in truth he had not even thought about his niece in ages. He reeled in his spinner and checked the bait.

"She married that Jew boy," Edward said, with the high-pitched self-righteous tone he got when he was being bigoted.

"What difference does that make?" Brendan asked. "Stan is a good husband."

"No. The girl broke Sarah-Jean's heart. She abandoned her family and her God."

"Her God? Didn't the Jews have him first?" Brendan asked as he glanced up. Millions of stars filled the cool night sky. He took a deep breath, trying to inhale some of the sense of calmness he usually enjoyed out on the water at night.

And then he noticed a star that seemed to be growing brighter.

"You don't know what—" Edward began.

"Hey—hey, look at that!" Brendan interrupted and pointed at the growing light. It seemed to be skipping through the night sky. It was unlike anything he had ever seen.

Edward craned his head and saw the radiant ball of light. He stiffened. "Almighty God, be with your unworthy servants in our hour of—"

"Get ahold of yourself, Ed. Probably a meteor or a plane."

But then the light stopped its forward motion and began to descend toward the men. It grew larger until it was the size of a full moon hovering a hundred feet over them. A searing glow from the craft's underbody illuminated the boat.

"Aw, shit-pepper," Brendan whispered, staring up at an orange glowing sphere maybe three hundred feet wide with a blue-green underbelly.

Edward lifted his hands the way an evangelist might on TV. To him the light held the image of an angel. "She's beautiful, brother. Filled with the spirit of the Lord. Feel the holy wind about her wings."

But Brendan felt only warm air like jet wash coming from the object. He saw no angel. This was some kind of craft. He could almost make out a row of windows. There! There was a figure in a window watching. Damn the lights. They were growing brighter. Brendan turned away from the craft.

"The Lord went before them by night in a pillar of fire to give them light." Edward fell to his knees but continued to stare up at the object.

"That's no angel, Ed," Brendan yelled. "Don't look at it." Brendan shielded his face, but he could see his brother gazing up with a beatific smile.

It's got to be some kind of experimental craft, Brendan thought. Eglin Air Force Base was not too far away. He'd see to it the base commander got an earful when he got home.

Suddenly the water around the boat began to froth white and the boat's hull started to vibrate. *But this is a Whaler, unsinkable, indestructible, overpriced. Definitely overpriced—but it can't go down*, Brendan thought. *But it's going—!*

Instinctively he reached for the keys on the center console, gave them a twist to start the engine. He glanced back to the huge outboard on the transom. Nothing. The motor was dead. He turned and saw the compass spinning wildly. And while that might have held his attention, he snapped back to reality with the sound of an agonizing scream. Brendan turned toward his brother and froze.

Edward hung four feet off the deck in the cone of blue light, his body stiff and lifeless.

"No!" Brendan bellowed but found he was just as helpless. He could not move his legs or arms. He was paralyzed, not out of fear but from some unknown force as mysterious as that which held his brother floating in the air.

Now a new sound filled the night. Not the hiss from the craft above or the churning of the water below but one Brendan recognized as the low roar of Air Force jets approaching, the same planes that routinely buzzed night fishermen like himself. Only he couldn't make out any flying lights; though he strained his eyes in the direction of the base, he saw nothing.

Then from the blackness came an orange flash. His heart sank and for the first time, he felt true terror. They had launched a missile and he was sitting under the target.

Brendan had heard that things move slowly when your life is at an end. He felt surprised at how true it was; from the light of the sidewinder slowly skipping across the water, to Edward falling like a rag doll onto the deck, to the alien craft glowing brighter than the sun, then moving at an impossible rate of speed straight up. To the normal eye and sense of time, the craft would appear to have simply vanished. But Brendan had seen it.

By the time the missile screamed over them, inches overhead, Brendan held his brother in his arms. A minute later the fighter jets roared over. Edward was alive but obviously delirious. His body shook in convulsions, his skin felt hot and blistered. He kept repeating the words "the boy, the boy."

"Easy, Ed. You're gonna be okay. You took a fall."

"The boy."

"I'm gonna get you to the hospital. I'll call Sarah-Jean. You're going to be okay—aw shit."

Edward was going into shock. Brendan checked his brother's eyes. They had rolled back, so only the whites showed. His body continued to shake.

"Hang in there, you old son-of-a-bitch. I know you can hear me. Fight this thing." Brendan wiped away a tear. He hadn't cried in fifty-five years and he wasn't about to start now. He slammed his hand hard against the dry locker and pulled out a raincoat. He wrapped Ed in it to keep him warm. To his surprise the boat's motor started. Keeping a wary eye on the stars above, Brendan headed full out toward shore.

"Stay with me, brother."

CHAPTER 7

PERUVIAN ANDES, 13,500 FEET

Dr. Jerry Sorich's eyes fought to adjust to the darkness of the cave and to the thin beam of his flashlight. He slipped in the mud and swore as he bumped into the rock wall. He lifted his head so that the light in his hard hat shone on the cave wall—and swore even more violently when he saw what the light's beam revealed.

Staring back at him were three painted figures with large heads, huge black eyes and no mouths. They looked similar to the rock paintings he had seen from Australia's Upper Paleolithic period.

But Jerry was not in Australia.

He was in Peru.

Jerry touched the cold wall. The texture of the clay was comparable to Australia's Central Kimberley region. And while he thought back to his summer sabbatical examining prehistoric Aborigine culture, he remembered the name of the god whose image the painting represented: Vondjina, the mouthless mythical being of the Milky Way.

The Aborigines had special reverence for this god above all other gods, for this was their ancestor who came from the stars.

But why would Vondjina be hidden in a cave in the Peruvian Andes?

"Eva, come look at this."

Dr. Eva Yi, Jerry's partner on the global warming study, was at the opening of the cave in the shadow of the great Andes Mountains. Her dark hair fell to the side and revealed her Asian high cheek-bones. Eva pulled a narrow metal tube from the earth and checked inside. There was a cartridge with a soil sample about a foot long. She marked the sample LT34 and sealed the container. It was the thirty-fourth soil sample she had taken from the Lake Titicaca region. They would test it for pollutants, chemical anomalies and metal polarity—everything to determine what the region's atmospheric fluctuation had been for the past forty thousand years.

She paused to look at the majestic view of Lake Titicaca below. Its surface was smooth as glass and it seemed to reach out forever like a great inland sea. She knew it had, in fact, been a finger of the Pacific, before immense geological forces lifted it to 12,500 feet above sea level. Today the lake was 130 miles long by 30 miles wide. Its shoreline was dotted with ancient temple sites. Small towns and farming villages had grown up around it, sustained by its fresh water.

"Eva, over here!" Jerry called again.

"Yeah, yeah," Eva said under her breath. "When you gonna do some real work?" She pulled a clear plastic tube out of the soil and inserted a plunger, marked the sample LTCD34, a number corresponding to the region and the soil. This one was to analyze the air for chlorofluorocarbons, methane, nitrous oxide and carbon dioxide levels.

"Eva?" Jerry's voice seemed more urgent.

"Coming, Jerry!" she yelled back as she zipped up the samples in her heavy nylon backpack. And then she added, under her breath, "This better be good."

Eva hiked into the damp cave. A swirl of birds flew out. From one step to another, the light faded to darkness. She fumbled for her flashlight.

"Jerry, where are you?"

"Over here."

Eva started again toward his voice. Then suddenly her sweat-soaked Syracuse Orangemen T-shirt reflected Jerry's light as she came around the corner.

"Come here, come here. Look at this, for God's sake. What do you think?" He pointed at the wall.

Eva tossed her hair back, cocked her head slightly and studied the drawing, then the rocks in the cave.

"Geologically speaking, I'd guess twenty thousand years tops."

Jerry nodded. "That's what I thought, which brings up an interesting problem."

"Like?" Eva asked, putting down the heavy pack.

"It's nearly identical to one I studied in Australia. It also dated back twenty thousand years—which as we both know was when the last major glaciation reached maximum. The question is, could this artist and his people have crossed over a major southern bridge to this continent?"

"Jerry," Eva sighed, her brown eyes sparkling in the light. "You know we have real work to do here."

"Just answer me."

"Fine. You want an answer? No problem. There is absolutely no way I find your hypothesis even remotely possible."

"Wait a minute. You can't blow me off that fast."

"Oh yeah? Facts, Jerry. The sea level was down maybe three hundred feet at glacial maximum. At best that could extend the coastline twenty or more miles, but it sure doesn't drain the Pacific."

"Okay, how about an ice bridge though Antarctica?"

"Aw, Jerry, for Christ's sake."

"Well, how about it?"

She sighed again. "Jerry—that would take freezing two major

bodies of water, Australia's Tasman Sea and South America's Drake Passage."

"But it could have happened. I mean, it's possible," Jerry pressed.

"Sure. I mean, it's completely crazy, but it's possible. There's never been any proof one way or the other. But okay, say hypothetically twenty thousand years ago both seas froze."

"We got an ice sheet to cross."

"Yeah, right, Leonardo here has an ice sheet to cross. Why? Why would he leave sunny Australia with magnificent grasslands and forests to trek over a huge snow sheet to South America?"

"I don't know."

She shook her head, and in the reflected light from the flashlights her hair sparkled. "Jer, you have only one character flaw."

"What's that?"

"You're always questioning the stuff that's known."

"Maybe because what is known is so often wrong."

Eva laughed. "But there's archeological evidence that early *Homo sapiens* walked over a warm tundra bridge from Siberia to Alaska then headed south through Central America and finally arrived here."

"Exactly," grinned Jerry. "Wrong."

"What?"

"Some *Homo sapiens* did cross to North America, but those sites date back only twelve thousand years. Here in South America there are excavations that date back thirty two thousand years. The closest region these earlier people might have come from? Australia! Those sites are confirmed at thirty-eight thousand years. So there must have been an even earlier southern ice bridge." He paused as if for dramatic effect. "Eva, do you know what this means?"

"It means, if you can prove it, you might make tenure."

"No," Jerry grinned. "Better. Look, the greatest mysteries in anthropology today are the unexplained gaps."

"Gaps?" Eva asked.

"Time and evolution." Jerry answered. "Our nearest relatives, genetically speaking, are chimpanzees. There's only a one or two percent genetic code difference between us and them."

"I thought we were talking about ice bridges?"

"Just listen—here's where it gets interesting. The genetic gap between us and our common ancestor has never been fully explained. What caused this two percent genetic code difference?"

Eva shook her head, feeling like the indulgent teacher not wanting to dampen her favorite pupil's enthusiasm, but needing to get back to the day's lessons. "Missing links? Missing skinks? Missing cuff links?"

"No, no! I'm not talking about undiscovered missing links, but real objections to Darwin's theory of evolution. The *how* and *when* that human and chimp diverge. Where is the hard physical evidence of genetic variations? The earth should be littered with half-breed remains. But it isn't."

"What do you mean? I thought it was a given that we descended from *Homo erectus* and all the subsequent variations."

Jerry's laugh was short and deep like a cough. Somewhere in the depths of the cave there was a small answering rattle. "I agree Africa was mankind's birthplace. Because each human ancestor group has C-14 dated sites showing a migration out of Africa. But when *Homo sapiens* archaic replaced *Homo erectus* it was not through interbreeding. *Homo erectus* was simply replaced. Then 150,000 years later *Homo sapiens neanderthalensis* superseded the archaic. The only branches to ever overlap were modern *Homo sapiens* and Neanderthals."

"Yes, well—"

He put a hand on her arm. "Wait. A hundred thousand years ago, Neanderthal and modern man lived at the same time in the same area. They hunted the same prey, buried their dead in the same way. They existed as equals side by side. It wasn't for a short time either, but for more than fifty thousand years, so we can prove we did *not* evolve one species to the other. That's not to say Neanderthals did not evolve, they did. Starting three hundred thousand years ago to thirty-five thousand years the brain size of Neanderthal increased from a thousand milliliters to fourteen hundred, the same size as modern man."

"Jerry, you're a size queen," Eva sighed. "If survival of the species was based solely on brain size, elephants would rule."

"Eva, what I'm saying is that Darwin's theory of evolution, survival of the fittest and all, is wrong. We know Neanderthals were stronger—they had thicker bones and larger muscle mass. They also had keener animal senses of sight, smell, hearing, and since they had the same size brain, we have to assume they were just as smart. So when the ice age came and species survival was at its toughest, Neanderthal should have succeeded over modern man. But for some reason, Neanderthals simply died out. I don't believe you can achieve that level of change except through replacement—one population taking over from another. But there is no proof of warfare between them."

"Maybe it was a virus like plague?"

"Maybe. But I believe it was because fifty thousand years ago we changed and they didn't. Think of it as some kind of brain mutation or a new neurological connection. Whatever it was, it permitted articulate speech so we could pass on information more efficiently and discover superior technologies like finer blades and projectile weapons. So when modern man finally left Africa we were equipped with the intelligence to build better shelters, more efficient hearths, tailored clothes, whatever we needed to survive the new ice age."

Eva sighed. "But Jerry, if *Homo sapiens* did not directly evolve from Neanderthals then how was it that modern man appeared throughout the far reaches of the world at about the same time?"

He gave her his most wicked grin, and his teeth shone with a strange band of colors in the darkness. "Exactly! There had to be a southern as well as a northern bridge with each ice age." Jerry clapped his hands, almost dancing in his excitement.

"Okay, even if all this is true," Eva said. "You still have one more problem."

"Shoot."

"If you're right and each of man's ancestors did migrate on their own out of Africa—well, what the hell was going on in Africa? New species-R-us?"

"Who knows," Jerry shrugged. "Maybe the Bible was right, God was there."

Eva laughed and reached into her pack and pulled out a Polaroid camera. She took aim at Jerry. "Smile. It's the last picture of you before they lock you up. Show it to Alexis and Stan on visiting days. Tell them all about your South American vacation."

The flash of the camera blinded both for a moment. Jerry leaned against the wall to get his bearings. Instead, his hand slipped and he fell back. The cave sloped and Jerry found himself sliding backward, down, down, till Eva's light was gone.

"*Evaaaaaa!*"

CHAPTER 8

Eva had just put her camera away in the pack when she turned toward Jerry's shout, but he was gone.

"Jerry?" she yelled.

No answer.

Eva examined the spot where Jerry had slipped. It was a narrow tunnel with slick walls descending 150 to 200 feet down, then turning at a right angle. She ran her hand against the rock. It was smooth, almost polished in texture.

"Jerry!" she called again. Still no answer. "Shit," she whispered under her breath. The closest village was seven miles away. She had no rope in her pack, but she did have a first aid kit. If Jerry was hurt she needed to get to him.

Eva pulled out all the geological samples from her pack and kept only the first aid kit, hand compass, camera and flashlight. She arranged the Geo samples in an arrow toward the tunnel's entrance with the snapshot of Jerry. If someone did come looking for them, at least they would know where to start.

Eva sat on the edge of the tunnel and took a deep breath. She had never been the brave child. Eva had always played it safe—the quiet, smart type. Even she felt surprise at her actions now.

"Geronimo," she whispered and pushed off. A small corner of her mind not occupied with the terror of sliding off into darkness noticed with surprise that the tunnel had not originated from natural causes. It was perfectly squared, making her think of a modern air duct. She felt her ears pop as she descended another hundred feet.

The air below became cooler and damp. She held her flashlight tightly to her chest and felt the smooth tunnel suddenly end. She screamed as she fell through the air, then landed with a splash. Soaked but not hurt, she swung her flashlight around like a scared child.

"Jerry?" Her nervous cry quavered.

She waded to the edge of the pool and almost forgot to climb out as the beam of her light revealed that it was also man-made. Very Incan in design, it had sharp geometric edges with a gold python snake lining the border. The room was a huge cavern, all man-made.

She took off her pack and looked through it. The Polaroid camera came out dripping and ruined.

"Great."

She pulled out the first aid kit and was relieved to see that the seal was still good.

"Jerry, where are you?"

Still no answer. She put everything back in her pack and shone her light across the room. There were seven large hallways connected to this great room. Which one? She put her light down on the floor to pull herself up out of the pond. When she bent to pick up her light again, she caught the glisten of wet footprints leading away and across the polished floor. Eva followed the footprints down the hall.

"Jerry!" she called. Only her echo answered.

The prints led to the center of the room where she found a large stone table with seven chairs on one side. Each had intricate gold inlay work. The whole room had the look of a primitive but royal tribunal. She ran her hand over the chairs, then whispered, "Gold."

"The find of the century," the voice behind her said.

Eva spun around and shone her light on Jerry's face.

"Jerry!" she yelled, then hugged and kissed him. "I was so worried. Are you hurt?"

"I didn't know you cared," Jerry grinned.

Eva pushed him away. "I don't, but I thought you were dead."

"Let me get this straight, you like me better dead?"

"Don't ask."

Jerry laughed. "All right. I missed you too. I was looking for a way out when I heard your scream."

"Did you find a passage?"

"Not yet, but I found something you're not going to believe. In fact," he giggled, "I hardly believe it myself."

"Like?"

"These chairs." Jerry held his light on the top of the chairs so Eva could see that an animal had been carved on each: an elephant, lion, crocodile, jaguar, bear, monkey and camel.

"So?"

"Take a good look."

Eva held her light on the carvings. "Very nice."

"Nice? Eva, since when did South America have African elephants and lions? How did these people know about them?"

"Oh, wait a minute. You're not still on that ice bridge thing. There's no way these tunnels date back twenty thousand years. Primitive man couldn't have carved them."

"At last we agree on something. Come here."

Jerry took her to one of the halls leading from the great room. Eva's flashlight shone down a tunnel that looked more like a catacomb. There were mummified bodies wrapped much as the Incas had wrapped their dead, only the heads on these mummies were misshapen. They were larger and elongated as if at birth they had been pressed between two pieces of wood. The seven bodies were placed in the traditional upright sitting position, legs crossed, backs straight, hands folded over their chests and heads tucked down, as if they were merely asleep.

"Human?" Eva asked.

"Humanoid," Jerry answered, holding his light on the closer figure. He lifted the faded cloth and pointed. "I counted the normal ten ribs, but the teeth look to be shorter, finer."

"Perhaps they filed them down. So many cultures did."

"Could be. But the eye sockets seem larger."

"Better to adapt to life underground."

"Okay. But how do you explain this?" Jerry lifted the cloth back from the mummy's hand. "Four-finger Sam."

"Genetic flaw," Eva answered.

"Every one of these mummies carries the same genetic flaw?"

"Same family, probably rulers. Like the Egyptians, they were all interbred."

"Okay, we have a lost tribe, whose art is very much like the Incas, but whose knowledge extends beyond the continent. How?"

"Look . . . at the time of the Fourth Glacial Age twenty thousand years ago"—Eva pointed back to the chairs—"that elephant would have been a mammoth, the lion a saber-toothed tiger. Paleolithic people could not have built this. They had a hard time working with stone, much less with gold."

"So what's your best guess? Who were these people?" Jerry pressed.

Eva looked around at the seven mummies. "I would venture, related to Incas, if not Incan. About 1200 A.D."

"Agreed."

"Really?" Eva looked surprised.

"Yeah." Jerry picked up a small gold amulet beside the male mummy. "See the geometric pattern, it's so very Incan."

"What about the figures there?"

Jerry held the amulet in Eva's light and studied it. He hadn't really paid attention to the figures. There was a boomerang-shaped object covered with stars riding above what clearly looked like a modern jet plane. Below that a man's face with another growing out of it. Next to him was a creature that was half man and half bison.

"I hadn't really noticed. But look at this. Part man, part bison."

"Yeah. So?"

"Remember that Chouvet cave in France with all those Stone Age paintings of bison running?"

"Sure."

"So they discovered a chamber off that cave which contained a mysterious drawing of a creature that was part man and part bison. Archeologists called it the Sorcerer."

"And I suppose it looked exactly like this?" Eva said, lifting the amulet into the light again. Her forehead wrinkled and she squinted . . . Then her jaw dropped.

"Hey Jer, this is an airplane."

"Nah, must represent a bird."

"Jerry, I'm the skeptic, remember? This's aerodynamic. Look—delta wings, streamlined canopy, engines, tail with stabilizing fins. If a kid had made this out of Play-Doh, there would be no question what it was. It's clearly a plane. And here, look, on the rudder. It's some kind of ID."

"Let me see." Jerry held his light on the spot and swallowed hard. "Geez, if I didn't know better . . . But it can't be."

"What?"

"Well, that sign. It's clearly the Hebrew letter for *beth*, or B. Eva, this is crazy. They didn't have jet airplanes here, or in the Middle East, thousands of years ago. I mean—I've heard strange things."

"Like what?"

"Like, oh—you're really going to think I'm nuts."

"You're already there."

"Okay, in 1898 an Egyptian tomb of Pa-di-lmen was opened. It dates back to 200 B.C., maybe older. Among the artifacts found was a bird figure. Keep in mind, it's 1898. There were no airplanes. But in 1968, the artifact was rediscovered by a cleaning crew who thought some kid had lost his toy in a Cairo museum. Only a passing archeologist recognized it as authentic. Made of lightweight sycamore, aerodynamic, it had the back tail wing of a modern plane. Now it was common for Egyptians to build scale models of everyday items and place them in their tombs. The plane was tested in a wind tunnel and found to be a perfect low-speed glider."

"So there were flights from the Middle East to South America."

"Don't tell me you're becoming a believer in the Nazca lines?"

Eva paused before answering. "You're still mad about that?"

Jerry tensed up. "It's really not a thing you forgive overnight."

His mind flashed to the famous huge animal drawing made in the Peruvian desert. And how, when the plane turned just right, the sun seemed to hit the drawing and it glowed. The effect was due to the desert varnish, a brown glint of mineral oxidization. Jerry had been fascinated by the Nazca lines since boyhood. They were one of life's greatest mysteries. Who made them? Why were they best viewed from the sky? What was their purpose? Jerry had no answers but flying over them fulfilled a lifelong dream. Until Eva spoiled it.

"It was funny, Jer."

"No, Jerry Seinfeld is funny. Slipping the Cessna pilot a hundred bucks to do a three-sixty roll was *not* funny."

"I didn't think you'd get sick."

"Can we stop talking about it? We need to find a way out of here."

Jerry slipped the amulet into his pocket. He and Eva reentered the great room. "One of these halls must lead out. I'm just guessing, but I believe we came though an air vent."

Eva panned the room with her light. "Wait a minute, I have an idea." She put down her pack and pulled out the compass. "We know which way the mountain faces, all we need to do—"

Jerry interrupted her. "No good, the compass doesn't work down here. I checked."

Eva turned around the room and found Jerry was right, the compass failed to change direction. "There must be a high degree of metal in the rock. Okay, well?"

"Choose one."

"That one." Eva pointed to the hall nearest the pond where she had fallen in. As they passed the huge gold python bordering the pond, Jerry turned to Eva.

"See, the snake is very familiar in Incan art, they say it represents their king, the Son of the Sun."

Eva shuddered. "Let's just hope we don't find any live snakes."

"I would worry more about live kings," Jerry countered.

CHAPTER 9

DREAMLAND BASE, GROOM LAKE, NEVADA

The white Lear jet circled the Groom and Papoose mountain ranges before descending toward the dry lake bed. It had been a twenty-minute trip from the Las Vegas airport to Area 51:S4. The plane held only two passengers, though it seated twelve.

Dr. Chris Keller pulled his battered meerschaum pipe from the pocket of his tweed jacket and began to stuff the bowl.

"You're not going to smoke, are you?" asked Valerie Ross, an athletic-looking short-haired young woman. She gripped the back of the seat in front of her to lean closer.

"Does tobacco bother you, Ms. Ross?" Keller smiled under his full beard.

"Yes. Yes, it does," Valerie said with a serious face.

"Okay. I won't send you into your first meeting with black lung."

"Thank you," Valerie answered. She relaxed her grip on the chair. Keller laughed and sat back.

"What's so funny?" Valerie asked, leaning forward.

"It's just . . . I haven't seen your kind of uptight, since Colonel Wesley's days."

"Wesley?" Valerie asked.

"Yes. Were you briefed on MJ-12 history?"

"Only regarding the *visitors*."

"I see. Well, perhaps it's better forgotten."

"No, tell me. I mean, please . . . if you would."

Keller smiled, fingered his pipe absently, then stuffed it back into his pocket. "Well, here's the short of it." Keller paused as he felt the plane's landing gear kick down. They would be touching down momentarily.

"Over the past forty years our group had been led by a Colonel John Wesley. Members came and went, but Wesley was a constant, a real security nut who frankly had it in for the visitors. He had few confidants—I believe your friend Dr. Fire was one. She started as Wesley's psychiatrist. Regardless of their relationship, I know he trusted her. Which is more than he did with most of us."

"Did you like Wesley?" Valerie asked as the plane lurched and the wheels touched down on the tarmac.

"Like and respect are two separate things." The plane braked and Keller bent forward with the shrill whine of reverse jet engines. "Let's just say, I respected him. He certainly died well."

"Is that important?"

Keller smiled. "Sometimes that's all there is."

"How did he die?" Valerie pressed.

"Vaporized. A weapon he had intended to use on the aliens was turned against him." Keller couldn't help but notice Valerie's facial expression. He assumed it was shock, though it could have been intrigue. "I assure you he went extremely quickly. The whole business was over in less than a second. But the struggle for Dreamland was not without casualties. It took years to rebuild, both in personnel and structures."

Keller glanced out the window. "Still," he pointed out as the plane taxied past several hangars, "good did come from it."

"What? What could possibly be worth—"

"In there," Keller interrupted.

Valerie looked. "What? The hangar?"

"Inside."

Then Valerie saw them. A series of strange-looking craft. One was the classic saucer shape, another resembled a top hat design, a third, more of a pointed triangle, a fourth, a soft-edged boomerang shape—and there were still more.

"Wow—they're really here."

"Well, their craft are here. Nine of them, total. Each one slightly different. Kind of a variety pack."

"Operational?"

"No. The scout ships were stripped of their power sources to get the mothership equipped for departure. But they still represent a wealth of back-engineering projects. Andros's promotion was based on negotiating for them."

"I see. So he traded human lives for alien technology."

"My dear," Keller chuckled, "we've done that for forty years."

The plane rolled to a stop beside a new brick office building. The jets throttled down to a low purr and a string of very fit Black Beret security men formed a line. Two pushed rolling stairs to the plane's hatch.

Waiting on the tarmac were Andros and a tall, remarkably beautiful, fiftyish blond woman, Dr. Katherine Fire. "Ah, the welcoming party," Keller said and stepped out. Valerie grinned and waved like a schoolgirl to Fire. At that moment Valerie looked more like a love-stricken teenager than a microbiologist from the Frederick Research and Development Center in Maryland.

"Colonel Andros, this is Ms. Valerie Ross, new head of our biological unit."

"It's a pleasure," Andros said and held out his hand. They shook and Andros continued holding her hand.

"Sir," Valerie said, looking nervous.

"Oh, no sirs," he laughed. "I'm not that old. Call me Mike."

"All right, Mike," Fire smiled. "You can let her go."

Andros smiled back. "Right, sorry. It's just, I think you're the youngest member of MJ-12 we've ever had. Not that—"

"Not that it matters," Fire finished. "Come on, we've got work to do."

Valerie blushed and picked up her bag. Fire put an arm

around her. They looked more like mother and daughter than colleagues as they headed into the building.

"Well," said Keller.

Andros turned to his old friend as Keller continued. "There go a couple of cute kids. Look, we have an hour before the meeting, I'd like to go over the new EMF propulsion data."

"Sure," Andros agreed, though it seemed clear his mind was still on Valerie. There was something about her—something he could not quite put a finger on.

Dr. Fire punched in a code before posing for the base's new security camera. Standing on a steel grid with a security gate blocking the building's door, she waited for the light indicating the camera was on. She could see Valerie's curiosity about the system.

"It works on the principle of the thermogram. An infrared camera and computer trace the radiation patterns emitted by facial blood vessels that identify each of us. It's more accurate than fingerprints and retinal IDs."

The light came on and Fire held very still for the camera.

"What about plastic surgery? Or if you're running a fever?" Valerie asked.

The gate lock beeped and Fire stepped through. Valerie was next. She stepped up to the camera and stuck out her tongue.

"It doesn't read facial expressions or external heat," Fire told her. "This thing works solely on internal patterns of radiation. It can even separate identical twins."

"Wow. It's like my mom always said, it's what's inside that counts."

"Absolutely," Fire laughed.

The gate buzzed open and Valerie stepped through. She noticed that it was not the only security system for the base. The corps of very tough-looking Black Berets who had met the plane were now resuming their positions around the complex. Valerie recognized them by their dark fatigues and the triangular patch of crossed lightning bolts on a field of gold and blue. They were the Black Berets Fire had warned her about. As long as she kept her ID badge on, they would leave her alone. But if the badge was out of sight, they were known to tackle you and hold a gun to your head until the colonel arrived. Considering what she was carrying, Valerie did not want that. In the privacy of Fire's office, a long-awaited and highly clandestine operation was about to begin.

"Where's my little present?" Fire asked with a slight smile.

"Here." Valerie pulled a small can from her bag and handed it to Fire.

"DMH, feminine hygiene spray. Oh, that's good. Very funny. Look, the warning—fatal if swallowed."

Valerie laughed, "Fatal for a one-mile radius. If—" She took the can back and twisted the bottom to unlock the seal. Out popped a liquid nitrogen cartridge with three tiny test tubes mounted on the icy sides. "Well, just don't defrost. Unless you're ready to use it."

"Brilliant."

"Thanks. But it needs a better name. I'm calling it K1397." She handed the can back to Fire, who held it up to the light. She could see the amber color of the poison and the strange manila-colored particles frozen in it.

"There's a fruity-garlicky odor released as the lungs initially collapse. The toxin works through the epidermis and moves throughout the body in the cardiovascular system. The toxin builds until the subject becomes nothing more than a canister of biological nerve gas."

"Fantastic. How fast?" Fire asked, holding the poison with new respect.

"Well, depends on the individual's health. Anywhere from six minutes to six hours. For example, during the time that medics took Mr. Ramirez to Riverside General, his IV puncture killed two of the ambulance crew and an hour later his last gasps terminated eight in the emergency room."

"You were always the best and brightest."

"True," Valerie grinned.

Fire leaned over her and covered Valerie's soft lips with her own. "Val," Fire whispered, running her hands over her young firm breasts, teasing the nipples. "We'll need to test this. Test it on an alien immune system."

"Yes," Valerie agreed, then paused, processing the thought. "Um, how?" Valerie looked into her lover's eyes and Fire answered with only a smile.

HOME DEPOT STORE, SYRACUSE, NEW YORK

It was evening by the time Stan made it to the huge hardware store. He wandered through the high-stacked aisles, remembering the old saying that you don't value something until you lose it. There was even a song he recalled singing at some concert back in college. *You don't miss your water, 'til your well runs dry.*

The cliché had taken on special meaning. *Could he keep his son safe?*

He wheeled the red shopping cart down aisle seven. Stacked across the shelves were dozens of home alarm units. He picked up a mid-priced unit, one with several features, such as a smoke sensor and multiple magnetic trips for doors and windows. Below the alarms were bins with security accessories. He grabbed extra window magnet trips and checked off *alarm* from his extensive shopping list.

As he turned down the last aisle, the cart was piled high with everything from new dead bolts for the doors, a house alarm, baby monitors, a motion detector laser, solar window strips that could detect the smallest pen light peering in.

Stan felt just a little funny when the woman ringing up his total asked if he had been robbed.

"Um, not yet, no," he answered.

She looked him over. "Uh-huh," she said.

Stan felt a hot flush of something between anger and embarrassment. "Even paranoids have real enemies," he told her.

And he did. He was sure of that.

This us-against-them attitude had given him back his drive.

There were things worth fighting for and Stan now had one. It was time for him to get his life back together.

He had agreed that Annie could take Max in the morning to see Dr. Aponte. He didn't really expect the doctor to help his son, but the hug Annie gave him was well worth his concession. How he had missed Annie's touch. That had been a major problem with his affair with Alexis—he still loved his wife. If only they could make love again.

He looked up from his reverie to see the woman at the cash register blinking at him expectantly. "Excuse me?"

"I said, cash or charge, sir?" she repeated loudly, the way you might talk to an idiot. Stan flushed and handed her a credit card.

When he had signed the slip he pushed the high-piled cart out to his old Volvo. He needed to be home.

CHAPTER 10

PERUVIAN ANDES, 13,500 FEET

The message for help had been found. But the arrow and photograph that Eva had left stirred feelings other than helpfulness. The tall Indian holding Jerry's picture was angry. He glared behind him at the boy holding the lit torch.

Like his chieftain, the boy had identical markings of Vondjina, the mouthless mythical being of the Milky Way, carved into his cheeks.

The chieftain yelled at the boy before he left, kicking the sample tubes lying on the cave floor. The boy wiped his eyes, then picked up all the stranger's things and placed them in a colorful basket.

"Owwy," Eva said as she pressed a new bandage onto her blistered heel. She and Jerry rested for a minute on the tunnel floor. She began to feel the effects of a mile-and-a-half climb uphill. Her legs ached, her back was sore, her pack had chafed her shoulder and a headache had started behind her eyes. But the blisters were the most impressive, each about the size of a quarter.

"You should have worn thicker socks," Jerry snapped.

"The socks were fine until I fell into your pond trying to save your sorry butt."

"Can we get over this? I'll buy you dinner. Soak your feet in champagne. Just stop complaining."

"Okay, okay."

Eva pulled on her sock and boot and the two headed again up the hallway. After another twenty minutes of hiking, breathing musty air, feeling the grit blend with their sweat, Jerry lurched to a stop and Eva, two steps behind and looking at her feet, bumped into him. "Hey—"

But Jerry reached back and took her arm. He pulled her up even with him, and what she saw took her breath away. "Oh," she said.

"Oh and a half," Jerry answered and for a moment they just stared.

The hall suddenly opened up into a room which Jerry could only think of as a library. Thousands of gold strips lined the wall, each only millimeters thick and three feet long with a strange form of writing stamped on them. The strips were placed next to each other like so many pages in a book.

"Didn't you say the Incas had no written language?"

"Yeah, that's what the research says." Jerry whispered. He knelt down next to the metal strips and ran his hand under them. A sound like wind chimes filled the room. His heart raced. He picked one and held it in his palm. Like an altar boy stealing money from the offering plate, he knew it was wrong, but did it anyway.

Eva held her light so that both could see clearly the printed characters. "Do you recognize it?"

"No. It's unlike any writing I've ever seen. It may be even older than Phoenician cuneiform. It's not hieroglyphics. I just don't know."

They both stared for a minute at the gold strip with its odd writing. *What did it mean? Who was the author?*

Eva finally turned her attention to the other things in the room. Like so many paintings, there were gold plaques at the top of the wall. There were no animals or geometric Incan designs on these plaques, only simple lines stamped on gold with a symbol pressed into the center. Up close they seemed meaningless, like oddly shaped ink blots. But as Eva stepped back she recognized one. "Jer, that's a map."

"What?" Jerry looked up.

"Look, North America." Eva pointed to a plaque. The shape did not match the land mass on conventional maps. Instead of California, Nevada and Utah there was only an inland sea. The mountain ranges showed as islands. In the South, the Mississippi River was a finger of the Gulf of Mexico overflowing half of Texas, all of Louisiana, parts of Arkansas and Missouri. Florida from Lake Okeechobee south was under the Atlantic and the Chesapeake was more than twice its current size, while New York's Long Island had disappeared.

"That's not North America."

"It is according to historical climatology. Look, that one's Africa, over there Europe. Jerry, these are the continents after the last great flood of 8000 B.C."

"But how could—" Jerry started, then just shook his head. He had no answers, and from Eva's baffled look neither had she.

"Wow, Antarctica's coastline." Eva pointed to another plate. "It's been under ice for a millennium. Our TOPEX satellite just charted it. In fact, Jerry, all these maps have the perspective from space. Look. That distortion is the earth's curve." Eva pointed to a curve on the plaque and then pulled her notebook from her pack and began a compilation picture of the strange plaques.

"You know what you're saying?" Jerry asked, standing.

"Yeah, this is a much older and more technologically advanced race." Eva sketched in the characters over the land masses.

"But we can't tell anybody. I mean who would believe it?"

"After all we've seen," Eva protested, "it makes perfect sense."

"Yeah, but Eva, it's one thing to say the Incas had a form of writing. It's even neat to speculate that they had ideas about airplanes. But if I say they had their own satellite system, I'll never work again."

There was a muffled thunderclap from above. Both Eva and Jerry flinched.

"Did you hear that?"

"Yeah, the surface must be close. Come on."

Eva put away her notebook. As she turned toward the hall leading out of the library she froze.

"Jerry, I think I see light."

Jerry was right behind her. Down the hall there was definitely light. "Follow me. I can smell the rain."

Eva laughed. All she could smell was damp earth. But that in itself was significant. The region had changed. Since the last great flood, the area had been nothing but desert, less than two inches of rain per year. Its only water source was Lake Titicaca, fed by the snowmelt from the Andes. But now, because of global warming and its effects on ocean currents like El Niño, there was flooding from California to Chile.

The hall came to an end. A flight of stairs rose up into an abandoned temple. The rock surface caught the sun and glistened. Eva stopped and studied the rock. "Solid granite, Jer."

Jerry laughed. "Yeah, and the world of archeology will claim the Incas dug through it with flint pickaxes."

"No, not these tunnels." Eva ran her hand over the glossy texture of the rock. "Look carefully. This isn't megalithic block construction."

Jerry stepped down and ran his hand over the wall. "Yeah."

"Well, as a geologist, I know rocks. You can see it in the sunlight."

"What?"

"That shine, it's a thick almost glasslike surface."

"So?"

"Jerry, this rock was heated and molded. That's how they made these tunnels and chambers."

"Impossible."

"No, very possible. I've seen it. Since the 1950s our government has worked to build bunkers underground. In 1983 the Rand Corporation came up with the brilliant idea of detonating underground nuclear bursts to create huge subterranean cavities. I spent a summer testing the rock for strength and weakness."

"What about radiation?"

"When the magma cools, the radiation is sealed into the rock's surface glaze. Makes you wonder what they're doing with all those chambers from underground testing in Nevada and New Mexico."

"Come on." Jerry started up the stairs again. They came out on what looked like a sacrificial well. All around them were the remains of an old mud-brick temple.

"Mud?" Eva said as she looked up at the towering walls several hundred feet high that ended in the traditional flat-topped pyramid shape. But because of the rain, the sides had grown deeply gullied.

"Some temple. It looks more like a melted chocolate bar."

"Mud brick was an idea imported from the lowlands not long after the fall of the Incas." Jerry scratched off the clay revealing granite underneath. "The Indians here must have been trying to cover up this temple."

"Then they know?"

"It would seem so. The Spanish came here in the 1500s. I think what was left of the Incan empire did their best to cover up these sacred temples and tunnels. Remember the Spaniards were hot to steal their gold and convert them to Catholicism."

Jerry walked over to the temple's grand entrance and stared out at the lapping waves of Lake Titicaca. The increased rain had brought the lake right up to the temple steps. Their only way out would be to wade through the reeds and leave from the water side.

Eva sat down on the steps next to Jerry. The rain seemed to be coming down more heavily. Eva admired the clouds rolling down the mountains towards the rust-colored valleys. "It's beautiful here."

"That it is. Do you know the legend of Lake Titicaca?"

Eva washed her arms and face, luxuriating in the feel of the rain and the wind after the tunnel. "No."

"Well," Jerry pointed out over the water. "It's said that one day the sun rose out of Lake Titicaca and Viracocha, the father of the sun, came forth. Viracocha was the supreme lord, creator and ruler of all living things. His descendants were called Incas. The sons of Viracocha."

"Quite a guy."

"Yeah, and when he left, he took his flying egg and ascended to heaven, vowing to return."

"And that was the end of the empire?"

"No, merely its decline. When the Spaniards arrived, it was the end. But what is amazing is that the Incas were only in power for three hundred years, from 1200 to 1500. And during that time, they took a nomadic people and constructed huge buildings and miles of stone roads, farmed terraces into mountains, and built city water aqueducts. It's the kind of advancement in a society that has never been equaled."

"Shhhh. Do you hear that?" Eva said suddenly.

"What? The rain stopped."

"No, not the rain. That . . . that hissing sound."

Jerry paused, then stiffened as he heard it. "What is it?"

Whatever it was, the hissing was getting much louder.

Then they saw it. A second sun in the sky, sinking down toward the lake. It was white hot and it hurt their eyes to glance at it.

"Dear God," Jerry whispered. "He's returned."

But before Eva could ask who, she already knew the answer. The huge glowing craft dropped down to sea level over the lake.

There was nowhere to run and very little they could do to hide. The alien ship blocked the only exit out and the light from it seemed to be getting brighter. Jerry and Eva backed against a corner.

"Eva, we've got to get underground."

"After you."

They ran for the well. Once in the underground hallway, they realized they had left their flashlights above.

"Jerry, stop. We can't go on. Not without light."

"Okay. I'll go back."

"That's crazy. We'll just stay here. We're safe here."

A bright blue flash down at the end of the hall cut them off. Eva pointed and screamed. The blue was followed by a steady orange glow. "Jerry, what's that?" she asked.

"I don't know. But let's *not* find out."

They raced up the stairs and back into the temple ruins. Gathered around them were dozens of angry Indians.

"Oh, thank God," Jerry said and turned to Eva. "Help has arrived."

But Jerry was wrong. A few minutes later both he and Eva were being carried back down to the well, bound and gagged. The last thing Eva remembered before she blacked out was that the strange glow was suddenly brighter.

CHAPTER 11

DREAMLAND BASE, GROOM LAKE, NEVADA

In the heart of the Dreamland office complex a meeting was in full swing. Twelve chairs sat around a black marble table filled by middle-aged occupants—except for Valerie Ross, who was not seated and not middle-aged. She stood in the back of the room, pouring a can of Mountain Dew into a glass. She looked up, trying to pay attention to Colonel Andros. Unlike most women, she found him utterly unattractive.

"Aside from these two craft leaving our air space," Andros continued, "We know two fishermen were booked into Pensacola General Hospital suffering from high doses of EM radiation burns. One is critical, the other stable. I want them both questioned. Second—"

Andros paused while Valerie took her seat beside Dr. Fire. He thought about how far the group had come since Wesley's death, how relaxed and informal the meeting was, considering the stakes. He credited this to relocating the group from the secret Country Club facility in Maryland to the remodeled Area 51:S4 base. Most members lived in the residential suburbs of Las Vegas and commuted, though five top military officials still had to fly in from D.C. As a whole, the group seemed less stressed. Even so, Andros knew there were still divided loyalties among the Black Berets. They were, after all, Wesley's men. But he would work on them later. The decisions MJ-12 faced now were more difficult than any of the earlier ones.

Colonel Andros turned to the Black Beret beside the door, a large man who looked like an NFL linebacker who had decided to take fitness training seriously. "Captain Sweigart, show Lieutenant Neister in."

The Captain opened the door and Neister entered in his full-dress uniform. He was followed by two more Black Beret guards.

"Thank you. Lieutenant, kindly recap what you reported earlier."

"Sir. My men and I were attacked by an unknown craft in the Antarctic eight hours ago. One was killed in his attempt to fire on the craft."

"What were you doing in the Antarctic, Lieutenant?" asked Dr. Keller.

"The Navy has an ongoing project to study rising sea levels."

"Caused by global warming?" Dr. Fire asked.

"Yes, ma'am. An average of three point nine millimeters per year."

"Did the craft in any way affect your study?" Andros asked.

"God, yes." Neister laughed, but stopped when he realized everyone was staring coldly. *Did I hit a raw nerve? Who are these people?* "I mean," he began again, "the craft generated a killer quake, a nine point three. And that, well, that broke free a megaberg."

"How big is this megaberg?" Keller inquired, making some notes on a pad.

"Six hundred feet thick, twenty-three miles wide and forty-eight miles long."

Everyone seemed surprised. There were murmurs among the members, until Andros spoke up again. "Its effect?"

"Well, besides a slightly larger rise in sea level this year, a cooler ocean will influence weather patterns. But then, you already know what a mess the weather's been."

"True," Andros agreed. Neister noticed several other members making notes.

"Is there anything else you wish to add?" Andros asked.

"Yes, sir." Neister paused to pull out a wrinkled sheet of paper from his pocket. "Right after the craft left, our computer printed out a series of numbers. We couldn't make heads nor tails out of it at first, but now we believe the numbers are latitude and longitude. It's somewhere in Peru."

"Thank you," Andros said and took the paper from Neister before nodding to the Black Beret captain. "We appreciate your time, Lieutenant. Captain Sweigart will show you out."

The Berets left with Lieutenant Neister. Andros turned and faced MJ-12, holding the paper printout.

"Well, this is news. Our Deep Space Network using HAARP tracked the craft to Lake Titicaca at twenty-one hundred hours. Evidently the visitors intended for their actions to be followed."

"Could be a trap?" J. D. Baker, the heavyset NSA officer, suggested.

"Trap? Since their return, we don't know what they're doing. But why would they need to set a trap?" Dr. Keller remarked.

"We're never going to know with that attitude," Fire said.

"Agreed," Andros added. "I want a team to investigate the Peru sighting and one to check out the fishermen's story. Let's assume none of their movements are accidental."

"What about the new rumors at Dulce?" Fire asked. "I mean, since we're assembled. I thought—"

Andros, staring hard at Fire, had not intended to bring up Dulce. But better him now, than her later. "Well. Our security at Dulce has reported, besides the genetic hybrid program, there are rumors that the visitors have started working on—"

"Nightmares," Katherine Fire interrupted with disgust. "Level six, the Bug Eyes have experimented cross-breeding humans with animals. Making all sorts of hideous creatures."

"That doesn't make sense," Keller commented. "We've known them to be a highly analytical and technologically oriented species. What purpose could mutating humans serve?"

"None," Andros answered. "And I want to point out that none of this has been verified. It's based solely on memories from abductees, which we know can be readily manipulated."

"I don't see a moral difference between a half-breed human and Bug Eye or a half-breed human and animal," Baker said angrily. "It's pretty clear they're playing God, to create new species. The question to ask is *why*."

"He's right. Why create new species unless they're going to do away with the old? Is there any way to investigate the Anthill?" the Naval Intelligence Officer asked.

"Short of storming it? No. And I don't think we're ready to go to war. Not yet. The best way to learn the alien agenda is to investigate their most recent movements. That will determine our next action." Andros stood up and circled the table. "Our teams will need full support from the CIA and NSA."

"You'll have it," the directors agreed.

"Dr. Keller," Andros continued, "I want you to head up the Peru group. Ms. Ross, you'll join him."

Valerie glanced at Fire, but said nothing.

"Katherine," Andros went on, "I want you to lead the investigation of the two fishermen in Florida. Do a full psychiatric review. Find out what happened. Take a couple of Berets. This must be kept out of the press. Use whatever means of disinformation it takes to convince the fishermen that they saw nothing. Are there any questions?"

The room was quiet. Andros paused before returning to the head of the table. "Okay, we're adjourned until the investigations are completed."

The group stood to leave. Fire turned to Valerie and whispered, "You'll love Peru. Just don't drink the water. Oh, I almost forgot. Before we leave, we need to run our little test."

"But how?" Valerie protested. Where could they find a living alien immune system?

"Such dirty little secrets are always well hidden. Come with me." Fire and Valerie continued whispering as they walked down the hall.

SENSORY PERCEPTION LAB, SYRACUSE, NEW YORK

"Welcome to the Sensory Perception Lab," said the heavy red-head with the friendly face. Max stared at the colorful fish in the twenty-gallon tank. The redhead bent down and put her hand on his shoulder.

"You like fish? My son loves to fish."

Max said nothing. He just stared at the small yellow-and-red-striped fish zipping up and down the glass wall, as if somehow, some way, the creatures might find a way to escape.

"Max, we have work to do. Come with me now." And not waiting for an answer she reached down and pulled Max away from the tank and toward the dozen other children about his age gathered around tables.

"Children, we have a guest today. His name is Max and I want you all to be his friends."

A petite black girl came over to Max and stared up at him with a wonderfully bright smile.

"I'll be your friend."

"Thank you, Sally," the teacher said, then waved at the group gathered around her. "Okay children, it's time to get to our work stations."

And the children darted off in various directions leaving Max alone again. He looked around and saw the group had broken into pairs. A couple of children worked with colored balls, while others worked with musical instruments, and still others tested sensory perception with vibrating shapes. There were six work stations in all, each with specialized toys to help the children.

Max moved to sit in a chair closest to a window. He could still hear the rain outside, but the sounds of the children rang much louder. He was not sure he liked their sounds. They seemed confusing. If only he could understand them.

"Max, today you're going to have a hearing test," the teacher said, holding out her hand. She led him to a nearby table with a set of heavy black headphones. She placed them over his ears and smiled kindly. The sounds of the other children were muffled. Max could hear his own heart beating.

But a beep suddenly interrupted the quiet, a beep followed by the voice of a man. "Raise your hand if you can hear me," the voice said.

Max turned to the teacher. She too had on a set of headphones. Was she hearing what he had heard? Max did not raise his hand. But his look indicated he had heard something. The teacher paused and wrote again in her notebook.

"Very good. We will now play the sounds of animals. You are to raise the hand on the side you hear the sounds in," the man's voice calmly said.

Max studied the teacher in the following period of quiet. His instincts told him she was a good person, though why she had hidden this little man in the headphones he did not understand.

Suddenly he heard the sound of high-pitched chattering from a monkey in his left ear. Max swung his head to the left expecting to see a very angry ape. At least he perceived the monkey as angry. But where was it hiding? Max turned back to the teacher and again found her writing on her pad. Perhaps she knew what was happening to the monkey. Maybe she even felt his anger, as Max felt it. The hatred grew and seemed real. Max closed his eyes and while his face did not show the emotion, deep inside he felt the animal's rage.

DREAMLAND BASE, GROOM LAKE, NEVADA

Inside one of the new buildings, behind a door marked LABORA-TORY, a screaming monkey shrieked. He had pushed himself against the wall of his cage as Fire and Valerie entered Andros's vacuum-sealed genetics lab.

"Sonny," Fire explained to Valerie through the intercom in her white bio-suit, "is Andros's only surviving experiment."

Valerie studied the chimpanzee. She could see his head was larger than normal, his fur oddly thin, and his eyes liquid dark.

"Don't let the little bugger fool you. I tested his IQ myself. While he lacks the opposable thumb and a larynx to speak, he's smarter than most men on the street."

Fire took out the K1397 can and popped open the bottom. "Just one whiff, right?" She rolled a tiny test tube in her gloved hand until it became liquid.

"That's it," Valerie agreed. "I have two antitoxin pills in case we need them."

"Why would we need them?"

"Well, the bacteria travels airborne unless injected directly into the blood. Airborne kills in hours. In blood it takes only a matter of minutes. So what we avoid is a rip in the suit or skin."

Sonny suddenly screeched again, then pushed away from the wall, baring his teeth and gums.

"Get back," Fire demanded. "I forgot to warn you, this little hybrid bastard has a working vocabulary of four hundred words. Sometimes, I swear, it's as if he can read your mind."

Valerie backed up to the door, while Fire held out the tube and popped it open. Sonny continued his approach. "Come on, boy, come and get me."

She held out her hand toward the strange-looking chimpanzee. But just as Sonny charged, she cracked open the vial and soaked his face. Sonny stumbled backward, then began to roll around, shrieking. His hands clawed at his eyes.

"That ought to do you," Fire declared as she stepped back to the air lock. She punched in the security override and the door opened.

Once outside the lock, Valerie peered back into the lab. Sonny had stopped moving and was now breathing heavily in the corner of the room. His eyes watered and he looked sick. As if he felt her gaze, he looked up and whimpered.

"Will it work?" Fire asked casually.

"It's already working," Valerie answered coldly. "If that's the best the alien immune system can do, I would say it's over. He'll be dead in a couple hours."

"So quickly?"

"You sprayed his eyes, so it's entered his bloodstream. How are we going to dispose of the body?"

"We're not," Fire said and took Valerie's hand and headed for the showers. "If we're lucky, a certain colonel will find his dear pet. And when we return from our investigations, I will take control of MJ-12."

Fire opened the stainless steel door to the decontamination showers. Valerie entered, then paused. "Katherine, how are we going to deliver it? There's no way to get it into the Bug Eyes' Anthill."

Fire smiled before answering. "Wrong. Good things come in small packages." She pushed Valerie on into the industrial steel shower stall with heavy soaps spraying down from a center spigot. A minute later the buzzer blared and they passed through a heavy door to a second shower. This one, a little more relaxed, was tiled in pastel pink.

"Why so mysterious?" Valerie asked, as she peeled off her suit and stood under the warm water.

"I'll give you a clue." Fire said, stripping next to her. "The Pied Piper."

Valerie made a face. "Rats? You're going to use rats?"

"Why not? We know the Bug Eyes have countermeasures against all our advanced tactical weapons. But rats—they dig, they chew, they crawl through air vents, they always find a way in. They're the most successful carriers of lethal infections our world has ever known."

Steam rose around them in the stall. Fire let the hot water run down her back and rubbed her face with the disinfectant soap.

"Okay, say they get through, how will it work?" Valerie asked, scrubbing her skin till the white turned a light pink.

"Dead or alive, rats continue to carry the disease. Not just in bites; urine and droppings are just as deadly. Step in it, touch it, breathe the air that passes over it, you absorb the poison. We used lesser toxins at test sites in Central America in the eighties and again in the early nineties at a southwest Indian reservation. Both worked."

"You did the Navajo reservation?"

"We had to find a place with similar climate and terrain to the Dulce base and we learned not only the efficiency of Mickey Mouse but the time for complete infiltration—three weeks."

"So the project is a go?"

Fire put a hand on Valerie's soapy ass and drew her close. "This isn't just a project, Val. It's our survival."

Valerie found herself looking once more into those confident, compelling eyes, and then feeling Fire's lips on her. A shudder that was part ecstasy and part surrender went through her entire body and she felt herself melt to the floor with Katherine as the shower steamed around them.

CHAPTER 12

LYMAN HALL, SYRACUSE UNIVERSITY, SYRACUSE, NEW YORK. 10:15 A.M.

Classes had been canceled that morning so Stan returned to his office to finish typing data from the latest study that had come in. It was from the National Oceanic and Atmospheric Administration's Geophysical Fluid Dynamics Lab in Princeton, New Jersey. They had just released a study which showed that increasing levels of carbon dioxide in the atmosphere had created for the first time an Arctic ozone hole. Though much smaller in area than the one in the Antarctic, its effects would reach far more people.

Stan could just picture future TV ads—a happy couple parking their sexy gas-guzzling car and walking out on the sandy beach while a jingle rang in the background for Hawaiian Tropic 3000. And along the bottom of the screen: *A Surgeon General Warning: Suntanning may result in injury, birth defects and cancer.*

Stanley suddenly felt a pair of hands come across his shoulders and Alexis leaned over to nibble at his ear. "Working hard, love?" Her breath sent a shiver down his back.

"I'm sorry," Stan mumbled and rolled his chair back. "I just can't."

"Oh, that's not the Stan Katz I know," Alexis said and slid up onto his desk. She rubbed her long leg against his shoulder.

"Alex, we've got to talk. I mean I'm flattered. You're a beautiful woman. We've had a great time, but look, you could have any strong, healthy man. Why me?"

"Because." She wrinkled her nose and tossed her fiery red hair to one shoulder. "I really like you. I don't know what it is. Maybe your smile or quirky sense of humor."

"My humor?" Stan laughed.

Alexis giggled, then turned more serious. "I know your passion, your caring—"

"But we shouldn't," Stan argued, "I mean I can't. This may be the new trend. Single, professional wannabe moms. But I have a family. I don't want another child, a new family."

"It wouldn't be your responsibility. I would take care of the child, entirely. Look, you know me. Can you really see me going to a fertility clinic?" Alexis reached for Stan and held his face in her palms. "Wouldn't you feel better if the father of my child was at least someone I knew?" She leaned forward and whispered, "I want you, Stanley." She slid off the desk and rubbed his back.

Stan pushed himself up from his desk. He wanted very much to run away, but he did not. Instead he closed his eyes and felt her warm hands moving across his back and neck.

"See how tense you are? You need to relax." She reached to tug at his zipper. He fought off his desire to take her. "I can help relieve your stress," she whispered, slipping her hand into his pants.

"No." Stan's voice cracked. "Please—" He stepped away and glanced back at his computer. "What about our work? We haven't heard from Eva and Jerry. You're letting this baby thing interfere with the project . . . with your judgment."

Alexis smiled and stepped closer to Stan. "You're right. I'm sorry. But—" She pulled out her cellular phone from her handbag. "It's not like they couldn't have rung me up. Day or night. I know. They have my number."

Alexis slid her fingers inside Stan's shirt and raked his chest hairs.

"Alex, cut it out."

"You can't expect me to give up so easy." Before Stan could protest again, she fell to her knees and took his sex in her mouth, her tongue licking gently at first, then sucking hard as he grew more rigid. She then abruptly stopped and added.

"You know you're right. Perhaps we aren't good for each other."

Stan could contain himself no longer. His hands ripped at her dress until it fell to the floor. He caressed her breasts and she felt his tongue lick her hard nipples through the lace of her bra. She ran her hands through his hair, then pushed him back and began kissing him as she took his clothes off. As she kissed his neck and shoulders her lipstick rubbed off on his shirt. Telling him would ruin the mood, so Alexis just pulled his shirt off and flung it to the floor.

Now both were naked and Alexis arched her back with desire as Stan caressed her. He moved from soft and melting touches to a fierce passion, lifting her legs until her knees touched her chin. The rhythm of their lovemaking continued until Stan turned her over and took her from behind. Shivers passed through Alexis's body. But Stan was not finished; he moved so Alexis would straddle him on top. He remained in her as she moved up and down. Her movements became quicker as they both cried out in climax. Alexis fell on top of Stan in a warm wet embrace.

Stan kept his eyes closed for a long moment. *Oh God, what have I done?*

He desperately wished there were a way he could undo it, but it was done.

SENSORY PERCEPTION LAB, SYRACUSE, NEW YORK

"Relax. Max is just fine," said Dr. Natalia Aponte, a slim dark-haired woman of thirty leaning back in her office chair. Her office was small, filled with books and filing cabinets, with the tendrils of a single, small green vine crawling up the venetian blinds on the window.

"Where is he?" asked Annie.

"We have a classroom with several special children. Max is with them."

"Really? With other children? I mean, he's so different. Is that okay?"

"He's fine. These kids are different too." Natalia smiled. "Would you like to see him?"

"Yes."

"Well then." Natalia stood up and opened her office door. "Let's go check on your little man."

They were headed down the hall when Dr. Aponte turned to Annie. "I take it you don't let Max socialize."

"Well, it's kind of hard when he doesn't talk. Children can be so cruel. It's not wrong of me, is it?"

"Annie, no one is judging you. I know how hard it is to raise a special child."

"You do?" Annie asked.

"Yes, I do." Natalia smiled, then paused to open the classroom door. They entered the room filled with special children. "My daughter is in this class with your son."

Annie's eyes searched the room for Max. He was in the section with the colored shapes working with the same instructor. Natalia smiled and took Annie's hand. "He's fine, Annie. They're just finishing up. Let's give them a minute. I'll introduce you to Maria."

They walked across the room to a brightly colored area with musical notes painted around the cubby. Inside was an assortment of musical instruments, from horns to bells to Casio electronic pianos.

There was a small, frail, dark-haired girl sitting very straight with her hands on the piano keys playing a beautiful, simple melody. An oxygen tank sat beside her and a tube ran up to her nose. Natalia put a hand on her daughter's shoulder. "Maria, this is Mrs. Katz, Max's mommy."

The little girl looked up and smiled. Her teeth seemed unnaturally white against her Mediterranean olive skin.

"I am pleased to meet you," Annie said and held out her hand. She felt a slight squeeze from Maria as she shook it.

"Why don't you play something more for us," Natalia asked. Maria's smile showed how eager she was to return to playing. New music came from the electronic piano. A range of emotions crossed Maria's face as her fingers danced on the keys playing a very complex rendition of "When You Wish Upon A Star."

Natalia then took a step toward Annie. She whispered under the music. "You see the day Maria was born was both the happiest and saddest day of my life."

"How so?"

"She was born six weeks early and weighed less than four pounds. The doctors gave her only a forty percent chance of living. Her lungs, they said, would never fully develop. Even now, at five years, she's still too short of breath ever to play. At night she sleeps with a pediatric respirator."

"I'm sorry," Annie whispered back.

"Don't be," Natalia answered. "Because of Maria, I understand special children. I could not ask for a more loving daughter. And you can see she's found an outlet for her energy. I'm very proud of her. As you will be of Max."

Annie nodded and wiped away a tear. How dearly she wanted her son to make such gains.

"The most important thing is to never give up," Natalia added and gave Annie's hand a gentle squeeze. Annie had not felt this kind of sisterly bond since her friend Carol had died. She was gaining reassurance and confidence in the hardest thing she had ever worked at—being a mother.

"Dr. Aponte, we're ready," the teacher who had been testing Max announced. Natalia gave her a nod, then turned to Annie. "Let's go see your son."

They walked over to where Max was staring at a block, a bright red star shape. He looked up with no expression and Annie, feeling a rush of emotion, hugged him. She held Max close. Though he did not respond to her hug, she felt he was pleased to see her.

The teacher who had been testing Max talked privately to Natalia for a moment and showed her the notebook with all of his given responses. Natalia went through it, then turned to Annie.

"Annie, let's go sit down."

At the far end of the room was a couch. Max stayed at his mother's side as they all sat down. Natalia looked one last time at the notes before speaking again.

"Okay," she said and made eye contact with Annie. "Hold on, it's not that bad."

Annie bit her lip and nodded.

"I mean it, Annie. Look, you know Max's physical condition from his MRI, right."

"Yes," Annie managed to whisper.

"The tests we did today were simply to determine where to begin."

"So?" Annie asked.

"Let me explain. The neocortex or what we call the thinking brain is the most recent in our evolution. It literally grew out of the emotional brain, or amygdala, part of the limbic system, which is centered deep in the brain. The reason for this is so that the primitive emotional brain can hijack the thinking brain during a burst of fear or rage or other emotional emergency where an instantaneous response might save one's life. That's the usual. But Max seems to react differently."

Natalia paused to touch Max's cheek. She smiled at him, but he failed to give her any emotional response in return. "As an example, a simple act like a smile normally will get a similar response in return. But with Max, it's as if he lacks the wiring to show his emotional brain. It's like his thinking brain has full control but no way to express it."

"Do you still think programming can help?" Annie asked.

"Absolutely. And we're going to start by keeping it simple. Something that stimulates both the neocortex and the amygdala."

Natalia paused and thought for a long moment. "Okay, I got it. Do you have a toy phone?"

"I think so."

"Good. It's important that it ring. We know his hearing is reliable. He is to hold the receiver to his ear and you talk to him. Smile, tickle him as you talk, try to reach his emotional brain through his intellectual. I want him to smile. And we both know, right now, a smile would be worth a thousand words."

"Yes, it would be." Annie hugged Max.

"Annie, one last thing. You'll be working with him six hours a day on this. It can become very stressful. It's important that you don't lose your control. When you feel your patience wearing thin, walk away, take a couple of deep breaths, go wash the dishes, whatever. It's going to take time. But the rewards are worth it, trust me."

"I do," Annie said. "Thank you."

Annie left with Max and walked to her Blazer. The rain was still falling in light sheets. The road had a slick shine to it. But instead of being depressed about the weather, Annie saw the rain as cleansing and renewing the earth, as hope reborn.

CHAPTER 13

PENSACOLA GENERAL HOSPITAL, PENSACOLA, FLORIDA

Palm trees lined the parking lot of Pensacola General. A thin, middle-aged woman stepped out of her old Chevy Nova and began walking toward the hospital entrance at the new wing.

Sarah-Jean Hall had called the hospital to check on her husband's status. Ed had been moved from intensive care, but she worried, felt an aching emptiness. Until the accident, she had never thought about what life would be like without him. She had not been on her own in more than forty years and suddenly the thought of losing him seemed impossibly hard. Who would she argue with, pray with, love? The hospital doors whooshed open and Sarah-Jean entered. She headed for the elevator and room 313.

Dr. Fire held Edward's hand and listened to his pulse with the stethoscope while the blood pressure cuff deflated.

"How'm I doing, Doc?" Edward whispered through a dry throat.

Fire smiled and grabbed a pen from her lab coat and wrote down his vitals on an official-looking clipboard. "Blood pressure one seventeen over seventy. Not bad, Mr. Hall. Tell me, how do you feel?"

Edward gave a wave of his hand at the oxygen tube running to his nose and at the saline IV hooked up to his left arm.

"It's a whole lot of nothing," he muttered.

Fire leaned down and carefully examined the red rash covering Edward's arms and face. All that was left of his EM radiation burn now looked more like a severe sunburn than anything unworldly.

"But I need to see the boy," Edward said.

"What boy would that be?" Fire asked.

"The boy the angel showed me. I must find him."

"What angel?" asked Fire, glancing toward the door where two Black Berets, McKenzie and Getz stood. They were both dressed in business suits and looked more like lawyers than the toughest security in the world.

"Don't listen to that crazy bastard," Brendan shouted from a bed behind the drawn curtain.

Fire pulled back the hospital drape. "And you must be the brother."

Brendan coughed as he sat up. "Brendan Hall. Who the hell are you?"

"I'm Dr. Fire. I was asked to determine if there was a need for a psychiatric review."

"Oh, there's a need all right. That son-of-a-bitch is nuts. Now I believe in God—angels too. But he's been telling everyone he's been dancing with angels. Well, I know what we saw and it wasn't any angel of God."

Fire looked surprised. "Really? Why don't you tell me what you saw, Mr. Hall."

"Don't listen to him, sister," Edward whispered. "My brother walks with the devil. He knows nothing. God forsakes those who do not heed his call."

"Oh, knock it off, Ed. That was no angel and you know it. It was some kind of aircraft, Doc. At first I thought it was an experimental out of Eglin, but when our fighters began firing on it,

I knew it wasn't ours. In truth, I don't think it was even from earth."

Fire took more notes, then asked, "Let me get this straight. Your brother thinks he saw an angel and you think—what? UFO?"

"Yeah. Now you're gonna think we're both nuts. Well, I'm not. I know what I saw. I never lost consciousness, not like Ed."

"When did your bother lose consciousness?" Fire asked sitting on the chair at the foot of Brendan's bed.

"Okay, it may sound strange, but it started with the light. Like a star at first, then it was more orangish in color."

"Venus?"

"No, not Venus. It made the night bright as day. Ed was in the thick of it, when this, this ship throws down a beam that just lifts Ed straight up—and holds him. He screamed like I haven't heard since we were kids, then nothing. I thought he was dead. He didn't move. He looked like a rag doll hanging from strings."

"What happened?"

"Well, the fighter jets came, Ed dropped to the boat and started mumbling about some boy he had seen. A minute later his eyes roll back and he's out of it."

"Do you know who the boy is?"

"Not a clue."

"Of course he doesn't know," Edward interrupted. "The angel gave *me* the vision. The boy is our salvation. Our salvation! But he is in grave danger," Edward whispered as loud as his hoarse voice would let him.

Fire glanced at him. "I'll get your statement in a minute, Mr. Hall." She returned to her questioning of Brendan.

"This craft—what did it look like?"

"It was covered in bright light—so bright, it was like looking directly at the sun. You just couldn't."

"And the Lord said, Thou canst not see my face, for no man shall see me and live. Exodus 33:20," Edward called out.

"You're wrong, brother. I did see a face."

"You did?" Fire questioned.

"Yeah, above the triangle of lights on the bottom were what looked liked a row of portholes, I saw something looking down."

"Tell me about it." Fire made a few more notes.

"It had a head and eyes, that's all I saw. I couldn't tell you if it was a human or a monster. But that ship—it was strange. I am sure we don't have that kind of technology."

"The U.S.?" Fire changed the page on her clipboard.

"No. Mankind. UFO, alien, whatever you want to call it, it wasn't from this world . . . Doc, you think we're both nuts?"

"Nuts? No. I have no idea what you saw, Mr. Hall, but there are similar symbolisms surrounding the UFO phenomena and religious experiences. A UFO is a machine, a technological artifact that embodies advanced science and advanced beings from another world, an aim we hope to re-create for our own future space travel. And like a religious experience, the need for exploring space grows from our desire for oneness with God, to reconnect with the cosmic order. In fact, the Latin *religio* means to reconnect." She paused and glanced back at Ed before continuing. "Religion, I believe, is the process by which man strives to link himself with the divine. Salvation is that moment we reconnect with God."

"But, *the boy is salvation,*" Edward whispered.

Fire stood up and moved over to his side. "Mr. Hall, I don't know what boy you are speaking of. Or how he fits into your story—you were, after all, alone with your brother on a boat. There's been no report of children missing at sea."

"He wasn't at sea. Oh, you're getting it all wrong. Lend me your pen—I'll draw you the face of this boy."

Fire turned to a clean sheet of paper on her clipboard and handed it to Edward. "You remember it?"

"I can't close my eyes without the Lord reveals the child's face." Edward began sketching. "Are you a religious woman?"

"Here he goes, Doc," Brendan warned. "He'll pass judgment on you faster than the Almighty himself."

Fire smiled. "I attended St. Mary's Catholic Girls School while growing up."

"Well, I trust you know the story of Lamech, Noah's father."

"Yes, I've heard of him."

"Do you know how Noah came to be with his father?"

"Why don't you refresh my memory?"

"I will, sister." Edward continued drawing the face of a small boy. "Lamech came home one day and saw a strange child at his door. He asked Bat-Enosh, his wife, who the child was. Without hesitation, she told him the boy was his. Lamech had been away on a long trip and he didn't believe it. He felt the boy looked much more like the sons of heaven than like man. His eyes—"

Edward began drawing in the large dark pupils on the child's face. "His hair—" He made quick soft strokes of wispy hair on the child. "His skin—" he continued, making no shading on the flawless face of Max. "Gave the boy an appearance that was unlike anyone in the area, much less like the Lamech family. But Lamech did accept him. Why? Because a wise man named Enoch felt the boy was the key to the great judgment when mankind and all flesh would be destroyed because it had grown corrupt and wicked. Lamech went home and recognized the child as his own and gave him the name Noah."

"Yes," Fire laughed, "and what a lovely shipbuilder he grew to be."

Edward stared hard at Fire, then handed back her clipboard. "The tongue of a serpent mocks the word of the Lord. This boy is our Noah. I'm certain."

Fire shook her head and turned her attention to the drawing. She stared at the face of the small boy.

Was it? No—it couldn't be . . .

She did not have a current photo of Max Katz. Andros had been careful never to disclose where the boy lived. But she knew the hybrid lived and now she had a drawing. Wesley had left her with a thick file of alien hybrid photos. They were all similar in appearance. She had studied the file for thousands of hours over the last thirty years. It had been part of the master plan to build a bio-weapon to protect mankind from these creatures.

If the old man was right and he did have a vision from the aliens, that meant the Bug Eyes were now looking for Max Carol

Katz. She could use this. Rats, at their best rate, took three weeks to spread the virus. A boy going into the complex could infect the aliens in one night. All she needed to do was poison the boy first, which meant she had to find him.

"Do you know this boy's name?" she asked Edward.

He shook his head. "No, ma'am."

"Just stick his picture on a milk carton," Brendan laughed.

"Quiet, heathen," Edward countered.

"He's my husband. Let me in!" Sarah-Jean demanded as she stood at the door.

"I'm sorry, no one is allowed to enter," the Beret answered, holding a firm hand across the doorway.

Fire turned toward the commotion and nodded to the Beret to let the woman in. "Please join us. I'm Dr. Katherine Fire."

Sarah-Jean smiled and pushed past the Beret. She shook Fire's hand. "I just want to see my husband, Dr. Fire."

"Of course you do. Which one is your—" Fire stopped as she saw Sarah-Jean clasp her hands over Edward's and they began to pray softly together.

"I see," Fire said.

"She's just as crazy as him, Doc. She believes this nonsense about angels and visions."

"Really?" Fire looked intrigued and turned back to Sarah-Jean. "Excuse me, Mrs. Hall, have you seen this vision yourself?"

Sarah-Jean looked up. "No, but I believe Ed. If he says the Lord spoke to him, He did."

"So you've never seen the boy?" Fire held up the drawing Edward had made. Sarah-Jean turned back to Fire. She was already shaking her head no, when she glanced at the paper and stopped.

"My goodness." Her voice trembled. She took the drawing from Fire and held it, then turned to her husband. "Is this your vision, Ed?" He nodded.

"You do know the boy?" Fire asked again.

"Yes," Sarah-Jean whispered. "That's our grandchild."

"What?" Fire asked, though she had heard it clearly enough.

"Max. He's our grandchild," Sarah-Jean answered.

"Well, that explains it," Fire laughed, trying to cover her own surprise. Then, as if to explain the situation to herself as well as to them, she said, "It's a simple transference from known reality to angelic hallucination."

"But I don't know that boy," Edward protested.

"Mr. Hall, how can you not know your own grandson?"

"Because he doesn't, Doctor," Sarah-Jean said. "Ed has never met him, nor even seen a picture of Max. He burned the only letter and photo my daughter sent regarding the boy."

"Son of man, thou dwellest in the midst of a rebellious house," Edward began. "Eyes to see, and yet see not; ears to hear and hear not."

"You feel this boy is evil?"

"No," Edward said as he wiped away a tear. "I've wronged him. I have borne false witness against my own blood. The Lord has raised a mighty savior from the house of David. And I have denied him." Ed began to sob as Sarah-Jean hugged him.

"Forgive me," he whispered.

"So I take it you're estranged. Do you have any other children?" Fire asked coldly from behind her clipboard.

"No, Annie is our only child." Sarah-Jean answered.

"I see."

Brendan waved at Fire to come over. "Listen, it would do a world of good if we could get out of here."

"I'll see what I can do," Fire replied, then stood to leave the room.

Down the hall Fire turned to her trusted Black Berets. "Today, gentlemen, is a good day. Mrs. Hall is about to lead us directly to the only known hybrid living among humans."

"How can she do that?" Getz, the taller of the Berets, asked.

"Because you're about to make her a widow and as a widow, she will seek comfort from her only child, Annie Katz, the mother of the hybrid. Do we have an understanding?"

Fire waited only a second for it to register with Getz and McKenzie, then added, "Good. You know what to do."

CHAPTER 14

211 DEMONG DRIVE, SYRACUSE, NEW YORK. 5:12 P.M.

Annie stepped over the clutter in the house. Stan's projects were running from room to room. Every security device he had bought had been only partially installed, leaving a wake of electronic gadgets still in and out of boxes. But Annie knew Stan felt better since beginning his project. And most important, he had left her alone to work with Max on programming.

Annie held out the toy phone as Dr. Aponte had suggested. "Ring, ring," Annie said, turning the bell; she put the receiver in his hand and held it to his ear. She leaned close and whispered, "Hello, Max. Answer me, sweetheart."

Max stared blankly ahead. He did not seem to register the phone, the gentle voice of his mother or even her fingertips as she tickled his stomach.

"Perfect little boy. Show me you can smile."

But Max did not. Annie did her best to shrug off her disappointment. There had been three days of programming with seemingly no effect. But once again, she began "Ring, ring," and put the receiver in his hand and lifted it to his ear.

"If only you could smile, Max," she whispered. "It would

make Mommy so happy." Annie continued the programming for the next hour. Then it was time to get dinner ready.

Annie walked across the oakwood floors to the kitchen, the only room in the house she had spent any money on. It had modern appliances, a stainless steel gas stove in a central island with a heavy brass hood. The dishwasher and refrigerator that fit into the custom cabinets were antique white. The real color in the room came from her potted herbs, which lined the bay window above the double sink. The smell of fresh basil, cumin, oregano and rosemary gave the room the fragrance of a summer garden.

Dinner, Annie decided as she pulled out her pots and pans, was to be a simple meal of chicken and rice. But, as with all of Max's meals, Annie blended everything together, creating a pitiful baby food mush. Stan would be home soon, and if she wished to avoid more fighting, it would be easier to have everything on the table. That was much like her own childhood, she suddenly realized, and wondered how Max might be affected by his parents sitting and eating in silence, avoiding direct eye contact. If there was conversation between them, it was a few words about the weather or news.

So this rainy evening Annie hurried to set the table, and was running the blender when the phone rang in the next room. She did not hear it ring and she did not see who answered it, but a few minutes later when she looked for Max she was surprised to see him standing by the phone.

"Max, it's time for dinner. Daddy will be home any minute," Annie said as she walked over to her son.

A warm red drip ran down Max's chin and hit the small puddle forming on the white tile.

"Max. You must be hungry, we worked— Oh my God," Annie said as she saw the blood on the floor. "Oh God." She ran to Max's side. "What happened, baby?" She could see it was dripping only from his left nostril.

She picked him up in her arms and for the first time noticed

the very real phone receiver dangling in his hand. "The phone?"
She picked it up out of instinct and held it to her ear. "Hello?"

There was no answer. Instead, on the other end of the line
was an odd series of bleeps and chirps that sounded like a strange
form of music. "I know that," Annie said aloud, before it even registered where and how she knew it. It had been the telemetry signal she had recorded at the observatory five and half years earlier.
It seemed a lifetime ago. "Hello," she whispered. But there was
no response. "It's not possible," she thought. The aliens were
gone. She had seen them leave. They were gone with no plans to
return. This was some kind of trick.

The Government.

Annie turned back to the phone. There was a small gray box
next to the phone. Another of Stan's security devices. Only this
one worked. The phone company had installed it. Caller ID.
Annie stared at the small green LCD screen. It would normally
list the number where that call originated—but now all it showed
was a blank screen. To the phone, there was no place of origin.
It was a dead line after the dial tone had clicked off. "You bastards!" Annie yelled into the receiver. "Leave him alone!" She
slammed the receiver down.

Max looked up at his mother. There was a change in his
face. Very slight. Annie was not even sure she had seen it. She
was emotional and rightfully so. Her son was covered with blood.

"Max, oh baby. Let's get you cleaned up." She picked him up
and carried him into the bathroom. She wiped his face, wrung
out the rust color from the white washcloth and held the cloth
under the cold water for a minute, then wiped his face again, his
head tilted back. The bleeding had stopped. Annie looked into the
bathroom mirror.

"Mama," she said aloud, surprising herself. She had caught
her own image and had remembered her mother, Sarah-Jean,
holding her after she woke up with her face matted with blood.
It was something the aliens had done. They had made it bleed.
But like a faded memory or dream, the pains of her childhood

had been pushed far away into her subconscious, and she was determined to keep them there.

"Annie, I'm home." Stan called out in the quiet house.

"In here," Annie said from the bathroom and continued to dry off Max's face.

"Hi. What's going on?" Stan asked from the hall.

"Max, ah, had a nosebleed."

"Was it serious?"

"Well, not really. You know how kids are."

"Did he fall down?" Stan asked.

"No—" Annie paused, not sure how Stan would react if she told him everything.

"So what happened?"

"Well," Annie smiled. "He, um, answered the phone."

"The phone?"

"Yeah, kind of a miracle. You know I've been working on programming him to do just that. Well, surprise, he did."

"So . . . Did he hit himself with the receiver?"

"I don't think so. I was in the kitchen cooking dinner, when—oh God, dinner!" Annie passed Max over to Stan and raced back toward the kitchen.

"Hey, big guy, your mom's lost it." Stan smiled and took a few seconds to look his son over. The bleeding had stopped. That was clear. In fact, the only evidence that Max had had a nosebleed were the brown stains on the washcloth.

Annie pulled a blackened chicken from the oven. "It's ruined. Oh, damn," Annie sobbed. "It's ruined."

Stan went over to her and put a hand on her shoulder. "It's okay. It's just chicken."

"You think it's just chicken, but it's . . . it's not about chicken. I mean, everything has changed." Annie found she could not control her emotions. She was crying when she really didn't want to, but she could not stop herself.

Stan hesitated for a second, then put his arms around his wife and hugged her. Much to his surprise Annie buried her head in his shoulder and sobbed. "I don't know, Stan. I just don't know. I can't stop crying. I can't control—" She snuffled and wiped at her stream of tears. "What's come over me?" She looked up at Stan, surprised to find his embrace felt good.

"It's okay," he whispered. "Everything is going to be okay." Stan had not held and comforted his wife in years and now she was in his arms.

"No, Stan," Annie whimpered. "It's—the phone call. Something happened—"

"The phone call?"

"Max answered—I took it." Annie paused again to weep, spitting out only a couple of words between sobs. "It just—"

"Who was on the line, Annie? What'd they say?"

"Nothing—strange clicks. It seemed . . . so strange." Annie began to cry more and she curled back into Stan's embrace.

"Was it—them?" Stan asked softly.

Annie paused, then nodded slowly.

"Oh Jesus," Stan whispered and looked down at his son.

Annie tried to block her thoughts, but again she remembered her terror. *A huge blue tank filled with hundreds of floating fetuses. So different with their enormous eyes and bizarrely proportioned heads. It was disturbing to look at them and she remembered running. She ran knowing her baby would be returned to her, but returned as one of them.*

Tears streamed down Annie's face. She had known all along that Max would be different, *part them, part her,* only now after the call, she finally acknowledged it. Stan held her close and she felt safe, safer than she had ever felt before, which was strange.

Because if she had learned anything today, it was that *they* were back and they knew where Max was.

Across the room, Max stood watching his mother and Stan. Something had happened from the sounds on the phone. He could smell the strange burnt odor of dinner. He could feel his mother's sadness and Stan's warmth. He could feel himself changing. *He felt alive!*

Like the caterpillar, born with the same DNA as a butterfly, an external force had triggered Max's transformation. He did not know why the sounds on the phone had begun this change. But he knew that it was the sounds, that with each strange click a new sense in his body was activated.

Max *felt* things.

Wonderful things. Smells, tastes and touches, feelings; emotions—joy, sorrow, anger, pity, love. Max looked at his mother and thought how happy she would be if she saw him smile. But she didn't see him. Her head was buried in Stan's shoulder. The sounds had done something to her, but he wasn't sure what.

Only he could feel them, like distant thoughts. He could sense how it pleased both of his parents finally to be in each other's arms. His mind flooded not only with his own emotions, but with those of his parents. For the first time in his life, Max had begun to understand people. He had taken the first steps in his need for total communication.

PERUVIAN ANDES, 13,500 FEET

The strange light filled the huge cavernous room. Jerry looked down and could see his feet and Eva's dangling over the pool they had both fallen into. The golden python lining the border of the pool seemed alive in the flickering light. He could feel Eva continue to struggle against the leather bindings that held them both to the wooden beams. The beams formed an X that crossed over the center of the pool. Jerry knew it was only a matter of time before she would have welts on her hands and slivers from the hard wood. He knew this, because he already had them. And if the pain wasn't enough, Jerry had guilt. He had failed to protect Eva. He had been unsuccessful in stopping the Indians from stripping off her clothes. Though she had not been raped, Jerry blamed himself for her violation. It was, after all, his curiosity that had led them to the cave. And while he too had been ceremoniously disrobed, he did not suffer the same embarrassment. Instead, he found himself becoming quite interested in the ceremony. It was as if he were outside his body watching the ritual take place below in an elaborate theater.

"Damn it," Eva said. "I'm cold, I ache, I want to go home. Tell 'em to let us go."

"Unfortunately, I don't believe that's the plan. This falls more into the ancient Moche custom."

"What custom is that? Stealing stupid Americans' clothes?"

"No, disrobing a defeated enemy before a ritual sacrifice."

"Come on, Jerry. If they were going to kill us they could have done that at the start."

"True—I'm probably way off base."

"Just in case, what is, ah, this Mocho custom?"

"Moche. Well, it's believed that the Moche presented their victims to the high priests and then slashed their throats and drank their blood. It's really no worse than the Aztecs pulling out the beating heart of a condemned man, or the Olmec sacrificing children for the spring rains. Mesoamerica was built on a river of blood."

"But we're in the twenty-first century. Why are they still doing it?"

"I'm working on that."

"No Jerry, no more Mr. Archeologist. I don't want to know why, I don't even care. What I want is for you to get us out of here."

Jerry had no new ideas. They were securely tied and guarded. If an escape was possible it would have to come later. There was really nothing he could do but watch the ceremony proceed. He strained to hear the conversation of the chief and his high priests. If only he could recognize a word, something to tell him the base language, then he might know what customs to expect.

Jerry found himself taking mental notes on the ceremony. The chief wore a silver conical helmet with a gold crescent-shaped headdress and a nose ornament that hung down low enough to cover his mouth. It was shaped like a fingernail moon. The chief paced beside the large stone table. *Pacing? Was the boss man nervous?*

The pacing produced a rattle from the chief's knee-length jade dress. The only pause in this sound was when he stopped to lift his gold scepter. The top of the scepter was an inverted four-sided pyramid, so highly polished it acted like a mirror, reflecting the light as clearly as any high-intensity flashlight.

And the source of the light—Jerry had never seen such strange illumination. The light emanated from a stone box at the base of the heavy table. It flickered like fire, but the core burned much hotter—almost pure white. Light escaped from the pattern cut into the box. Jerry was not sure, but the pattern appeared to be a bird inside a triangle.

Four priests came out of the third hallway. They moved in slow procession carrying on a platform one of the strange mummies.

"Hey, look at that," Jerry whispered.

"Jer, I can't see anything," Eva countered. Her view was limited to the back side of the pool.

"Sorry—well, they're moving out the mummies."

"Eww." Eva made a face. "Not over here."

"No."

"Good."

The priests placed the finely wrapped corpse carefully into the first of the seven golden chairs.

"Jer, you don't really believe they're going to kill us?"

"I don't know. I see aspects of several Indian cultures working here. It's almost as if they are following some earlier mother culture. Pre-Inca, pre-Moche, pre-Mayan, pre-Aztec."

"Oh, good. So we'll be going to a Mesoamerican afterlife."

"Look, if it helps any—I believe these people are descendants of whoever built these caves. That would make them master engineers, architects, astronomers and historians. As for human sacrifice? It's anyone's guess. But I was thinking—"

Eva struggled against her ties again. "Jerry, shut up."

The sun sank behind the Andes Mountains, casting the sky in deep purple hues. The first of the evening stars was visible.

The shoreline was dark and near the temple it was pitch black.

The dozen Indian warriors guarding the temple saw the lights descending from heaven, like pearls on a string. They seemed to be bright stars falling silently at first, then with the roar of beating wings. The warriors were too late in realizing that this was not their god.

"Alpha, this is Tango. We have targets in sector one," the commander of the Black Beret team rattled into his headset. Like the rest of his men, he wore the latest in Kevlar full-body armor. Inside their helmets they each had a heads-up infrared display, satellite radio linkup and a filter system to remove all chemical and biological agents from incoming air.

"That's a go, Tango. Repeat go. Subdue targets and secure area," Dr. Keller radioed back. He and Valerie watched as the two leading UH-60 Blackhawks settled down and the Black Beret teams fanned out.

"Without light," Keller explained, "our boys can see better than their targets." Keller pushed the button on the side of Valerie's helmet that activated her infrared display.

The two watched the Berets move through a field of blue-green brush and surprise the dozen reddish-orange figures. There was little struggle as the brave warriors went down.

"Dead?"

"No, just gas. They'll be out a good twelve hours."

"Primary area is secure," the voice on the radio crackled.

"That's a roger, Tango. Meet you inside," Keller responded. "Take us down." The third chopper began its descent.

Valerie stared out her window as the ground seemed to race up toward her. There was a hard thump and the loud whine of the rotors as the door opened. Keller held out his hand and helped her out. She could see the silhouette of the battered old temple against the reflected starlight. But she barely noticed what many others might have thought of as a beautiful scene. Only one thought crossed her mind.

Why would the aliens come here?

CHAPTER 15

The chief caught Jerry's attention again with a wave of his scepter. Jerry watched as several priests returned, rolling what looked like two large oblong tubes set at a forty-five-degree angle. They appeared to be made of gold, or a gold-colored alloy. Jerry did not recognize the markings on the sides, though if he had to guess, perhaps ancient Sumerian. But they were a long way from the Middle East.

A long braided cable ran from each tube and was carried by a priest following behind. Strange for a sacrificial altar, Jerry thought. In fact, the cables seemed oddly familiar. If he didn't know better . . . no, that was impossible, a bundle of braided fiberoptics?

"What are they doing now?" Eva asked.

"They're, ah, just setting something up."

"What?"

"I'll tell you when I figure it out."

The priests rolled the strange tubes over next to the heavy center table. All seven mummies were now assembled in the chairs. Other priests carefully unwrapped the fabric from around the heads of the mummies, revealing their deformities further.

Jerry knew that the early Indian Olmec sculptors were fascinated with dwarfs, hunchbacks, sufferers from Down syndrome. They felt wonder at any fellow human born with a deformity, and considered it a manifestation of the will of their god. Often the Olmec elite would mark themselves with physical deformities to set themselves apart from the peasantry. This quirk was passed on to other cultures such as the Mayan, Teotihuacan and Aztec. But while Jerry could understand the acts of body tattooing and skin piercing, these mummies were a far cry from the ancient Indian perversions.

The heads he and Eva had thought grossly misshapen under the heavy burial cloths were now being unwrapped and something pulled out—something *crystal?*

Jerry had heard about crystal skulls being found in various places throughout the Americas, the first in 1927 in a Mayan ruin in Belize. Several more crystal skulls had been unearthed in the mid-1950s in Mexico's Aztec ruins. The last was reported in the late 1960s by a deep-sea diver who claimed to have found it in a sunken pyramid off Bimini, Bahamas. All, Jerry believed, were nothing more than elaborate fakes, made solely for the purpose of quick sales to private collectors. Only these Indians by no means fit the profile of collectors.

Jerry noticed that the room had become very quiet. The chief stood before his tribe and spoke in a hushed voice.

"Jerry, I'm scared." Eva whispered.

"He's just talking. I don't—"

Jerry stopped in midsentence as the chief raised his scepter and the room's light source went from bright white to light blue. The crystal heads of the mummies suddenly took on an eerie glow.

"Oh my God," whispered Jerry.

"What? What is it?" Eva demanded. She struggled against her ties again. "Jerry, I don't want to die. I don't want to *die!*"

Inside the temple, several more Indians had been knocked out by the gas. Valerie stood next to Keller at the top of the well leading down into the cave. The Black Berets took their positions as they went below.

Valerie held a palm-sized magnetic sensor. "Well, it may not be radioactive, but the needle is pegged on the magnetic signature."

"That's what we're looking for." Keller waved his hand down. "After you."

Valerie smiled, then showed her athletic ability by jumping military style behind the Black Berets. Keller was right behind her. The hall seemed surreally lit from the enhanced reflected light on the wall.

"Look at this," Keller said into his headset. His gloved hand ran along the glazed wall. Valerie paused to look at the rock.

"Yeah?" she asked.

"You see any shovel marks?" He didn't wait for an answer. "No. Smooth as a baby's bottom."

"So?"

Keller shook his head. "So? What's with your MTV generation? This was not made by primitive Indians."

"You're saying it's like the Dulce base?" she asked, running her hand over the glasslike surface.

"Just like. From what I understand."

"So why did the aliens come here?"

"Why indeed. Come on."

Valerie caught herself wondering if the Bug Eyes were onto Fire's plans. Perhaps this was to be their evacuation site. Too bad she had not brought some K1397 with her. She could have contaminated the area herself. Her thoughts were interrupted by the small voice in her headset. "Alpha, this is Tango."

Keller answered, "Go ahead, Tango."

"We have a hostage situation."

Keller stopped dead in his tracks. Valerie turned and saw his face go slack. Obviously he had never taken another life. He was carrying his Glock like a soldier, but she figured him to be one of Andros's boys—a weak engineering nerd.

"Repeat, Tango," Keller said.

"Hostage situation, main cavity. Approximately a hundred unfriendlies, two hostages, nationality unknown."

"Any sign of the visitors?" Keller asked. There was a long pause before the radio crackled again and then it was only one word. "Unclear."

Keller glanced at Valerie, then bit his lip. If he had not been enclosed in his Kevlar body armor, she imagined he would have lit up his pipe and sat back to consider his strategy. But instead he surprised her.

"Tango, go ahead. Secure the area. Repeat, we're still go. Alpha out." Keller turned. "You don't have to do this."

"Please, you're not going to stop me from joining the fun." Valerie lifted her Glock .45 and pulled back the slide to chamber a round.

"Fun?" Keller questioned. But she was already four steps ahead of him and headed down the strange sloping hall.

Jerry stared in disbelief at the seven glowing skulls on the mummies seated around the table. Beside them, the high priests were standing by the strange tubes that were powered up and producing the thin, three-feet-long gold strips that had lined the library wall, with the strange form of writing stamped on them.

When one of the strips was complete the chief would hold it up and present it to his bowing warriors, then place it on the stone table next to the last.

"Eva, I think we've found the authors of that library."

"Forget it, Jerry. I'm about to get us out of here."

Jerry craned his neck and saw Eva had just about wiggled her bloody hands out from under the leather straps holding her to the heavy wooden beam. "You did it," Jerry said, surprised.

"Yeah," Eva gasped as she pulled her hands free. "Now, you ready to go?"

Eva slowly turned around and held on to the heavy wooden beam. Jerry was still tied and because he stood between her and the bowed warriors, no one noticed she had slipped her bonds.

No one but Tango, leader of the Black Berets. He and his men had silently penetrated the main cavern. Moving among the shadows they had come to within twenty feet of the fountain and forty of the chief. "In position. Let's do it."

There was the clatter of several tin cans hitting the walls and table. A thick oily fog spilled out from the canisters and quickly filled the room. The warriors were on their feet and the chief had turned his attention to his golden scepter. A bright light was building around the head of it and the chief's face was growing darker as he raised the scepter—

Jerry spotted the red dot of a laser sight on the chief's forehead. "No—" he screamed, but watched helpless as the chief's head snapped back as though struck by a hammer, and his scepter dimmed.

"Run, Eva," Jerry coughed through the oily fog. *"Run!"*

Eva pulled on Jerry's leather ties, but found the very act of standing up becoming impossibly difficult. "I can't," she said. The smell of slightly metallic cinnamon was suddenly replaced with the cool sensation of water floating over her. She felt relaxed, calm, and her lips formed a serene smile as she slipped along the side of the pool and finally under the water.

Jerry struggled with his legs. For some reason, they didn't work anymore. He saw Eva in the pool. She was drowning and there was nothing he could do but hope that the methodically advancing black-clad figures would save her. He couldn't.

211 DEMONG DRIVE, SYRACUSE, NEW YORK

Annie stepped out of her hot bath and felt a little better. She could hear Stan in the bedroom with the TV on. This was the first night in a long series of nights that he was not running back to the office. It felt good to have him home. It felt— She paused and realized she had become overly sensitive lately.

She reached for her warm terry cloth robe. There was something about the texture of terry cloth that made her feel safe. She tossed the blue bath towel at the clothes hamper, but missed. When she bent to pick it up she found Stan's office shirt. It had caught her eye primarily because of the red on white. The same color as Max's blood on the washcloth. Only this was a shirt and lipstick.

"Stan?" she muttered, as it began to sink in. "Stan!" she said a little louder, now marching toward the bedroom. "Stanley Jacobs Katz!" She held out the shirt with such a combination of hurt and anger that Stan just stared blankly.

Busted.

He could see the lipstick. He hadn't seen it when he had taken the shirt off, but it was clearly there now. "Oh," he said. "Uh-oh."

"Stanley, why? No, who? No." She shook her head and sat down on the foot of the bed. "How could you?"

"You"—he paused, then finished sadly—"didn't need me."

"The hell I didn't." Annie stood up and threw the shirt at her husband. "You can't blame this on *me!*"

"Annie, I'm sorry. I truly am sorry." Stan stood up and took a step closer to Annie. But she stepped back.

"Sorry? How can sorry—" Annie started to cry. "You want a divorce? That's what you want! Because this marriage is over. I mean, how am—"

"No. I don't want a divorce. I love you."

"You have a hell of a way of showing it."

"You haven't been— Look at us, Annie. When was the last time we made love? Talked? Laughed? Cared? This is not one-sided. I was there for you, but you turned me away. Yes, I found someone else—but it was never like with you and me. I wanted it to be you and me. I don't care about her. It's over."

"Over? That isn't going to work, Stanley. You can't betray me, say it's over and expect it to be all okay."

"What do you want, Annie?"

"What do I want? What do I *want?*" She wiped her tears. "I don't know what I want. I guess—start by sleeping downstairs."

"Fine. It won't be the first time," Stan mumbled and turned away. He left Annie and grabbed a blanket and pillow from the closet. Downstairs, he did not pull out the couch into the sleeper. Like all sleeper sofas it was more comfortable to sleep on as a sofa than as a bed.

But Stan was in no mood to sleep. He wanted to talk. He wanted to explain. He wanted everything back to normal. But of course they couldn't go back, and there had never been a normal.

Stan paced the room then turned and headed down the hall to his son's room. *How would he explain this to Max? Mommy kicked Daddy out. Mommy hates Daddy. Daddy's real sorry.*

The door to Max's bedroom was open a crack so Stan peeked in, glad it was dark so that his son could not see his tears. He hadn't meant to hurt Annie, hadn't meant for things to get out of hand. Worst of all, Stan realized he would lose his son—not in some covert government game or strange alien abduction, but in a Syracuse court, where his infidelity would bring only more pain.

"Max?" Stan whispered. His eyes adjusted to the darkness and he could see the sheets kicked back from the boy's bed and the bed empty. "Max?" Stan clicked on a light and blinked as his eyes readjusted. The light only confirmed it.

Max was gone.

"Annie!" Stan yelled from the bedroom. "Annie, come here—now!" Stan turned and raced to the foot of the stairs. He looked up at his wife standing on the landing. She was still mad, but he didn't care. "Max is gone."

"What?"

"He's not in his room."

"Oh God," Annie said and flew down the stairs. "I'll look in all his hiding places." She began opening closets, looking under tables. But Stan was right, the boy was gone.

Stan checked the front door—locked. Windows, closed. They met in the kitchen as Annie reached for the phone to dial 911.

At the crack of distant thunder, they both turned and saw the back door standing open. "Did you—?" Stan started, but

Annie was already shaking her head no. She put down the receiver and both ran into the rain and black of night.

"Max!" Annie screamed.

No answer.

How do you find a child who cannot speak? She scanned the yard for movement and found only the sway of the large oak tree. She could see Stan down at the edge of their property. Their back yard butted up against two hundred undeveloped, heavily wooded acres. When they bought the house, they had fallen in love with the idea of Bambi coming to visit. But now the beautiful woods were an area of terror. Their son was lost in there. Lost and alone. She ran down to join Stan.

"Come on. We'll find him," he said and took her hand as they entered the woods.

CHAPTER 16

Peruvian Andes, 13,500 feet

Jerry realized he was lying flat as he awoke from a faraway place, a cool dark place, where his sleep had been blurred with nightmare. He remembered Eva slipping underwater in the pool, lacking the strength to pull herself up, and then her body gagging in convulsions as her lungs filled with water. He had to find her. He had to help.

Jerry lifted his head and felt a deep throbbing pain race from behind his eyes and down his spine to an electroshock at the base of his feet. Struggling against the pain, Jerry took a deep breath and became aware of his terrible rasping thirst. His tongue was thick and dry. He felt as much like roadkill as one could and still be breathing. Breathing . . . There was cool air coming from the oxygen mask covering his face. His eyesight was blurred, but his other senses were functioning. He could feel the warm thermal blanket over his skin and there was an antiseptic taste in his mouth. He understood someone was taking care of him, but he had to find Eva.

Not wanting to repeat the pain of seconds before, Jerry chose to turn his head. There were strange sounds all around him. The loudest was on his right. He gritted his teeth to avoid screaming, and pivoted. Then he saw her.

Eva lay naked on her side on a gurney. A man stood over her with his back to Jerry. He was dressed in a solid black uniform which gave no clue to his identity. There were several medical machines running. One held the steady ping of a heartbeat. Eva's heartbeat. She was alive.

Jerry felt a joyful tear roll down toward his ear as he mumbled a quick prayer of thanks. Everything was going to be okay. Everything. It was then, when he reached to wipe the tear, that he found his wrists handcuffed.

Adrenaline is a funny thing, nature's way of helping you realize you're caught. Jerry not only understood this, but was struggling with it. Perhaps it was the adrenaline or the drugs finally wearing off, but one thing was certain. Jerry's head was clearing and his eyesight improving.

He now recognized the room they were in. He had called it the Inca's library, though in truth he had known the Incas had very little to do with it. And he could now see that the man in the black uniform was not a man, but an attractive young woman. What Jerry could not see was what the woman was doing to Eva. She held something in her hand, something like a needle, twisting it just between Eva's shoulder blades.

In the main chamber, the thick oily smoke still permeated the room. The Black Berets were in the process of mopping up, moving the warriors' bodies into neat rows against the wall.

Keller, however, was unaware of anything but the RPSU monitor. The remotely piloted science unit was a triangular machine about the size of small dog, with four wide wheels, a set of diamond-grade drills and more computing power than two mainframes. It had been designed by NASA for future space probes because of its ability to withstand extreme heat, cold, radiation and atmospheric pressure. Right now, however, it was drilling a core sample out of the strange light source under the table.

The glowing crystal skulls on the mummies had faded and the machines had stopped producing the strange strips with the ancient writing. Keller had collected the strips and placed them in his duffel bag.

He had wondered about the use of the crystal skulls. He had heard that a team at Hewlett-Packard was working on replacing the microchip with quartz crystals and finding that crystals using laser optics were almost a million times faster than any chip using an electrical pulse. Was this an alien computer? If so, why shape the crystals like human skulls? And what was this writing?

With a beeping sound from the RPSU unit, the diagnostic system came on line. In a moment they would at least know what the power source was. Keller watched closely as the remote monitor fed the numbers crossing the top of the screen. It registered surface pressure, core temperature, escaping radiation, electromagnetic field levels. The bottom half of the screen was a computer graphic of the drill's progress through the target.

"How's it going?" Valerie's voice crackled though the headset.

Keller turned and saw that she had joined him. "Good. We're almost through the casing. Any luck reviving the girl?"

Valerie smiled. "Yeah, but luck had nothing to do with it."

"You're awfully young to be that overconfident."

"Arrogant, then." She stepped closer. "I know what I'm doing. They're ready to answer our questions." Valerie glanced at the screen. "That magnetic signature is through the roof."

"Yes. It seems like—a fixed source of electromagnetic energy." Keller watched as the computer graphics showed the drill entering the core. A high-pitched hum came from the machine twenty feet away.

"My God," Keller mumbled as the periodic table showing the chemical makeup of the power source raced at the top of the screen. The atomic weight rose steadily: 103, 104, 107, 109, 114. It held steady at 115.

"Jesus God. It's 115." Keller turned to Valerie. "Do you know what that means?"

"What?"

"I've only theorized about element 115, because it would be impossible to synthesize here on earth. Fact is, it would take millions of years and an infinite amount of power to bombard atoms with protons enough to produce a substance that superheavy. We always suspected the *visitors* mined it naturally, maybe next to a larger sun, or a binary star system, or even a supernova. But I never thought we would get our hands on it. It's— The most advanced element we've ever created is 109, with an atomic weight of 266, electron configuration of 32-15-2."

Valerie put her arm around Keller's shoulder. "Doc, you're babbling. What's it mean?"

"It means, Ms. Ross, that we finally have the power source to run those nine scout ships back home."

"Oh."

"Yes, oh. After a hundred years of aviation, from the Wright brothers to the Aurora, we're still approaching flight the same way, pushing air over a fixed wing. But with this electromagnetic energy we can take the next step. It's—it's a completely new understanding of flight. It's a big, big step. The equivalent of, well . . . take computers fifty years ago. They weighed sixty tons, took up a whole building and cost ten million dollars."

"Now they fit in the palm of your hand."

"Precisely. With that kind of jump in aviation, a jet would fly a thousand miles on a single gallon of fuel and carry ten thousand people." Keller stared hard at Valerie. "You don't get it?"

"Sure I do. You finally got batteries for your toys."

Keller laughed. "To the point, my dear. Okay." Keller typed in some new commands for the RPSU. "Tango, this is Alpha one. Pack it up and let's get out of here."

"That's a roger, Alpha one," the head of the Black Berets answered. His men began boxing the artifacts and brought in a special crate for the power source. Valerie picked up a gold strip from Keller's bag. She looked at the strange writing. "What about our interrogation?"

"Yes, very good." Keller turned back to her. "Where have you put our guests?"

Valerie smiled. "A cozy little dungeon down the hall." She took the strip of alien writing with her and headed back toward the Inca library.

211 DEMONG DRIVE, SYRACUSE, NEW YORK

"Max!" Annie yelled, stumbling through the woods in the dark. She could see Stan off to her left, his white shirt occasionally moving past the pine trees into clearings. "Find anything?" she shouted over to him. He was twenty feet away, but in the dark twenty feet seemed impossibly far.

"No, nothing," Stan returned.

"Damn." Annie pushed her way through new heavy brush but as she came out the other side she felt the ground give way and before she could catch herself she slid downhill in the mud. She let out a loud scream and clawed at the side trying to grab hold of something, but the roots all slipped by or broke off. Then with a splash she landed in a fast-moving river of muddy rainwater at the bottom of a ravine.

"Stanley!" she yelled as she bobbed up from the icy water. "Help me!" The river of mud carried her quickly away. "Help!" The taste of gritty earth filled her mouth as the stream washed over her. When she surfaced again she was coughing. *Swim, Annie,* she told herself and instead of fighting the current she moved with it downstream, slowly making her way to the other side.

Bam, crack! There was an incredible pain in Annie's shoulder and side as she slammed up against a fallen pine tree. It must be shattered, she thought, but she looked at her fingers and found they could still move. The muddy water whipped past her. At least with the tree holding her, she was not being carried farther downstream. She caught her breath and then called out, "Help! Stanley, help!"

Her eyes scanned the ridge above, but she saw nothing moving in the dark. "Where the hell is he?" she mumbled and stared in the direction from which she had come. What if he hadn't heard her? What if—no, she could feel her panic rising, her heart pounding. *No, he must have heard. Okay. Stay calm. Okay. Scream!*

"Stanley!" Just then, she saw the white shirt against a bush on the other side. "Stan, over here!"

She grimly waved. "Stan!"

He turned in her direction and paused, then waved back.

"Oh, thank God," she said and watched him move toward her at the top of the ravine. Only now they had a very real problem. They were on opposite sides of the river of mud. She would have to swim to him if he was going to help her. Annie waited until Stan stood directly across. There was a ten-foot drop from where he stood at the top, down to her at water level. It was too far to reach even if she were on the other side.

"You okay?" he shouted.

"Yes," she answered, feeling happy not to be alone anymore. "But I'll have to swim back. If you came in, we'd both drown."

Annie did not want to let go of the pine tree. The other side had nothing to grab. As far as the eye could see there was only a wall of mud. She would have to continue downriver. "I'm scared," she called out.

"I know. But you're right. I can't help, unless you come to this side. There will be a handhold ahead. There has to be."

"Okay. Okay, But don't lose me."

"Never." Stan stood up as Annie kicked off from the tree. She could feel the river again pulling her downstream, but this time she could see Stanley running along the bank.

INSIDE ALIEN SHIP, LOW ORBIT, SPACE

Max was cold and wet standing in the gray fog-filled room, but he did not complain. He had followed the bright light that called him into the woods. Then when he had stepped into the beam of light, his breath seemed to be sucked away. His stomach twisted and he felt like his skin was shaking. But the whole time he had kept his eyes open and had seen the world below him—trees, the tops of houses, the lights of the city—disappear. Then suddenly he was in a round room. There were two windows to the side and he could see the stars. They were more clear than ever before. Bright round points of light against a black sea.

Do not be afraid, came a voice in his head. Max turned and saw two short men standing behind him. They were dressed in gray one-piece suits and had large peaceful dark eyes.

Max was not afraid.

One held out his hand and seemed to smile. *Come.*

Max took the being's hand and started toward a doorway. The next room was dome-shaped and had railing running along the wall. There were naked people in this room. Some were lying on tables, others seemed asleep in chairs. There was a chattering of clicks and hums as doctors worked on them.

Max sensed the silent communication between them. A woman over to the right screamed in her mind, *Stop, stop. You have no right.* The doctor told her he did have a right. That she was theirs and what she had in her was theirs. And that despite the woman's protests, they would take it. The woman's screams ended when the doctor leaned close and stared deep into her eyes.

Come, said the small man to Max. They moved to a table that was empty. Two more little men joined them and all helped remove Max's wet nightshirt and his Batman underwear. With little effort they lifted Max onto the table. Max turned and saw a large black man with a beard lying on the table next to him. While the little doctors worked on him, the man seemed to be asleep.

Then the small man, the one Max now felt was a doctor, leaned in by him and blocked his view of the room. All he could see were the liquid black pools of the being's eyes. Max felt a sense of peace come over him. The doctors then turned him over on his side and began their examination. He felt their fingers run down his spine and heard in his head their thoughts. They were counting his bones, then checking his arms, legs and ankles and finally his head. They worked a long time on his head. There was a long silver rod that they held behind his ear that gave a tickling sensation. Finally the being said, *It is done.*

What? Max asked and in his mind he heard.

Time to begin.

Begin what? Max asked again, but this time there was no answer. He held still for what seemed a very long time. Finally the doctor helped him up and off the table. They put his nightshirt back on and to his surprise it felt warm and dry. The doctor then took his hand and led him out of the room.

They entered a hall. At the end Max could see a blue light coming from the wall.

Max's shuffle quickened and he found deep in his memory a strange feeling. *I know this place,* he thought. *From my dream.*

The bluish glow from the wall grew more intense as they came up on a huge glass fishtank. There were symbols embedded in the wall panel by the tank. Max stopped the little doctor and stared at the symbols. He could understand them. Read them without stumbling. No struggle. It was as clear as if he heard it.

This was life support.

That is correct, the doctor said.

Max assumed it was for the fishtank. He wondered if such a big tank would have big fish. Max took a dozen more steps and stood on his tiptoes to peer in. His face was bathed in blue light and his eyes widened with surprise.

There were no fish. The tank was different from the one at school. Here the water was alive. Bubbles everywhere and hundreds of floating—*babies!*—babies in small clear tubes bobbing on thin lines. Each baby had its own light rising from the bottom of the tank. Max stared at the babies.

How beautiful, he thought. Their gray skin was wrinkled and they had large peaceful eyes. Then a feeling hit him. It hit harder than any emotional thought before.

I'm home.

Yes, answered the small doctor beside him. *Come.*

The doctor led Max past the tank and into the next room. Here, Max saw a raised tier with many machines staged around it. Several small creatures stood in the center. They looked like the doctor—except one slightly taller with lighter gray skin.

Hello, Max, the taller one said without moving his permanent smile. Max stared up at him, wondering how it knew his name. But before he could ask, the being said, *Come to Father.*

Father, Max repeated and in his heart he felt it true. He climbed the stairs and stood before the reptilian being. He felt the long thin fingers brush the hair from his temple. *Behold,* Father said and suddenly Max's mind swirled with visions. A huge wonderful calm ocean, a large white bird and in the distance majestic green mountains. It was beautiful. Peaceful. A place for the children.

Why? What is going to happen? Max asked. *Why me?*

You will know in time.

Just then, the small doctor placed a hand on Max's shoulder and led him back down the stairs. *It is time to go.*

Max turned and looked one last time at the being on the raised tier. *Father,* he thought and tears came from his eyes. The doctor tugged at his arm and Max followed. He wiped the tears, annoyed at the sticky wet on his face. Then, looking at his hand, he realized what tears meant.

He was crying, really crying.

He smiled.

CHAPTER 17

PERUVIAN ANDES, 13,500 FEET

Jerry stared at the black uniforms, his face reflected in the glossy sheen of their helmets. Even though the closer of the two showed curves in the uniform that indicated a woman, Jerry was beginning to think of them as twenty-first-century storm troopers. The commander, the taller one, so intent on asking the hard questions, paced behind the woman.

"Look, I'm telling you," Jerry said, trying again to get it through their thick dull heads, "I don't know. I can't figure out the writing. I really wish I could." How he wished he could see their faces. It would help ease the fear building in his stomach.

"How long are you going to ask the same questions? We're telling you everything," Eva added. She sat next to Jerry on a stone table in the library. Both had blankets over them, but Eva was still shivering.

"We're sure you are. But you have to understand that what you have said is, well, unbelievable," Keller continued. "Now, not to dwell on it, but the writing—you're clear that it came from those machines out there."

"Yes," Jerry said, and pointed to the thousands of gold strips on the wall. "I know it's not Incan, Aztec, Mayan or any other ancient Mesoamerican language. But if you look at the maps on the wall—"

Keller turned to the library wall while Valerie kept her Glock pistol trained on her captives.

"You think those are maps?" Keller asked, stepping closer.

"Yes," Eva answered. She started to stand but Valerie threw her foot against Eva's shoulder, shoving her back down. "I told you to sit."

"Look, I'm not a dog and you can stop being a bitch. We just want to go home."

Valerie pulled back the slide on the Glock and held it to Eva's ear, then whispered softly, "I could put you to sleep now, but we want answers."

"Then shoot," Eva dared, staring at her.

"Shut up!" Jerry cried. "She saved your life."

"No, Jerry. She just prolonged the misery." Eva turned, and Jerry could see tears streaming down her cheeks. "I don't care. I just don't care." Jerry put his arm around Eva and pulled the blanket up over her shoulders.

"Professor Sorich, we're all very tired," Keller began again. "I would like to end this as fast as you. Now, I don't recognize these plates as any kind of maps—"

"That's because they're ten thousand years old," Jerry answered. "Eva's a geologist. She identified them as the continents after the last great flood."

Valerie glanced at the maps. "They look like ink blots to me."

"We don't have any reason to make this up," Jerry countered. "Take them, run a computer comparison. I think what you'll find is this is maybe some kind of warning."

"Warning?" Valerie questioned.

"Of what?" Keller asked.

Jerry could see he had sparked their interest.

"It's not news that humans have produced a greenhouse effect on our environment. Now I don't know what the writing says, but just finding these maps is significant. These things don't just happen. We were meant to find them."

"What are you saying?" Valerie asked.

"I'm saying, maybe these maps aren't just our past, but our *future*." They stared back at him dumbly, and Jerry shook his head and tried again. "Listen, if we were any other tourists would we have found these caves? Would we have recognized the maps? No. And how did you know to come here?"

"That's classified," Valerie answered.

"Right, we saw the alien ship." Eva tossed her head back and looked up at the woman soldier.

Valerie turned to Keller. "Security breach. You know the procedure."

"No. They're not about to talk." Keller wanted to stop the escalation of ill will. "It would ruin their professional academic standing."

Valerie shook her head. She had seen Keller for what he was—weak. But it didn't matter now, she had already planted a microtransmitter on Eva. They could track her at any time and send in a wet team. Just as Fire had planned.

Jerry stared at the woman's gun. "None of this happened. We saw nothing, really."

Jerry watched as the man and woman stepped back and whispered. Finally the woman stormed off.

"Hey, Eva, she's as pigheaded as you," Jerry joked, thinking it would raise Eva's spirits.

"Then it's not over," Eva said wearily.

211 DEMONG DRIVE, SYRACUSE, NEW YORK. 9:25 P.M.

Annie reached up from the bank for Stan's arms above. They were both covered head to toe in mud and she could feel his hands starting to slip as he tried to gain a grip. For the last hour, she had clawed her way along the rain-filled ravine, sometimes finding a place to hold on, only to slip and fall back into the river. Fatigue had set in and her muscles ached.

"Stanley, I'm not gonna make it," Annie said as she watched his grip slip from her elbows to her wrists.

"Yes you are," Stan told her. "If you drop, I might not find you again."

"I just can't," Annie cried, hands cramped from the hold.

"Give me a chance," he said and squeezed more tightly to hold on. "I'm not letting go."

Annie glanced down and saw the rainwater racing below. The last time she fell it had been up to her shoulders. Soon it would be over her head. The current had carried her hundreds of yards and she had no idea where she was.

An unspoken but very real fear was that Max had fallen in before her, that the time Stan spent trying to save her might have saved their son. Thinking about this gave her a burst of adrenaline. "Okay, Stan." She could see the strain on his face. "Give it one more try."

"On the count of three!" he shouted.

Annie dug her feet against the muddy slope and tried to gain a toehold.

"One, two—"

The dirt crumbled and she felt herself drop.

"Thr-EE!" Stan screamed and fell back still holding her wrists. Annie cleared the lip of the bank.

"Oh, thank God," she mumbled and crawled a few feet farther before collapsing beside him.

"You okay?" he asked.

She nodded and he put his arm around her. It felt good. She looked at him and realized just how much he meant to her. It wasn't just saving her life, but that he never gave up. Maybe she had been wrong. The pain and betrayal of earlier in the evening seemed a lifetime ago.

They sat to catch their breath and listened to the forest. The rain, the wind, the smell of wet earth. Nothing gave a clue to where Max might have gone.

"Stanley, it's too dark, too dangerous. We need help if we're going to find Max."

Stan nodded. The lights from their house and the neighbors' had long since disappeared behind the thick brush. "Annie," he said helping her up, "we will find him."

DREAMLAND BASE, GROOM LAKE, NEVADA

The warning siren and contamination code was blinking outside Sonny's chamber. Andros entered the heavy double steel doors wearing a white bio-hazard suit. There were three Black Berets lying on the floor of the chamber. Two had followed their captain in, as good soldiers charging into battle. But their enemy was invisible and with every breath they took, it attacked. They were the first three casualties of a secret little war.

Andros had avoided their fate when he checked the contamination code and discovered that the computer had listed a high level of sarin, an organic chemical similar to some pesticides, but much deadlier. And while the Nazis had invented it, its most recent use had been in a subway in Japan. Unlike the sarin of yesterday, this one was mixed with several other unknown chemicals. Andros could only guess at their effects.

He leaned over the only Beret who was still conscious. The trooper wore captain's bars. It was Glen Sweigart, the Black Beret whom Andros had hand picked for his loyalty.

"What happened, Captain?"

Sweigart was covered with sweat. His breathing was shallow, rapid. "Sir, Sonny was sick. We tried—"

"I know you did. But now we have to help you. Tell me what happened. Were there any fumes?"

"Just a bad smell."

"What did it smell like?"

"Rotten fruit—garlic. Colonel, he died as we got to him."

Andros nodded. He knew sarin caused respiratory failure. Death was almost instantaneous. The fact that Sweigart had lasted this long meant that this bio-weapon was intended to have a delayed reaction.

"Your men . . . what happened to your men?"

"The syringe in the med-pack. They got a blood sample—and passed out. It's in the blood."

The Captain's body began to shake violently. Andros grabbed the med-pack kit and pulled out a blood pressure/heart rate kit. He held the Captain down while the arm cuff automatically inflated. The small electronic screen gave his rapidly changing vitals.

"Ninety over 60, 86, 73, shit, the blood pressure is dropping." Andros switched to the heart rate and watched it rocket: 120, 138, 142. "Jesus—easy, Captain." Andros held Sweigart down. The Captain's convulsions continued getting stronger. "Sweigart, listen to me. I need you to—"

But that's all Andros got to say. The Captain's eyes rolled up as his heart rate flat-lined. The Captain was dead and there was nothing Andros could do about it.

Andros stared down at his friend for what seemed an impossibly long time, then finally let go. He glanced around the chamber. What the hell had happened? Three good soldiers were dead—and Sonny. Why in the world would someone go to all this trouble to kill a monkey? What purpose was behind this bio-weapon? And most troubling—*who in MJ-12 was behind it?*

He paused as he realized he had no idea who had done this, or how many others might be sympathetic. In the shadow world of intelligence and black projects, relying on the wrong person could be deadly.

Andros let out a large breath. He had to do this by himself. The stakes were too high. He was on his own. He trusted no one until he could find the traitor.

He started for the door when he saw the sample of Sonny's blood lying on the floor. He picked it up and found the light reflecting off some manila-colored particles floating in the blood. "What the hell?" he mumbled, then headed for his lab.

211 Demong Drive, Syracuse, New York.
11:07 p.m.

Annie could just make out the lights of their house as she and Stan came out of the forest. After two and a half hours of searching, they had failed.

"I'll call the police and Fire Rescue. You see if any of the neighbors saw anything," Stan suggested.

Annie nodded. She was beyond tired, she was totally drained. But as they passed a huge old pine tree and headed for the house, she stumbled to a stop. A blindingly bright light streamed down in the clearing of their backyard.

Stan held a hand up to shield his eyes, then followed the beam up to the huge delta-shaped craft in the sky. He was stunned, then he heard Annie's scream.

"Max!" He glanced down to see Annie running toward the light.

Max had kept his eyes closed and felt a tickling in the pit of his stomach and then the wet ground under his bare feet. He was through. He could smell the rain, though it wasn't falling on him. The light flickered off above and he stood in the dark. He looked up and saw the huge black triangle rising silently into the sea of stars. Then in a flash of bright orange it streaked across the night and disappeared.

"Max! Max!" Annie shouted as she came upon him. Max turned and looked at his mother. He could read her thoughts instantly. He knew what she had been through and how worried she had been.

"Max, honey," Annie said and slid down next to him. She wrapped him in her arms and hugged him.

"I'm okay," he whispered in a small clear voice. He felt a thrill in hearing his thoughts come out with a breath.

Annie clutched him tightly to her and then it hit her. "What?" she asked and leaned back to look at Max. "What—did—you—say?"

Stan fell to his knees beside them and gave them both a hug.

"I'm okay now," Max answered.

Annie glanced at Stan. His expression mirrored her own thrilled shock. "He spoke," Stan muttered, and turned to Max. "You actually talked."

Max could feel his mother's and Stan's delight and he smiled. It was a beautiful, innocent smile. Annie grinned and hugged her son. This was the happiest moment in her life. "You smiled. Max, you can smile."

The little boy looked up and pointed at the stars. "Yes. I go home. Home."

A moment passed and it dawned on both Annie and Stan what he meant. Their eyes lifted to the night sky and both felt their stomachs drop. "Oh my God," Annie whispered, and Stan said, "Let's get inside."

Stan stood and helped her up and they headed back to the house, keeping a wary eye on the sky.

Annie sat at the kitchen counter with Max. She grabbed a heavy towel and wiped the mud off her face and glanced at her son. He was really there, home safe and sound, something she had not believed possible only minutes earlier.

There was the slam of a door closing, a ticking of locks being bolted and the zip of shades being drawn. Annie knew that Stan was in a panic to protect his family. But what had happened was already over. They had returned Max unharmed. In fact, they had returned him talking and showing emotion. Annie felt a great sense of excitement. She sat next to Max and looked into his dark eyes.

"You're really okay?" she asked slowly.

Max nodded.

"Did they"—she paused, trying to find a way to word her own fears—"touch you?"

Max nodded again. "Doctors."

"Bastards," she mumbled. They had no right to touch her

son. No right. Memories of her own childhood physical examination came crashing back. *She lay cold and naked on a low table, while long gray fingers poked, touched or made small incisions on the soles of her feet, calf and thigh muscles, back of knees, spine, arms, rib cage, neck. Finally they came to her head. The beings examined her eyes, nose and throat, forcing a wad of material into her throat until she thought she would choke. Removing it, they examined her teeth and gums. All the time, the little doctor had promised he would not hurt her, but she was terrified.*

This was a feeling Max couldn't quite understand yet, but he did see her thoughts in his mind. He tried to calm her. "I met Father."

"Father?" Annie asked, as she woke from her memory.

Max nodded slowly. "In the stars."

"Oh—no." She was not ready for this. She was not ready for what it meant. She wanted to believe the boy was hers and Stanley's, not some alien mix. "No, Max. Daddy is here. Your daddy is right here. Stanley!" Annie shouted. "Come here."

A minute later Stan stood beside his wife and son at the dinner table. He put a hand on Annie's shoulder and gave a small squeeze. "Yes, honey?" he asked.

Annie looked up at Stan. Her eyes were pleading but serious. "We need to know what they have done. A few more tests," she said. "Tomorrow. Please?"

Stan nodded. "Agreed."

CHAPTER 18

GULF BREEZE COMMUNITY CEMETERY, GULF BREEZE, FLORIDA

Sarah-Jean looked down at her black dress. She had not worn black since her mother's death when she was a child. For precisely that reason she had nothing black in her wardrobe. She had gone to the mall, hardly knowing what she was doing, just to find something to wear for today.

Everything had happened so fast. Edward and Brendan had survived their boating ordeal only to die a day later in a car crash. God had taken his good shepherd home. Sarah-Jean honestly believed that. She did not question why or how Brendan had lost control of his car. In fact, everyone seemed surprised at how well she was taking all of this.

Two dozen people had gathered for the funeral service. Most were Brendan's friends, but they had come by to see her through. Gulf Breeze was not just a small town, but a small Florida cracker town. And while friends did stop to pay Edward their respects, about one in three asked the personal question "Where is your daughter, Sarah-Jean?"

And she had forced a smile and answered, "Annie was unable to attend." But the truth was, Sarah-Jean had not let Annie know that her father had died. She felt sure Annie would refuse to attend the funeral and found that much harder to accept than a Christian telling a small white lie.

Sarah-Jean had sat on the hard-backed metal chair for the last two hours. The friends had come out to the cemetery from the church service and paid their final respects, and now at last she was all alone.

Edward's casket had been lowered into the plot and covered. She found herself staring at the gravestone, all she had left of him. A stone and a name.

She glanced out across the cemetery lawn and saw how all the stones lined up in neat little rows, one behind the other. It gave her the feeling that even in death there was order, though her life now seemed so disorderly.

"Sarah-Jean." Dr. Fire spoke from behind the grieving widow.

Sarah-Jean turned and recognized the nice woman doctor from the hospital. She stood up and held out her hand. "Hello. Thank you for coming, Doctor."

"I'm very sorry this happened, Mrs. Hall. I read about it in the paper. Is there anything I can do?"

"No, I'll be all right."

Fire smiled and patted Sarah-Jean's extended hand. "I know you will. You're a strong woman . . . Did your daughter come?"

Sarah-Jean turned away and looked down at the palm trees lining the cemetery hill by the river. Her voice was just above a whisper. "She couldn't make it."

"Really?" Fire could see through Sarah-Jean's subterfuge. "It would be a shame if—it is Annie, isn't it?"

"Uh-huh." Sarah-Jean glanced at the shoulder of her black dress and dusted off a piece of annoying lint.

"—if Annie never learned the message about her son."

"I suppose."

"Well, it's your decision, of course. But—be of good courage, and the Lord will strengthen your heart." Fire was pleased she had looked that up in the Gideon before leaving her hotel room.

Sarah-Jean nodded and whispered, "Amen." She forced herself to make eye contact. "Thank you, Doctor, for coming by."

"Don't mention it." Fire put a hand on Sarah-Jean's shoulder and pulled a syringe from her purse.

Sarah-Jean didn't feel the sting on her neck until it was too late. A moment later she was out cold and lying under the heavy oak tree.

Fire began to work, until she heard a laugh from up the hill. A tall black teenage boy in baggy pants and large T-shirt stood next to a winged statue on a headstone. Unaware of Fire, or the danger he was in, he stuck his cigarette in the angel's mouth and let out a high-pitched cackle.

"Don't hold out on me, baby." He grinned, then reached behind the statue. "Come on, Lena," he said, and pulled a thin dark-haired girl in a bright red top and loose jeans out next to him. He turned and stumbled. The girl fell to the ground with him. Fire could hear the laugh again, then the silence, as the couple began to kiss under the Gothic gravestone.

Fire glanced up the hill to the parking lot where her Berets stood watch. A wave of her hand sent McKenzie and Getz to chase the teenagers away, and she continued to work on the old woman.

She turned Sarah-Jean on her side, unzipped her dress and found just the right spot between the shoulder blades. It was important that the microtransmitter be placed just out of reach. A scratch with a hand could destroy the device, which was slightly smaller than a grain of rice. It was standard equipment in the CIA's microtechnology.

The smell of rubbing alcohol mixed with the dank earthy scent under the tree. With a twisting motion like that of an acupuncturist, Fire embedded the microtransmitter. When she was done, the slightly raised spot looked like a mosquito bite.

A minute later Fire had Sarah-Jean sitting by Ed's grave and was holding smelling salts under the old woman's nose.

"What happened?" Sarah-Jean whispered as she regained her strength to stand.

"You fainted. A combination of too much sun and too much strain. You really should be with family."

"Yes, thank you." She stared at Ed's grave. "I'd better go."

"Can I help you to your car?" Fire asked, holding out her hand.

"Please."

She held the good doctor's hand and walked past the rows of gravestones, pausing only once while Fire stomped a burning cigarette. They passed a line of palms and she thought more about her daughter, about family, about how much she missed Annie. They crossed over toward the parking lot and a few minutes later, they stood beside Sarah-Jean's old Nova.

"Thank you again, Doctor. I think you should know I've made a decision."

"Oh?"

"Yes. My Edward used to say, the hardest choice is usually the right choice. So I've decided to face my daughter."

"That's wonderful." Fire smiled. "I'm sure everything will work out."

Sarah-Jean shrugged and opened the car door. "Thank you and God bless you."

Fire watched as Sarah-Jean's Chevy narrowly avoided hitting two other cars before clearing the parking lot. It would take a miracle for the old woman to navigate the freeways, even with her bumper sticker, JESUS IS MY CO-PILOT.

Fire crossed a small lawn to a second parking lot and climbed into the sky blue Lincoln Continental. There was a steady beep from the microtransmitter on a small screen. "Well, gentlemen. Don't lose her."

DREAMLAND BASE, GROOM LAKE, NEVADA

Andros stood in front of his microscope still wearing his bio-suit. He peered in and adjusted the focus on Sonny's blood sample. The strange particles that had reflected the light in the vial were now unmasked as crystal formations around a man-made genetic marker.

Andros had come a long way from being the whiz-kid lab assistant who had helped Doctors Crick and Watson stumble across the double helix structure of the DNA molecule. He had gone on to graduate magnum cum laude in genetics from Johns Hopkins and had spent the past twenty years working in MJ-12's advanced genetic studies. If anyone could trace this bio-weapon, it would be Andros.

Andros stepped over to his computer and printed out the coded sequence. It was a formula for sarin plus several additives the computer did not recognize. That wouldn't matter, the formula had to be on file at the National Institutes of Health in Maryland. All biological weapon formulas were registered there. During the cold war the facility had been called the Frederick Cancer Research and Development Center. A harmless sounding name, but in truth, harm was their business. It headquartered the U.S. Army's Fort Detrick chemical and biological defense facility. Andros knew it housed some of the world's deadliest secrets: formulas for unspeakable plagues and horrifying chemical weapons. There had been rumors the facility had invented the earliest form of AIDS, and had tested it in sub-Saharan Africa, only to have it evolve away from its parent virus into something that scientists couldn't stop. While normal rational people might fail to credit such a military conspiracy, Andros did believe it. If he had learned anything in twenty years of top secret, black projects, it was never to underestimate military paranoia.

The basis for this could be found in the cold war. If the old Soviet Union researched germ warfare, you could bet the U.S. spent twice the effort and ten times the money to develop something 1,000 percent better. Good old-fashioned American ingenuity. Only these inventions had a twist: the final product could be disguised as an act of God.

Andros raced his finger down the computer printout scanning for clues. He stopped at the LIPOSOME readout. Liposome is a kind of DNA-filled bubble that fuses with cell membranes to deliver a mutated gene to a nucleus. It had been the key to successful germ warfare. It worked because a modified virus which would look like a foreign invader to the immune system would appear natural when the liposome was added to it. This was the stealth delivery system for all future biological weapons.

But this liposome was different. Instead of the standard human DNA code of a double helix structure of two connected spiral strands, each made of four building blocks called A, C, G and T, this one had seven with the addition of blocks H, J and L. Andros recognized this as a combination of human and alien DNA.

Whoever had designed this weapon had gotten their hands on alien DNA. Andros shook his head. That should have been impossible, but here it was. He knew there was only one source of alien DNA and that was under heavy lock and key—in the level-ten basement of NSA's Washington office. It was where they stored the bodies of the dead aliens after the Roswell crash.

SENSORY PERCEPTION LAB, SYRACUSE, NEW YORK

Dr. Aponte stared in disbelief as Max walked across the wooden bar on the floor. His concentration was like that of a tightrope walker on a thin wire, moving one foot after the other: slowly, carefully, precisely.

"Hop?" she asked and mimicked the move she wanted. Max glanced up at her then did as she asked, hopping and landing on the three-inch-thick beam.

"My God," said the heavy blond teacher next to Aponte. "What happened?"

"Parents wouldn't say. But in the last half hour he has improved from just being able to lift a leg on the bar to hopping. It's as if . . ." Her voice trailed off and the other teacher finished the sentence. ". . . he's a regular five-year-old."

"Yeah." Aponte nodded, then smiled. "Okay, Max. You're terrific, but we're going to move on." Aponte turned to her colleague and said, "Time to test the fine motor skills."

Max sat at a table drawing a triangle, copying the shape from a booklet beside him. It was not perfect. In fact it looked like a kid's drawing. Slightly off, but the general shape was right. "You're doing great," Dr. Aponte said, glancing at the drawing.

"It needs color," Max said, staring at his picture with a slight frown.

"Color?" Aponte did a double take. This was the first time she had heard Max speak, and instead of one word he had given her a whole sentence. "Color, right, ah . . . Why do you think it needs color?" she asked, hoping he would speak again, and since he was copying a black and white image his explanation might explain why it needed color to him.

"It can't fly. No orange."

"Fly?" she asked with a puzzled glance.

"Yes." Max nodded to give added emphasis.

"I see. Okay." Dr. Aponte nodded back. Obviously the boy thought it was an airplane. This showed not only that he had the fine motor skills to copy shapes, but the cognitive powers to perceive them as real objects. Another major breakthrough. Except she was coming to realize that whatever had happened to this boy, her programming had very little to do with it. It was just too huge an improvement. She opened a couple of desk drawers and finally found a box of crayons. "Here you go."

Max opened the box and carefully pulled out an orange crayon. He colored in the shape of the triangle with the bright orange then reached in the box and grabbed yellow. He drew a light coming from under the belly of the craft to the ground.

"That's terrific," Dr. Aponte said, admiring what she thought was jet exhaust. "Now Max, we need to do a couple more tests. So finish up." Aponte moved over to a different table and began setting up a series of building blocks.

When Max was finished he held up his picture for Dr. Aponte. "I'm done," he grinned.

Aponte came to his side and looked at the drawing. He had added new colors of green for grass and black for the sky. And off at the top were a dozen yellow dots. Aponte smiled to herself, thinking they looked like some star formation.

"Yes, Big Dipper," Max answered, staring up with big blue eyes. He turned the paper so he could see the picture again.

"What?" she asked. *Had he just read her mind? It can't be.*

Max suddenly looked hurt and shy. "You like the picture?" he asked slowly.

"Oh yes." She smiled. "It's great. You did fine." She must have heard him wrong, she told herself; dipper, picture, whatever. It was time to move on. "Okay, Max, I need you at this next table."

She showed Max the colorful wooden blocks. "Now I want you to build a wall. Understand? Can you do that?"

Max nodded and they both sat down on the child-size chairs in front of the table. Aponte took notes as he moved a series of six blocks into a straight line. A minute later, he began to place a second level of six on top.

"Good, good," Aponte said, drawing in her notes the way the boy had set them up. "Now, Max, I want you to think about this. With the blocks left how high can they go? A little or a lot?" She moved her hand up and down as she asked. There were only six blocks left. Max grinned and moved his hand up three levels. "Interesting. Okay, show me." Dr. Aponte said. She had expected two different approaches from a child this age; one would have lined up the blocks as a final row over the other two, the second would have piled all six straight up, one on top of the other. In all the years she had tested children on this logic question, they had always given her those two answers, but now Max had a new answer. He placed three blocks in the center of the foundation of the six, then placed two blocks over those three, and the last one on top.

"Very nice."

Max nodded and said, "It's a boat."

Dr. Aponte broke into a big full smile. Sure enough, it did

look like a boat. A sailboat. *What a clever boy,* she thought. *A very clever boy.*

"He what?" Annie asked, leaning on Dr. Aponte's desk. Stan sat beside her and placed a hand on Annie's shoulder.

"I said, he's changing. In the two hours I worked with him, I saw him do things that, well, no amount of *programming* could explain. He's very smart and growing more so."

"So, how do we explain it?" Stan started, but Dr. Aponte interrupted.

"Look, the fact that this is happening at all is a miracle. You want a scientific explanation? I don't have one, I guess." She paused and looked between Stan and Annie. "If it matters so much, get a second MRI. But, either way, you both should relax. You have a bright, wonderful boy. A *dreamchild.*" She gave them a huge smile, letting them soak in what she was saying. "Don't let anything happen to him."

Annie and Stan turned and looked at one another. Annie could feel the tears welling up in her eyes. She reached out and hugged her husband and whispered, "My God, Stan, we have our boy."

Stan nodded and held her close. He could feel the tears pouring down Annie's cheek. He ran his hand down her hair as if he were stroking a cat.

Not only did he have a son; he had a wife again, too.

CHAPTER 19

69 Tanglewood Drive, Las Vegas, Nevada

Colonel Andros cut his lights and parked his white Cherokee Jeep. The street was lined with brand-new model homes. Each was freshly painted, with green sod squares laid across the lawns-to-be. The neo-lawns were broken by trees pinned in place with wires, looking like so many child-size teepees. All the homes were considered phase C, priced to start at $120,000. Several were still under construction. This was the fastest-growing suburban development anywhere in the U.S. It was where the real people of Las Vegas lived, the people who serviced the casino community: schoolteachers, landscapers, cooks. Middle-class U.S.A. Only without the dirt. It always surprised Andros how clean the city of sin really was. Like Disney, it wanted to share the illusion of safe, clean, family fun.

Only a few homes on the street had their lights on at this time of night. Sixty-nine Tanglewood Drive did not. In fact it had a Century 21 Real Estate sign in front, with a SALE PENDING placard.

Andros drove by slowly and carefully. He was sure no one from the base had followed him, but fieldwork had never been his strong suit and he wanted to take no chances.

The National Institutes of Health had released the information he needed: an address and the name of the company that had ordered the parent source of the biological weapon used on Sonny. Of course the name, Pasteur Disease Center, had been used numerous times by the CIA for black bio-weapons projects. And the paperwork to confirm the existence of Dr. Lorian Rothchilde, head scientist, had proven worthless. Yale did not have her records, the IRS showed she had never paid taxes. But she did have a laboratory, or rather an address for the lab existed. At least according to the Fed Ex tracer the NIH had sent, it did. But hiding it in the suburbs seemed quite devious.

Andros shoved the fax back in his pocket and proceeded toward the one-story Tex-Mex–style house. Andros had expected the lights to be off and had brought a small, high-intensity flashlight, along with a satchel of other tools.

He found the door locked and the realtor's lock box busted. A sticker in the corner gave the warning of an alarm system. All the windows had ornate bars, making it a modern fortress. Andros decided to try the backyard.

He opened the side gate and entered, not using his flashlight. Instead he moved slowly, letting his eyes get used to the dark.

Without warning, the ground gave way and his knees hit something hard as he tripped. He stared down at the large black pit before him. He pulled himself up and caught his breath. A moment later, he could make out the outline of the drained pool and partially constructed wooden deck. His eyes adjusted to the starlight so he could see more clearly the back of the house. There were french doors to the patio. His luck was about to change.

Andros approached the doors, wrapping his hand in his jacket. He swung his fist and broke out the top pane closest to the alarm lead. Glass sprinkled down onto the reddish-orange Mexican tile. He reached an electric screwdriver inside and unscrewed the ground wire, disabling the lead without setting off the alarm. Then he simply turned the knob and opened the door.

As he entered, the first thing that hit him was the foul smell. "Ohhhh," he muttered, trying not to breathe the stink. He grabbed his flashlight and shone it around. With no furniture, no pictures, it looked as clean and unlived-in as any model home. He moved through the family room into the dining room. He could tell it was the dining room because of the low-hanging chandelier. The stink got worse. Andros pitied the real estate agent scheduled to show this house next.

His flashlight caught a glimmer in the kitchen. He moved toward it. Fighting off gagging, he flipped on the overhead light.

The fluorescent light nearly blinded him. When he stopped seeing blue dots, he saw the mess. The kitchen had been turned into a laboratory, with beakers, Bunsen burners, test tubes.

He took a step in and found his shoes sticking to the floor. He was standing in a gluey gray puddle. He followed the puddle's origin to a black Kenmore refrigerator in the corner. It was the fancy kind, two doors with ice maker and cold water tap. He felt the refrigerator's side and realized it had been unplugged. Hell of a time to save energy. Must be rotting food, it had to be.

He took a breath and swung open the door.

Something large stood wrapped in a towel. The shelves had been removed, giving about four feet of clearance in the fridge. He lifted the towel up with a penknife. The stink of decay kicked in his gag reflex, but Andros did not turn away. Instead he threw up, staring right at a rotting alien corpse.

That's impossible, he thought, rinsing his mouth at the sink and returning to stare at the corpse. Impossible, because the only person in all of MJ-12 with security clearance high enough to visit the NSA deep freeze, where all known alien bodies were stored, was himself.

So while he had suspected Ms. Valerie Ross from her training in biological weapons, he knew there was no way that she could have secured an alien body. In fact, even if he himself had wanted to, NSA would never have released it.

How could this happen? Who was the traitor? Why hadn't they covered their tracks?

Andros puzzled over it while he pulled out a garbage bag from his satchel and began the unpleasant task of placing the alien remains in it.

He had found the answer to alien DNA in the virus, but had discovered a greater mystery—an unaccounted-for alien body.

UPSTATE MEDICAL CENTER, SYRACUSE, NEW YORK

Annie searched the new images coming in on the MRI scan of Max's brain. Stan stood beside her in the control room.

"Okay. Match that with sixty-one-A from the last set," Dr. Feuer said to the radiologist. The video monitor flickered with side-by-side black and white images of the same section of the brain.

"Wow," said the radiologist before she could stop herself.

"Yes, it's remarkable," the doctor agreed.

"What is?" Stan asked squinting at the small screen.

"Look." Dr. Feuer pointed at the noodle-shaped wave of brain on the video monitor. "This is the same picture of your son's brain sliced at eye level. Only instead of just the extra folds and creases of his cerebral cortex as before, there are changes in the gyri-ridges themselves."

Annie shook her head. It all looked the same to her. "I don't get it. What's different?"

Dr. Feuer smiled and looked up at Annie and Stan. "For one thing, the brain tissue is now functioning."

"Doctor—" Stan began, but Feuer cut him short.

"What did you *do?*" she asked.

Annie glanced at Stan and felt her throat go dry. "Um, we, don't know. We were kind of hoping you could tell us what happened."

Feuer gave a short laugh. "You mean a medical explanation?"

"Yes." Annie answered.

"Don't have one," the doctor shrugged. "I've never seen anything like it. His brain functions were hindered because of a lack of neural-synaptic cyneurotonin. Well, now he has it. I don't know how. I haven't seen that kind of cortex rejuvenation since I stopped working with fetal tissue in Parkinson patients."

"Doctor," Stan began again, this time determined to get his question out. "Just, ah, what functions do this part of the brain control?"

"Right there," the doctor pointed at the MRI slide. "That would control his communication ability."

Annie and Stan glanced at one another.

"You say he began talking?" the radiologist asked.

"Yes," Annie answered. "Just in the last day or two."

"Well, this is the kind of recovery I could write papers on for the next ten years." Feuer laughed.

"No thanks," Annie said. She was not about to let Max become a lab pet. Stan put a comforting hand on her shoulder. "Let's get our family home."

NATIONAL SECURITY ADMINISTRATION HEADQUARTERS, WASHINGTON, D.C.

Andros had left Los Angeles immediately after finding the corpse in order to get to Washington during working hours. That was a problem with Washington—they still kept regular nine to five hours even in the black project divisions.

He exited the NSA elevator with Agent Crawford, a thin brunette with intense green eyes.

"Not too bad a flight, I hope?" she asked.

Andros smiled. "No, I slept until we hit the rain."

"Yes, they say we're in for another few days of it."

They walked down the clean white hallway to the fifth security checkpoint. Andros placed the steel suitcase, four feet long by a foot wide, on the table. He made no attempt to open it and neither did the guard.

Crawford signed for it, and passed her security card through a panel on the guard booth. "How's it going, George? Your wife have that baby yet?"

The heavyset guard smiled and answered, "Nope, not yet. Said she was gonna wait till the rain stopped."

"Good luck," Crawford laughed. She turned and held still for a retinal ID check. A green light blinked and a buzzer sounded and she and Andros walked through the security door.

At the end of the hall, Andros could see the heavy double door labeled simply NSA COLD STORAGE. His pace quickened as he headed for it.

"Whoa, Nelly," Crawford said, stopping at her own office first. "You'll freeze within six minutes if you go in there dressed like that."

Andros doubled back and entered Crawford's office. It was a surprisingly large room, with heavy thermal padding on the walls. "We keep it a cozy twenty-five degrees below in there."

"I see."

Crawford handed Andros a heavy blue hooded jumpsuit and a pair of thermal goggles, one of four sets she had hanging against the wall. "These should fit."

Andros looked around the office while he pulled on the suit. Standard government issue black file cabinets, a few lockers and, in the corner, a desk with a computer. About the only thing personal in the whole room was a poster stuck with push pins in the wall. It was for the TV show *The X-Files*. The caption read, "The Truth Is Out There." Only Out There had been crossed out and above it, hand printed, IN HERE.

"The truth is in here?" Andros asked.

"Yeah, well, there's more than one reason they keep me in a padded cell. Come on."

Andros followed Crawford from the room holding the steel case in his thick gloves.

"You know, I didn't believe you when you called, Colonel."

"I know you didn't." Andros said.

Crawford pulled her security card from the chain around

her neck and slipped it down a wall panel. The heavy doors buzzed open. Inside, the NSA cold storage appeared, a winter wonderland. The gymnasium-size room had large concrete bins rising from floor to ceiling. Everything in it had a light coating of ice.

"We took a lesson from Mother Nature. At twenty-five below, nothing lives, and nothing rots. They found a ten-thousand-year-old Siberian mammoth frozen at that temperature. It was fresh enough to eat, once thawed."

"Trust me, you don't want to eat this," Andros said and hefted the steel case.

"I hear you." Crawford grimaced and pulled out a sheet of paper from her jacket. "We want J-47."

Andros followed Crawford down the main aisle. Their breath froze in puffs of white. He was surprised at how fast Crawford walked, but then she was used to working in this kind of cold. Finally they came to row J and worked their way down to bin 47.

"Here we are," she said, pulling the bin out. There on the slab were seven child-size body bags. Crawford opened each to make sure the strange little gray corpses were still there.

"All accounted for. Thank God. It would have been my butt."

"I didn't really think this could have gotten by you."

Andros brought the steel case up and laid it on the slab of the bin.

"Hold on." Crawford waved him back and grabbed a thin orange hose that wound out from the floor. "Okay." She stood ready to hose it down.

Andros popped open the case and pulled down the zipper on the body bag. Even here in the intense cold, the smell was bad.

"Step back," Crawford said and began spraying a hot water mist on the alien cadaver. Within seconds the mist had frozen into a fine ice film, sealing in the smell and protecting the skin from further deterioration.

"Okay," she said and rolled the hose back into the floor. "That ought to do it."

Andros paused before closing the bag and reached a gloved hand down to touch a long gray finger.

"We'll take good care of him, Colonel," Crawford smiled. "By the way, this one couldn't be from Roswell. Not unless it was alive and kicking when they took it."

"Alive? Huh," Andros said, glancing up. "But how could Wesley have kept it secret?"

"Can't help you there. Come on, we've got a ton of paperwork to begin."

Andros followed Crawford back down the aisle to the door. His mind raced with questions. *Why would Wesley do this? Who did he trust? Who could have carried it off?*

There was only one name that made sense.

DREAMLAND BASE, GROOM LAKE, NEVADA

"Keller here, Colonel Andros! We found the power source, 115. Yeah," Keller laughed. He stood in the shade of the large hangar and talked on a wall phone. From where he stood he could watch the three engineers supervising the Black Berets unloading the helicopter's secret cargo.

"Hey, careful with that!" he yelled to the men wheeling down a large crate. The Berets waved at him and continued unloading.

"What's that?" Keller asked into the phone. "No, she left with Dr. Fire. Yes, she was all excited about some ancient writing we found . . . No—alien writing, I think. She believes it's some kind of warning. Sure, I'll fax it . . . They left about two hours ago. Why?" Keller glanced around at his men. His voice lowered before he continued. "I see. You're sure? Yes, I heard their pilot say he was headed for Syracuse. What's in Syracuse?"

Andros said nothing for a long moment and Keller realized he was holding his breath. When Andros finally spoke, it was only one sentence, but it sent all Keller's blood rushing to his stomach.

"You should consider this a condition Zeta Blue."

A minute ago Keller had been full of triumph and the excitement of his discovery in the Andes. Now he was being ordered to protect himself and the base from an internal security breach.

"Understood," he said quietly, and hung up the phone.

It would be crazy to go up against the Black Berets and they both knew it. But he could stash weapons and set up an escape route. About the only thing he was sure of was that those Berets who had been loyal to Wesley would act and it would be on Fire's command.

CHAPTER 20

The Lear jet set down on the rain-slicked tarmac of the Syracuse Airport. Dr. Katherine Fire and Valerie Ross left the plane with only briefcases and backpacks. They proceeded through gate G to the drive-through pickup lane. Fire was the first to spot the clean-cut Black Berets.

"There they are."

"Geez, they look more like Secret Service Ken dolls," Valerie joked. But there was truth in her observation. The men were now dressed in fashionable London Fog coats, gabardine pants and Ray-Ban sun glasses. They opened the door of one of the two rental vans. Both were late-model white Chevy Astros.

"Sergeants McKenzie and Getz, you know Ms. Ross." They both nodded. "Good. Climb in."

The four entered the van. Fire turned to Getz. "Where is Sarah-Jean now?"

"She arrived late this morning on an American flight and took a cab to a residential address." He handed her a piece of paper with 211 Demong Drive written on it. "We didn't see anyone when she arrived. But they're in residence. Power's on, dishes in the sink."

"Good." Fire nodded. "We'll take it from here. Now, Ms. Ross has a little assignment for you."

Valerie fished around in her backpack and pulled out a small hand-held radio receiver. There was a steady ping from the machine and green screen at the top that indicated location.

"I know you gentlemen are familiar with microtransmitters," she said, handing the receiver to McKenzie. "The subject is Dr. Eva Yi. She and her partner"—Valerie glanced at her notes—"Dr. Jerry Sorich, are to be eliminated. Security breach, extended visitor contact."

"Gentlemen," Fire added. "This is a wet operation in a civilian environment. I don't want loose ends. Clean and simple. Stop it here and now. Understood?"

The Berets nodded.

"Good, now where are the bio-suits?" Fire asked, going on to her next point of business, her job of infecting the hybrid.

"All your equipment is in the back," Getz answered.

211 DEMONG DRIVE, SYRACUSE, NEW YORK

Sarah-Jean sat on the damp swing on the wraparound porch. She had watched the cab drive off and the rain slow to a drizzle, but there was still no sign of Annie and family. She looked at the old Victorian house and hoped it was the right address. It surprised her that her daughter had not bought some ultramodern home, something to go with her need to keep up with progress.

Progress.

The subject had been the basis of their last argument, at least the last argument face to face. It had happened the day Annie went off to graduate school. Sarah-Jean had listened to her daughter explain that a doctorate in astrophysics was, in fact, progress. She said that only 2 percent of astrophysics graduates were women and her goal was to join them and become a radio astronomer.

Why? she remembered asking Annie. What's so wrong with

being a part of the majority? Why not be a housewife? Her fear was that Annie would become so overeducated that no man would want her as a wife. After all, in her day most women did not go to college. If they did, it meant they would become spinster teachers.

Then one day, Annie called and told them she had gotten married. It was a surprise, in part because they had not been invited. But then they learned why. Stan was Jewish. Perhaps Annie did not realize how that would affect her father, perhaps she did. But that night Ed made it clear: they had not gained a son, but lost a daughter.

Years passed and Annie sent occasional letters, but Ed refused to let Sarah-Jean answer them. Then came a note from Annie's girlfriend, Carol. She learned she was about to be a grandmother. She defied Ed and secretly sent Annie a package. It contained a letter and her childhood teddy, Gruffy Bear. But Annie did not acknowledge this gift, at least not right away.

It was a year before Sarah-Jean received a baby photograph, letter and new address. The address she had copied in her tattered diary. The letter announced the boy's name was Max. She assumed he looked like his father, since he failed to resemble anyone in her family. But perhaps the greatest news was that Annie had finally come to her senses and returned to the honorable job of motherhood. So much for *progress*, Sarah-Jean thought and wiped a tear from her face.

In her heart she was sorry about their rift and wondered if they could ever mend it. How could she explain to Annie her father's vision? Or learn if Annie even believed in God anymore? After all these years, rejecting her daughter had become easier. She wondered if Annie would do the same to her.

LYMAN HALL, SYRACUSE UNIVERSITY, SYRACUSE, NEW YORK

McKenzie listened to the steady click of his boots on the stairs as he made his way to the third floor of Lyman Hall. He glanced

, down at the palm-size scanner. The indicator showed the target was now ahead about two hundred yards. The hallway was empty except for a janitor mopping the floor.

He pocketed the scanner and continued down the hall. As he passed an open door, he could see lab tables set up but no students. The place was deserted. This was going to be too easy. He had a .45 with a heavy silencer on it. All he needed to do was step in, fire and leave. The janitor wouldn't even hear it.

A conversation echoed out into the hallway ahead. The Beret could make out the voices of two women and a man. He paused just outside the door and double-checked his scanner. Yes, that was the target twenty feet inside and to the right. He reached for his gun, but as his hand slid into his pocket, Eva and Jerry suddenly stepped into the hallway.

"Get some rest!" Alexis called out.

"Yeah, right. Who can sleep after a visit with ET?" Jerry said from the doorway.

Damn, security breach. The Beret made a mental note. An unlucky third had been added to the wet team's list.

Eva sang back into the room the five-note melody from *Close Encounters* and laughed. It all seemed so ridiculous, so far away. With a good sleep she could forget this nightmare. She was home now. Home and safe.

"Bye," she called and turned into the hallway and froze. The Beret stood only a few feet from them, his hand still in his pocket, his expression that of a cold killer.

"Oh, sorry," she said and grabbed Jerry's arm and started toward the stairs.

"What? What?" he protested, but Eva kept moving.

It was clear to McKenzie that she had made him. Whether she knew who he was, or only sensed what he was, it didn't matter. She was in flight. He would have to shoot both out in the open. Poor damn janitor, he thought. Oh, well.

He pulled the .45-caliber Glock just as Eva and Jerry came

to the stairs. He cocked the slide back to chamber a round and took aim. As his finger began to squeeze, he heard the sounds of a child laughing. He spun around and repocketed the gun. At the far end of the hallway, he could see a man with a young boy riding on his shoulders.

This was not going the way he wanted it, the way Fire wanted it, clean and simple. He turned to glance in the door behind him where an attractive woman with red hair typed on a computer.

"Excuse me," he said.

Alexis looked up and smiled. "Yes?"

"Dr. Keller?"

"No, Alexis Campbell. Sorry."

"My mistake. Thanks." The Beret turned and left. He had what he needed, her name. He would have to return for her, but now he had to catch the other two. He raced toward the stairs where Eva and Jerry had disappeared.

There was no sign of them as he flew down the three flights. He turned to the front door and spotted the couple outside. They were huddled together under an umbrella walking toward a gold Volkswagen bug convertible. It was one of only a dozen cars in the parking lot. The white van quickly pulled to the curb and McKenzie climbed in. He pointed to the VW pulling out and said, "That's them."

"Got 'em," Getz answered and followed.

Annie looked up from the front seat of the old Volvo and watched the white van splash through a huge lake of a puddle. "College kids," she mumbled and turned her attention back toward the science building. Stan had taken Max with him, saying he needed his son's support for this, and while she had a hunch what *this* was, she had not asked and Stan had not told her.

Stan ducked under the doorway with Max still on his shoulders. He saw Alexis sitting at her desk. "Hello," he said. "Hope we're not bothering you."

Alexis turned, recognizing the voice, then raised an eyebrow when she saw the boy.

"Well, isn't this a surprise!"

"Yes, well," Stan started as he lifted Max from his shoulders. "I just wanted to clear some things up. You know, what we keep talking about."

"Of course," Alexis said, as she moved from her desk to kneel beside Max. "What a handsome young man you are." She ran her fingers through the boy's fine hair, then glanced at Stan. "Not what I imagined. But then today is full of surprises."

"Really?" Stan asked.

"Yes, Eva and Jerry are back."

"Here?"

Alexis nodded. "You just missed them." She turned to her desk and picked up the gold amulet. "You won't believe the lovely adventure they had. In fact, I don't." She gave a little chuckle. "Jerry, it seems, stumbled on an unusual cave. That's the trouble with Greek archeologists. Can't keep them from sticking their face in what they love."

"You don't say. Anything in this cave?" Stan asked, holding Max between himself and Alexis.

Alexis laughed again and swirled the amulet around her arm. "If you believe it, they met God, or rather a Peruvian god, who turned out to be nothing less than an alien."

That word got Stan's attention. He looked up, distressed, but he could see Alexis did not believe the story as she continued her sarcastic tone. "Local Indians tried to sacrifice them, but they were saved by a strange commando team. Frankly, I believe they smoked some great peyote and tripped heavily."

Max wiggled free of his father's grip and moved around the room staring at the geo-satellite photos on the walls.

"What a dear boy. Why haven't you brought him by earlier?" Alexis leaned down to Max and whispered, "Tell me what you see?"

Max stared at the image of North America and pointed. "Us." He turned and pointed at the ceiling. "Stars."

"So very bright," Alexis said, astonished. She glanced at Stan. "He has your mind, and I suppose he favors his mother in looks?"

"I wouldn't—" Stan started.

"Oh, it's nothing to be ashamed of."

"I'm not ashamed—" Stan began again, but Alexis waved him off.

"Max, isn't it?" she asked and watched as the boy turned and looked at her. His eyes seemed piercing. "Come here," she whispered and held her hand out. The gold amulet on her arm seemed to catch his attention and he moved closer. "You like this, don't you?" She smiled and held the amulet out toward him. Max reached for it.

"Easy, son," Stan cautioned, not sure how he felt about Alexis's attention to Max.

Max took the amulet and held it. He stared at the strange engraving. The triangle shape was covered with stars, a plane under it and a man's face growing into that of another. He knew what all of this was and he smiled.

"Ah, see? I don't frighten all males," Alexis whispered and glanced at Stan to give a wink.

This wasn't what Stan intended. "Alexis," he said in a firm voice. "I need to talk with you."

"Good, I need to talk with *you.*" She rubbed her hands down her perfect hips and straightened her skirt.

"No. I mean, it's over. It's really over. I'm leaving the Geo study. We're not seeing each other ever again."

"Really," Alexis said, not intending this to be a question, but a statement.

Max found the drawing at the bottom, the creature that was half man and half beast.

"Father—Father—" Max said.

Stan looked down and put a hand on Max's shoulder. "Right here, son."

"Father—" Max said again, holding the amulet up. Stan took it and returned it to Alexis. "It's okay. We're going now. Alexis, I, uh, I told Annie everything."

"And?"

"And, well, she's forgiven me. I'm not giving up on my family."

"A family man like you? I wouldn't dream of it," Alexis said with a hint of anger. "Why your family is growing—every day, in every way."

CHAPTER 21

LYMAN HALL, SYRACUSE UNIVERSITY, SYRACUSE, NEW YORK

"What do you mean?" Stan asked.

"I mean, daddy dearest, I'm pregnant." The words stung as they hit, just as Alexis had intended.

Stan took a step back and mumbled, "No."

"Oh yes. Cells dividing, the miracle of life perseveres. You're quite the little provider," Alexis said, rubbing her abdomen. "This is *our* baby."

"Baby?" Max turned. He walked over to Alexis.

"Yes, your little sister, no doubt," she said with a certain amount of vindictive glee.

Stan stared dumbfounded, then in horror as Max reached up and touched his ex-lover's stomach.

"Baby?" the boy whispered, then paused, and waited. It was as if he were waiting for an answer and not getting one. "Baby?" he said again.

"Yes, baby," Alexis answered and pushed the boy's hand away.

"No—" Max said. "No baby." He turned to Stan and shook his head. "No baby, Stan."

"You're wrong. What does a child know? I spoke to my doctor, I'm pregnant."

"No baby!" Max said again.

"Of course a five-year-old would know better than a gynecologist," Alexis sneered.

Stan picked up his son. "As a matter of fact, he probably does," Stan said. "Goodbye, Alex." Still holding Max, he walked out of the room.

"You've got to be kidding. You believe the child? Stan Katz, come back here!"

But Stan did not. Alexis stood still for a moment, then in anger she flung the gold amulet against the wall.

211 DEMONG DRIVE, SYRACUSE, NEW YORK

"She's just sitting there," Valerie said. "I mean, if it was me, I would break in and start to go through my kid's stuff."

"I'll bet," Fire laughed, then glanced in the van's rearview mirror. There was still no sign of the Katz family. "Tell me more about Peru."

"Well, besides my troubles with Keller"—Valerie paused and ran her fingers through her hair—"I guess, most interesting was the discovery of the ancient alien writing."

"Any ideas what they said?" Fire asked.

"No. There was discussion that it might be some kind of a warning."

"Warning?" Fire questioned.

"Yeah, well, because of the maps on the walls. The two scientists thought it had to do with weather changes. Something about the icecaps." Valerie watched the rain slap at the window.

Fire was quiet for a minute, then turned to Valerie. "You know, this might not be a warning, but a threat. Perhaps the Bug Eyes learned of our plans and this was their reply. We annihilate them, they advance our extinction."

"Could they do that?" Valerie asked.

"Certainly. We've always contended that was their ultimate

purpose. Of course, we might be paranoid. Man has lived with the fear of being terminated; by God, the enemy, or now even self-inflicted destruction."

Valerie thought for a moment. She had a nagging question she was afraid to ask. Not that the answer scared her, but she could not gauge Fire's response. Finally she broke the silence. "You, ah, ever wonder *what* the Bug Eyes are?"

"How do you mean?"

"Well, it was something Keller said, but I don't want you to take this the wrong way."

"What? What did he say?" Fire asked, growing more impatient.

"Well, after he found the power source he said they could finally run a scout ship. Then we'd know if they were 'our future' or merely 'visitors' from some other world. I mean, I always assumed they were from some other system. You know, Vega, Pleiades, Zeta Reticlui. Somewhere else."

Fire interrupted. "And it would bother you, if they're from our future? What's the old cliché? We have met the enemy, and he is us?"

"Yeah, something like that."

Fire laughed. "Well, if it's any comfort, I don't believe they're our future, or our past. I don't believe they're gods, angels or Christ. I do believe they fear us and will use any means to beat us, physical or psychological. As for Keller, he's hooked on the Einsteinian mechanics of the thing."

"Einsteinian mechanics?"

"Mmm. As I understand it, if their ships cannot achieve light speed or better, then there is no way they could have come from another system. Which means, they're from here."

"You mean time travelers?"

"No . . . well, maybe. Look, there's a theory that has been going around for a long time." Fire glanced at Valerie. "They may be man's distant future, or, just as easily, they could be from our past."

"Past?"

"Sure. Say sixty-five million years ago, a breed of dinosaurs survived, evolved and became thinking beings."

"That's crazy," Valerie objected.

"Is it? Ten years ago, evolutionary biologists ran some primary tests on what a medium-size, plant-eating dinosaur would look like if it had evolved from then to the present day."

"And?"

"Well, based on environmental changes in the food chain, temperatures, UV radiation, they would have shrunk in size, say to four feet. Their skin would most likely be scaly and gray. They would evolve into bipeds, with a substantial cranial increase."

"And the eyes?"

"Double-lensed to protect from the UV radiation. Wesley of course dismissed it. After all, how could lizards create such advanced technology?"

"I agree," Valerie said.

"Really? Think about it. They've had sixty-five million years to evolve. Modern *Homo sapiens*—less than one million."

"So you believe?" Valerie asked, amused.

Fire laughed. "No. I don't care what they are, or where they're from. I believe only in *our kind's* survival."

"And the writing?" Valerie asked.

"We'll never know."

The radio between them suddenly crackled. "We have secondary target now at home. Advise. Over."

Fire picked up the radio. "That's a go, wet team. *Go.*" She put the radio down and glanced at Valerie. "So much for Dr. Sorich."

11 EAST GENESEE AVENUE, SYRACUSE, NEW YORK. 12:57 P.M.

Jerry had returned to his small apartment, a one-bedroom place filled with the unusual combination of ancient artifacts and new-age metaphysical trappings. These things would stir the mind from past to present. Tribal spears hung on the walls, and models of the space shuttle *Discovery* and *Star Trek*'s *Enterprise* dangled from the ceiling. A lighted teak bookcase featured a tattered Twelfth Dynasty Egyptian shield, a bust of Nefertiti and a partial Neanderthal skull. On the shelf below stood a fine collection of small Incan llamas and pre-Columbian pots and statues. In the hall leading from the living room to the bedroom were framed aerial photographs of Stonehenge and crop circles. This was Jerry's home and he was glad to be back in it.

As Jerry passed the kitchen, he remembered the cold Beck's beer sitting on the top shelf of the refrigerator. But it was not thirst, or hunger, that obsessed him. Instead, all he had thought about since the ten-hour plane flight home was a hot shower. His plan was to stand under the rush of the water massage until his skin had wrinkled enough to resemble a Chinese Shar Pei.

The plan might have worked if McKenzie hadn't been able to slip the front door's lock so easily. After that, it was only a matter of following the clothes on the floor to the bedroom where he could hear Jerry singing over the water running in the adjoining bathroom.

There are three ways to kill a target by Black Beret standards: one, execution; two, fatal accident; three, foul play. McKenzie had plenty to work with; in the bedroom alone there was a colorful assortment of crystals on the dresser. Two were large enough to strike and kill a man. Beside them was a collection of American Indian arrowheads. The Beret ran his fingers across the biggest and tried to decide if it was sharp enough to cut a throat. No.

He turned to survey the rest of the room. The largest piece of furniture was the waterbed. It was also the most likely place his target would sit after his shower.

The Beret lifted the corner. Yes, the bed was heated. Within a minute he had stripped the wires from the heater and punched pin-size holes through the plastic surface. The dark comforter soaked up water. He then flipped on the switch and the comforter became a fatal 210-volt blanket. Of course, there was still a matter of the wait.

The water stopped and Mckenzie stepped into the bedroom closet. He pulled back the slide on his Glock automatic. The gun was backup, a backup he decided he might need when Jerry passed by his bed and walked on to the kitchen. McKenzie stood still. He would count to twenty and if Jerry failed to return, he would come out firing.

Seven . . . six . . . five . . . Jerry suddenly reentered the room sipping his Beck's and holding a bag of pretzels. The Beret stopped his count and watched. Jerry flipped on the TV and moved to his bed. He retucked the towel around his waist and took a long sip of beer.

The local weather flashed on the screen, images of people sitting on their roofs, canoeing through streets, crying over their losses. Another storm was moving in. *Great,* Jerry thought, *more rain.* He stepped back toward the bed, then he suddenly stopped. *What was that?* His eye caught a dark spot on the carpet. He moved over to it and recognized it as an arrowhead, a Hopi design. He picked it up and glanced at the TV again. It featured a heinous story about the rape and murder of three sisters in Chicago.

He rubbed the arrowhead and thought about the old Hopi legend—how the world grew corrupt, wicked and warlike until the gods destroyed it with a great flood. Waves higher than mountains rolled over the land and all was consumed by the sea. A shiver went down his back. He was cold. He drew the last sip from his beer and turned to his closet. He wanted his robe, a nice warm flannel that he had bought on sale.

As he opened his closet to reach in, he was blinded by a light, a bright red light that stabbed through the dark and formed a perfect circle on his forehead.

"What the hell?" he gasped and stumbled backward onto the bed.

Jerry suddenly felt the sting of electricity race through his body. From his feet to the top of his head, there was an intense sensation, like a deep burning inside. He wanted to jump away, run, but with his greatest effort, he was still unable to move. He could see his hands and chest violently shaking. Then in a wonderful moment—all pain ended. He felt himself rising, as if surfacing in a pool—calmly, effortlessly, smoothly.

He looked down and saw the strange man step from his closet. The man held a gun with a red light pointed at the body on the bed. *My God, that's me!* Jerry thought, recognizing the body. In that instant the room became a brilliant white and he was free.

211 DEMONG DRIVE, SYRACUSE, NEW YORK. 2:16 P.M.

Annie felt the seat belt pull on her shoulder and she glanced up to see why Stan had braked so hard. There was a woman standing on their porch. A woman who looked a lot like Annie, only older. Before Stan could ask, Annie had already answered. "Mama."

Stan slowly pulled the car into the driveway. "What is she doing here? I thought—well, you said, she—"

"Take it easy Stan. I don't know, okay? I'll find out."

Stan looked in his rearview mirror at Max. "She'll find out. Great. Geez, we don't need this, I mean we're finally getting it together and—"

Annie swatted Stan hard on the shoulder and got eye contact. "Calm down. Okay?"

"Yeah. Okay." Stan parked the car and turned off the ignition. "We'll just, you know, wait here."

"Fine," Annie said and opened the car door. She stepped out into the rain and walked up to the porch. She stared a moment at her mother and said nothing. She'd had no idea her mother had aged so, but there she was, a few more wrinkles and a full head of gray. "Hi—Mama," she said, then stepped under the covering, but made no attempt to give a hug.

"Annie," Sarah-Jean answered, her voice void of emotion.

"What are you doing here?"

"I came—" Sarah-Jean paused and bit the corner of her lip. She tried to find the words, but there was no easy way to say it. "Annie, your father is dead."

Annie tried to contain her shock, but this had caught her by surprise. "What?" she asked, not that she had not heard, but she did not believe what she had heard. She held the mental image of her father reading his Bible beside the old Franklin stove.

"Car accident," Sarah-Jean said. "Both he and Uncle Brendan were killed."

"I see," Annie said and she leaned back against a banister. She glanced down and saw for the first time the small bag of luggage by the porch swing. "Do you want to come in?" she asked and unlocked the door.

Sarah-Jean glanced back at the car. "Your boy out there?"

"Yes," Annie answered. She waved at Stan to come in and ignored his stare of disbelief. "He's a good boy, Mama."

"I'm sure he is."

Annie turned to Sarah-Jean. "I don't want trouble between you and Stan."

"I accept that."

Annie nodded and entered her home. Sarah-Jean followed.

Watching this turn of events from their cozy white van, Fire turned to Valerie. "Well, she's in."

Valerie nodded. It was time to put the plan into action. "All right. We'll hyperdose the entire family this evening."

Fire grabbed Valerie's leg above the knee and gave it a little squeeze. "Beautiful *and* brilliant."

"Hello, Sarah-Jean," Stan said, forcing a smile. He held Max on his hip and gave a wipe at the raindrops on his glasses. The old woman sat twenty feet away, lost in an overstuffed couch in his living room.

"Stanley," she acknowledged with a short nod. Her eyes stayed on his son. Stan could feel something going on, something unsaid but very strong. He glanced between his son and Sarah-Jean and saw them studying each other.

"Stanley," Annie called from the kitchen.

Relieved to have an excuse to break this strange moment, he was quick to join his wife. "Yes, honey," he answered, then whispered, "What is she doing here?"

Annie turned away from the stove and made a little face. Stan didn't quite know how to read it, until Annie said, "My father's dead."

"Oh. I mean, I'm sorry."

"Yeah, I guess I am too," Annie whispered and reached out to Stan and hugged him. She glanced at her son and brushed the bangs from his eyes. "I don't know how I feel." She looked back up at Stan. "A part of me is very sorry, and a part of me is relieved and overall, I feel really guilty."

"Don't be. It's not your fault," Stan told her. The blame was his. Annie had alienated her family because of him. Regardless of their hostility toward him or his religion, he never should have let it happen. "Look, your mom is welcome for as long as you want her here."

"Thanks," she whispered. Just then, the tea kettle began to whistle and Annie pulled it from the burner. Stan glanced at Sarah-Jean in the next room.

"Tea's almost ready," Stan said, moving out into the living room. Sarah-Jean smiled again at Max and gave a funny little wave. Stan realized that he had not introduced them. "Oh, forgive me. Max," he said, moving closer, "ahhh, this is your grandmother, Sarah-Jean." It seemed strange to give such an intimate title to someone he barely knew. "Um, your mommy's mommy," he added. He took Max by the shoulders and stood him before Sarah-Jean.

The old woman held her hand out. Max did not flinch or make a face when she touched his cheek. "Max," she whispered as if this was to be their little secret. "God has blessed you. You know that, don't you?"

"Yes, well, indeed he has," Stan agreed, but felt a little

strange about her comment. "Listen, we've had a long morning. I'm going to run him a bath."

"Of course, dear."

"Mama," Annie called from the kitchen. "I have your tea ready now."

Stan watched Sarah-Jean move to the kitchen, when Max spoke up in a small voice. "Father, water."

"Okay, okay," Stan muttered. "One bath, coming right up."

CHAPTER 22

211 DEMONG DRIVE, SYRACUSE, NEW YORK. 4:20 P.M.

Max sat in the warm bath holding his red toy boat. He shook the boat and lifted his hand with two fingers extended like a man being pulled into the sky. He was reenacting the image he had seen when his grandmother's hand had touched him.

"Father, water," he said and understood that Father had taken the man from the boat and brought him to the light. The man was told of the danger. He was a good man, but he was dead and the old woman was sad. Max knew this without ever speaking of it. He merely stared into a person's eyes and knew their feelings, thoughts and desires. And with every hour he grew more in touch with his human identity by experiencing the feelings of others.

Now he glanced at Stan working by the bathroom window. He could see how troubled he was, how scared. Max had never felt genuine fear before, but through Stan he had begun. The pit of his stomach ached, his head hurt and his heart raced.

"Why?" Max asked, not finishing the question, but Stan understood.

"Son," he answered, snipping a pair of wires on the end of

the security device attached to the window, "I just don't want anyone to come in."

"Who?" Max asked, and suddenly his mind filled with a memory from Stan's past. Gunfire, blood-soaked bodies. A man and woman thrown against the wall and floor, scarlet pools forming. From the moment Max saw them, he knew everything about them.

The man had helped his mother remember her dreams about *Father*. The woman, Carol, had been his mother's best friend. She believed his mother, when no one else did. Both, killed by evil men. Evil men, who somehow Stan knew. *Guilt*—a new feeling for Max. How could Stan feel he was a part of this? The answer came to him in the shape of a drawing. These men killed for a drawing, a drawing that would run a horrible machine, a machine Stan had built. And that machine had been designed to be used against *Father*. *Why did Father scare him so?*

"I—just want you safe," Stan answered. "No one is going to harm my family. I won't let them. Not this time."

Max agreed. There was too much fear in his family. It was a bad emotion. Not what *Father* wanted, not what he wanted. Max stood up. "I will help you, Stanley."

"Umm, I guess, I mean, sure you can," Stan said and smiled. Max could feel his delight. "You can be Daddy's number-one helper. But first let's get you dried off and dressed."

Stan heard a creak from the floorboard as Sarah-Jean leaned in next to Annie in the doorway. "This is Max's room," Annie said, waving to Stan and Max working by the dresser. "I'm giving Mom the grand tour."

"Great," Stan said and returned his attention to the wire running from the light sensor on the window to a home VHS camcorder on the dresser. Max watched intently everything Stan did.

"What are you boys up to?" Sarah-Jean asked.

"Just, uh, some home security," Stan replied, reaching for a

Phillips head screwdriver from one of a dozen small tools he had placed in the pockets of Max's Osh-Kosh overalls.

"Is it really necessary? I thought you said this was a good neighborhood."

"Mother," Annie answered, "it is. Come on, I want to show you the sunset from our porch." She took her mother's hand and led her down the hall. Stan heard the old woman protest as they left. "I just don't think that's right, Annie. All these rooms with wires running about, it might start a fire."

"Mom. Stan is an engineer. He knows what he's doing. He's doing it for our own good."

Stan grinned and winked at Max. It was the first thing Annie had said in defense of him in a long time. The idea of a fire had not entered his mind. He had nailed the bedroom window shut and secured a light-sensitive strip. He debated pulling the nails, but settled for knowing there were fire alarms throughout the house. Ultimately, this was more secure.

"Okay, sport," he said and moved to where Max sat on his bed. He opened up a sheet of directions. "Now the trick is getting the wiring right for the camera to work."

Max peered at the paper. "Green wire, input," he answered.

"What?" Stan asked looking down at the Sony directions.

"You need green wire," Max said, pointing a small finger to the page. Stan stared down at the paper. He had not told his son their electrical problem, nor where to look. But there under Max's finger was figure two, the answer—in Japanese. Stan quickly turned the page for the English translation. It was the green wire. "How did you know that?" Stan demanded.

"I know," Max answered.

"You can read?" his father asked.

"Read?" Max looked puzzled.

Stan pointed at the page. "You can read the paper? You understand?"

Max nodded and gave a big smile. "I hear it."

"How?" Stan glanced around the room.

"In my head."

Stan tried to knock off his shocked look, but failed.

"Is it wrong, Stanley?" Max asked.

"No." Stan paused. "Just—well—different." Like so much with his son. Stan lifted Max's chin so their eyes met. "It's okay—it's good to be different." Max slowly beamed and hugged Stan, who wiped away a joyful tear.

How long he had wanted his son to hug him, to show emotion, to say, *"Daddy, I love you."* Though Max had not said that. In the quiet, Stan asked, "Why don't you call me Daddy?"

And for a long moment Max did not answer.

645 NORTH SHORE DRIVE, SYRACUSE, NEW YORK. 5:30 P.M.

Eva entered her building holding her bag in one hand and the mail and some groceries in the other. She fumbled with her keys for a minute before finding the right one and sliding it into the door. Her *Newsweek* dropped to the floor. She might have left it, but she had seen that the cover story was on global warming. Eva gathered it up and wondered if the press knew anything she didn't. She doubted it. Still, it amused her to see how they softened the impending environmental catastrophe.

Eva dropped her handbag inside the door, carried the bag of groceries to the kitchen and settled on her sofa. Her apartment seemed barren of all personal property. It might as well have been a time-share condo: ultraclean, modern, with pastel floral prints, glass dining table, white wicker chairs, a queen-size bed and a wicker dresser. About the only thing that said *Eva* was her computer table. Instead of the standard office desk, she had an antique, early American, Hampton Hall's Prairie writing desk. She had bought it at a barn auction in Sackets Harbor two years earlier. On top of it was the latest on-line IBM computer. She glanced at the screen to see if she had any e-mail. No, the screen was blank. Eva felt herself relax.

She kicked off her shoes and put her feet up. She gave a long stretch and heard her back crack. Rather than flip on the TV, she reached for the *Newsweek*. Reading had always put her to sleep. But instead of unwinding, Eva found herself staring at something that looked strangely familiar: a color enlargement of a microscopic parasite. In fact, there were several parasite pictures across the next two glossy pages, each looking curiously familiar. Where had she seen them?

The pictures were connected to the cover story on global warming, but it was an aspect she had not even considered. As the article pointed out, a rise of just a few degrees would give an assortment of deadly diseases new territory in which to flourish. The world's more densely populated regions of moderate climate would become warmer, wetter, more tropical. The perfect breeding ground for plagues.

She studied the strange shape of *Anopheles*, the tropical parasite that causes malaria. The sidebar said it was a killer of two million people per year in Southeast Asia, spread mostly by mosquitoes that die in temperatures below 66 degrees, but a rise in temperature would expand their environment ten thousand–fold. In fact, any place with an increase of rainfall and temperatures above 70 degrees would become their domain.

Eva looked at the next picture. It was of *Yersinia pestis*, a rod-shaped bacterium, better known as the base genus for the bubonic and pneumonic plague. The sidebar gave it a four-star deadly rating. Only in America could an epidemic be evaluated on an entertainment kill scale. "Two thumbs up," Eva mused. "An action-packed little killer that leaves you breathless." A literal truth; traveling through the lymph nodes, the disease usually ends with bacteria-produced lesions drowning the victim's lungs with blood. In the 1300s it had killed one-third of Europe's population. In the early 1900s it had killed twelve million in India. In 1994 it killed six thousand in just under six weeks, again in India. Throughout the centuries it never really disappeared. There would be declines followed by sudden outbreaks. Why? Like all great plagues, it survived in the wild. And as man encroached on wilderness, Mother Nature fought back. It was spread by fleas on rats, rats that had abandoned the woods for wheat fields, then accompanied the harvest into cities. The last case, however, was from rats leaving flooded lowlands for the higher ground in a city. There would be more of this, she was sure, in the future.

Eva sighed and turned the page. She glanced at the next set of color pictures of Hantavirus, streptococcus A and ebola.

The Hantavirus, named after a South Korean river, was first noted by doctors treating twenty-five hundred U.S. troops during the Korean War. The germ caused its victims' blood vessels to leak, leading to organ failure and death. It was rated three stars on the kill scale.

While streptococcus A had made world headlines when the British press gave it the catchy name of "flesh-eating" bacteria, it only rated two stars. The article noted that this was not a new plague, only a reawakened scourge that had yet to make its mark on a major municipality.

Eva glanced at the last virus. Ebola, a simple corkscrew-shaped parasite, had come from the jungles of Zaire and seemed biblical in its wrath. The victim begins with only a fever, but by nightfall is bleeding from all orifices while the organs liquefy, leading to an agonizing death. Ebola was given a four-star rating even though it had yet to kill on a mass scale.

Eva stared at the photo of the microscopic enlargement. Something about its shape—suddenly it clicked. "That's it," she said aloud, remembering where she had seen it and the others.

Eva got up and grabbed her nylon bag. She dumped it out and searched the mess for the single sheet of paper. "Where is it?" she whispered. Pushing aside dirty clothes, a hairbrush, toothpaste, soil samples, lab reports, she finally came to the crumpled ball of paper. She opened it and smoothed out the drawing.

It was the sketch of the unusual maps they had found in the Incan cave. She reached for the magazine and studied the glossy microscopic enlargment of the ebola virus, then glanced at the drawing. The symbols above Africa were identical. Not only that, but the others, *Anopheles, Yersinia pestis,* Hantavirus, streptococcus A, were all identifiable symbols on Asia, the Americas and Europe. There were several others on her map that were not listed in the magazine, one that looked like a crystal formation, but she was sure it could be identified. It would only be a matter of contacting the Centers for Disease Control. This was a great discovery. Jerry would be so pleased. Not only had she discovered what the symbols were, they were more evidence that these maps came from a far advanced race, a race that understood microscopic organisms and left the simplest clues. It was as if they wanted to help.

Eva tossed the magazine in with the rest of her mail and ran over to her computer to ring up Jerry's home e-mail address. She began her message, even though he was not answering. She figured he was dead asleep. She was half right.

"Dear Jer," Eva began, "I have uncovered the meaning behind the alien symbols on the maps. We were right about the weather connection and mankind's survival."

Eva continued typing on her computer, when she heard the lock on her door suddenly click open. Before she could turn, an incredible pain blossomed in the side of her head.

Getz checked the body for a pulse. There was none. A crimson flower showed on Eva's temple below her hairline. The Beret had shot her as she finished the sentence to Jerry. He glanced at the blood-splattered screen, but could make nothing out.

Getz picked up his hand radio. "Primary target has been eliminated." He looked around the overly neat apartment.

"Excellent," crackled his radio. "Retrieve the microtransmitter. We'll rendezvous at sixteen hundred hours," Fire ordered.

Getz slipped off his leather gloves and snapped on a pair of latex. He pushed Eva forward, so that her head hit the keyboard. He softly began to hum "Old Man River" while flipping open his four-inch Buck knife. He lifted Eva's T-shirt over her head and with a twist cut off her bra so her back was exposed. He ran his fingers along the soft flesh between her shoulder blades and felt the skin with the precision and disinterest of a doctor.

He came to a rise, just left of the T-5 vertebra. Pausing mid-song, at the line "Bodies all aching and racked with pain," he slid the knife in. There was little blood. Getz was a pro. He retrieved the transmitter with its fine hairlike wire and put it carefully in a small plastic bag. As he turned to leave, something dropped from Eva's hand. He reached down and picked up a piece of paper from the floor. It was her map drawing with the alien symbols. "Shit," he mumbled, and picked up his radio. "We have a problem."

211 DEMONG DRIVE, SYRACUSE, NEW YORK. 5:41 P.M.

In the white van Fire held the radio close to her lips. "What kind of problem?" she asked. She and Valerie were still parked down the street from the Katz house and Fire did not like it when there were problems.

"Primary target had evidence of visitor contact and was engaged in analyzing it," Getz replied.

Fire turned on Valerie. "How could you have missed evidence in their possession?" she demanded.

"I don't know. I went through everything. I *did*." She frowned. "Wait—Keller checked their environmental equipment. He must have missed it."

"Val, Val, be a big girl and take the blame if it's your fault. This is not a company where you run and hide. We're not children here."

Valerie had never seen the condescending side of Fire. She didn't like being scolded. She was far too smart to be treated like that. She grabbed the radio mike and demanded, "Cut the crap. Did she get anything?"

There was a pause of radio static, then "It appears so. She was e-mailing a letter, said there was a connection between the weather and the visitor writing."

"So they are tied together," Valerie answered. "It's a shame you killed her before we learned what she found."

Fire took the radio back. "All right. Do not terminate third target. Repeat, do not terminate. We'll rendezvous at the university. I'll interrogate target."

"Understood. Out."

Fire hung up the radio and looked at Valerie who was staring out the window. "What's with you?"

"You didn't have to treat me like that," Valerie said.

"Yes, I did."

Valerie turned to face Fire. "I'm not a child."

"No, and this is a not a child's game." Seeing the raw hurt on Valerie's face, Fire paused. She placed a hand on Valerie's knee. "Val—If this woman was onto something we'll find out. But in our business, we stop them *before* they get close."

"You only hired me to build a bio-weapon."

"No, Val, you were hired to be on the team. You are a team player or you are a team liability. And liabilities—" She patted the knee and smiled. "Well, let's not get grim, dear. But the team comes first. Don't ever forget that."

Valerie turned and looked toward the Katz house. In her anger she longed to run, but there was no escape. For the first time she saw what she had gotten herself into, and she didn't like it. She was in over her head and she wanted out.

But she also knew that if she hoped to survive, she had to stay long enough to finish the job.

CHAPTER 23

211 DEMONG DRIVE, SYRACUSE, NEW YORK.
5:58 P.M.

"So why didn't you tell me, Annie?" Stan asked, entering the living room where Annie and her mother were sitting.

"Tell you what, Stan?" she asked.

"Max says I am not his father." Stan tried to cover his concern in a semisarcastic tone.

Sarah-Jean nodded her head as if suddenly everything was making sense to her.

"And you believe him?" Annie laughed. "Honey, you know how kids are. They say things. Who knows what they're thinking? You're his father, honest."

"Maybe not," Sarah-Jean interrupted.

"What?" Annie and Stan both stared.

"Annie, I know this is going to be hard for you to understand." She turned to her daughter. "But Edward had a vision, a revelation about your son."

"Our son," Stan corrected.

"You cannot claim what's not yours. Edward saw an angel who told of this boy. His purpose, his danger."

"What kind of danger?" Annie asked.

Stan cut in. "Angel? Like a real angel, wings, halo, the whole nine yards?"

"Don't mock the Lord's messengers."

"Me?" Stan pointed at himself.

"Mother, what kind of danger?" Annie asked again.

"Those who would see his end, but promise deliverance. Your boy is our salvation."

"She's flipped, hasn't she?" Stan asked, making eye contact with Annie. "I mean, most grandmothers are happy with a hug or a kiss. Yours demands her grandson save souls."

Annie waved Stan off. He was only making things worse. "Mama," she tried again, "Max is just a boy. He's not a savior."

"Annie, it's the Lord's will. Do not turn your back on the Lord, like the Jew."

"Excuse me," Stan muttered, unbelieving.

"You were raised a decent Christian," Sarah-Jean continued, ignoring Stan. "Satan welcomes those who turn from the light."

Annie raised her hands as if to stop a physical fight. "Okay, all right. Mother, take a breath. Stan, I'll handle this . . . Now, you have no right to accuse Stan of anything . . . Stan, I just want to know what kind of danger she thinks Max is in."

"They will come for him. Four living creatures who wear robes of white and crowns of gold. In their hands, they hold lightning and thunder and carry unnatural death."

"What is she talking about?" Stan asked, trying not to show his outrage.

"Revelation, boy," Sarah-Jean answered. "It's a happy man who heeds the words of the prophecy."

"I'm overjoyed," Stan replied.

"Mother, please calm down. I—just can't—" Annie paused, looking for the right words. "Okay, what angel? When did Daddy see it?" she asked finally.

"Dear child, we all see angels. I do not question when or where, any more than I question faith. I admit the angel I see does not speak of your son, but—"

"Excuse me," Stan interrupted. "You see angels?"

"Yes. Certainly," she said, and raised a bony finger, swiveling it to point at Stan's nose. "You are a man of the Old Testament. You must believe in prophecy."

"That depends," Stan answered.

"Then your answer is no. Because like faith, either you *believe* or you don't. Nothing depends. I suggest you read Psalm 96 as if it were for today, and all those that follow, one for each year after. They are the prophecies of God."

"Fine, right, let me go jot that down in my daybook," Stan said with restrained anger.

"Mother, what danger are we in?" Annie asked again.

Sarah-Jean moved closer to her daughter. " 'Let the heavens rejoice,' " she began, 'the earth exult, let the sea roar and all creatures in it, let the fields exult and all that is in them; then let all the trees of the forest shout for joy before the Lord when he comes to judge the earth.' "

"Whoa, stop—I've heard enough. I can see where this is going." Stan moved closer to Sarah-Jean. "Fire and brimstone judgment time."

"Psalm 97. 'Cloud and mist enfold him. Righteousness and justice are the foundation of his throne. Fire goes before him and burns his enemies all around. The world is lit beneath his lightning-flash; the earth sees it and writhes in pain. The mountains melt like wax as the Lord approaches.' "

"Like I said, I've heard enough." He turned to Annie, "Honey, I don't think we'll be saving mankind this evening. In fact, I was kind of looking forward to a quiet dinner, some TV and turning in early."

"You don't believe. You spend hundreds of hours securing your home from common criminals, but you don't believe in soldiers of evil." Sarah-Jean paused. "Evil has many faces. Criminals, soldiers, politicians, anyone who lacks faith. Save yourself, your family. Believe. The hour of our Lord is at hand." Sarah-Jean turned to her daughter. "Keep your son safe. He is in danger. As we all are. Believe in the Lord."

"Mother. I just— He's just a boy."

Sarah-Jean turned to Stan. "You've done it, haven't you. You've poisoned her. She's lost her faith."

"Mother!" Annie yelled. "Leave Stan out of this. I—"

Sarah-Jean did not wait for Annie to continue. Instead she pushed past Stan and headed for the front door, grabbing her bag.

"Mother, wait—" Annie called after her. Stan put a hand on Annie's shoulder. "Let her go, Annie—you're not going to change her. Let her go."

Annie shook her head and moved to the front door. She watched as her mother became flecked with rain. "Mother, come back," Annie yelled, but Sarah-Jean did not respond.

Valerie caught her reflection in Fire's gold helmet. The image surprised her. She looked so juvenile. She felt more like a kid dressed up for trick or treat than a killer. But that was what she was; she held the vial of K1397 in her gloved hand, while Fire locked down her helmet. The suits were from a field research team of the Centers for Disease Control. They were designed for sub-Saharan weather, white with a mirrored helmet. They looked more like Apollo moon-suits than equipment for the CDC.

"Can you hear me all right?" she asked Fire through the headset.

"Loud and clear," Fire responded. "Oh, what great luck. Mohammed has come to the mountain."

"What?" Valerie asked. Fire pointed out the front window at Sarah-Jean walking toward them.

"I'll grab her, you dose her and she'll infect the whole family."

Valerie nodded and positioned herself.

"Stand by," Fire said and watched the old woman come even with the door. "Now," she yelled and Valerie slid open the door. Fire grabbed Sarah-Jean hard and pulled her in. The door closed behind them.

"Do it," Fire demanded and slammed the old woman to the floor. Without a second's delay, Valerie opened the tiny warm vial and splashed it on Sarah-Jean's face. It was done. The poison had been delivered. Valerie fought off a wave of nausea as she looked down at the old woman squirming, clawing at her eyes. She could hear muffled screams of pain through her helmet and felt regret. There was nothing pretty about it. But there was relief in knowing it was finally over. At least she would not have to give it to the child—that, she had dreaded.

"Can we go now?" Valerie asked.

Fire did not respond. Valerie turned and froze. From her angle, she could see inside Fire's helmet. She could see Fire's face. There was neither compassion nor guilt in that face. Instead, Fire's eyes were cold, lifeless.

Was this really her lover? What had she become?

"Drive to the next street. We'll drop her there," Fire ordered.

Valerie wanted to scream "No!" But she lacked courage. She realized she had been living out her fantasy of being a tough girl, when she wasn't, but there was nothing she could do. She made her way to the driver's seat, and did not look back.

Sarah-Jean fought the pain deep behind her eyes, like a thousand needles buried into her flesh. She gasped and her throat burned like coals. As she struggled, she glimpsed one of her attackers. It was not what she expected, though she wasn't sure what she expected; perhaps a ghetto street punk, or a homicidal maniac. Instead, she saw her own face—grossly distorted in a golden reflection. It was the head of a beast, just as the Bible foretold. Dressed in white, the beast held its foot against her shoulder, pinning her to the floor.

There was a horrible screech. It took a second for it to register as car brakes. The beast lifted her up. She could see out the window. They were in a van and, she thought, still in her daughter's neighborhood.

They've come for him, she thought. *These devil creatures.* She had to warn Annie. *Lord Jesus, help me*—and before she could finish, she was outside. Thrown onto the wet ground between two parked cars. The van disappeared down Euclid Avenue, leaving her with her pain.

Valerie drove two miles and pulled into the parking lot of a run-down convenience mart. The sky blue Lincoln Continental with Nevada license plates was parked on the side of the store. They would use it for interrogating the third witness.

"I'll set up the decontamination unit," Fire said, pulling a large metal suitcase from the back of the van. It was a portable shower, designed by the army's R and D for field combat, a perfect invention for urban terrorists fleeing a biological war. Within minutes, they both were clean and dressed as if to go shopping at the mall.

LYMAN HALL, SYRACUSE UNIVERSITY, SYRACUSE, NEW YORK. 6:18 P.M.

Alexis was writing the latest NOAA ocean current speeds and temperatures on a large world map hanging on the wall when the four entered her room.

She had not really heard them, but felt them, rather like the feeling you get when you are sure someone is watching you and turn and see that they are. So it was not a surprise when she saw the two clean-cut men and two women standing in her doorway.

"May I help you?" she asked, figuring they were looking for some other room, some other professor.

"Yes, Ms. Campbell, you can," Fire said, moving toward her while the others followed.

"Do I know you?" Alexis asked, her British accent emphasizing every word.

"No, I'll introduce myself. Dr. Katherine Fire, my assistant, Valerie Ross, and our associates."

Alexis could see the young woman was not pleased to have been introduced, though why that should be escaped her.

"How do you do. And what is this about, Doctor?" Alexis asked, pushing her hair back.

Fire held her hand out and Getz gave her a sheet of paper from his suit pocket. Alexis noticed his leather gloves and thought how inappropriate for warm wet weather.

"We need you to look this over and give us your best guess as to what it means," Fire said, holding the paper out. Alexis hesitated and Fire smiled. "I was hoping to avoid going through channels. I've heard you don't insist on university protocol," she said.

Alexis nodded. It made sense, and the "Doctor" almost certainly made Fire a colleague somewhere in the university.

"Of course, Doctor," she said, taking the paper. "May I ask what department you are with?"

"Unfortunately, I was recently kicked upstairs into administration," Fire said. "Can you help with this? It's rather urgent."

"I'll do my best." Alexis smiled and leaned forward against her desk. But as she examined the page, she recognized the writing as Eva's.

"Oh, you know Eva. What did she tell you?" Alexis asked, looking up fast enough to catch Fire's eye. For an instant, she could see hesitation.

"Eva"—Fire paused before continuing—"said you would have a better understanding, since this is weather related."

"Oh," Alexis nodded. She had not recognized the markings. "Well, I think she just put one over on you. I haven't a clue."

Valerie stepped closer. "Oh, surely you must. Eva said it was some kind of weather map. That it had to do with human survival."

"Well then, you know more than I. Perhaps I should give Eva a ring and she could fill me in."

"That won't be necessary," Fire said, glancing at Valerie with a look of irritation. "If you have nothing to add—you have nothing to add."

Alexis watched as Fire reached in her purse for something. She could see that the younger woman was clearly uncomfortable with this action.

"Look, I have all kinds of weather maps. But I don't see any resemblance to this drawing."

"Why don't you take a closer look," the younger woman said.

"I said *I'd* ask the questions." Fire glared at Valerie. The Berets glanced at each other with a look of amusement.

"I thought you were done," Valerie countered.

Alexis tried to calm down the two. "See here, map or not, the survival of any given species is based on weather patterns and these, of course, are inherently unstable. This accounts for evolution. What can't evolve becomes extinct."

"And man's evolution?"

"What evolution? Man's the only species to break nature's rule. He hasn't evolved since he climbed down from the trees."

Fire looked surprised. "Really? What about caves to houses?"

"Exactly. They're the same in principle. Instead of adapting to environment, growing fur and layers of fat for a coming ice age, he simply built fires and moved into a cave. Today, the world is growing hotter so he kicks on the air conditioning. It doesn't end. Advances in medical science have all but stopped the process of natural selection. In short, we're at an evolutionary dead end."

"At last I can agree with you," Fire said, leveling her 9mm Beretta at Alexis.

"Wait a minute, what's all this about?"

"It was about the map," Fire said, holding her aim. "I wanted answers about it, but you chose to fill the air with a bunch of nonsense. So it's over."

"You're going to kill me?" Alexis asked, feeling her head spin with the bizarreness of this action.

"No," Fire laughed. "You're going to kill yourself."

Fire unloaded the pistol clip into Alexis. Each of the fifteen shots hit her body with a slap of red. Valerie stared in disgust at the bloodiness of the execution.

"They call it a Colombian suicide—multiple shots because the will to live is so strong," Fire laughed. She bent to pick up the map from the floor. "Come on," she said, "let's go."

Valerie glanced back. The humor of the situation was lost on her. And it was getting less funny all the time.

She needed to find a way out.

CHAPTER 24

EUCLID AVENUE, SYRACUSE, NEW YORK. 7:10 P.M.

Sarah-Jean staggered as she headed up the winding street, taking shallow, rapid breaths. She could feel her heart beating so fast she imagined it popping from her chest. The colors of the outside world swirled like oil on water. As her blood pressure dropped she lost her equilibrium. She steadied herself, leaning over the hood of a parked pickup.

And as she stood gasping in the rain she was blinded by a light. A car came down the hill with its lights on. She needed to make it stop. She needed to get help.

In a blur, the light became brighter, until there was a screech of brakes, a car horn and more intense pain. She felt fire on her right side and a rush of air as she sailed across the street, where she fell like a limp doll against a tree.

The man in the Honda ran to her. He wore camp fatigues and was on his way north, back to Fort Drum. He had not seen Sarah-Jean as she pulled herself along the parked cars, nor as she stepped into the street. Everything had happened so fast. He leaned over the old woman and held her hand.

"I'm going to get help," he said in a reassuring voice. "I won't leave. You're going to be okay." He tried to remember his medical training from the Gulf war.

"Annie," the old woman whispered. "Help Annie."

"What?" he asked and leaned closer. It was then he noticed the odd chemical smell coming from the gash on the woman's side. He sniffed. It wasn't alcohol, more like ammonia, he thought.

As he made his way to his car's cellular phone, he felt the first wave of nausea hit him. His eyes and throat began to burn. Holding the phone, he dialed 911 and returned to the woman.

"This is the emergency operator; what is the problem?"

The man did not respond. He had put the phone down to hold the old woman as her arms flailed and legs kicked in final death throes. He could see that her eyes had rolled back.

"Hey, you!" a teenager called from the house whose lawn they were on. The girl took a couple of steps down the porch holding her baby in her arms. "What happened?"

"Get back," the man yelled. "Toxic fumes."

The phone, he thought and reached for it, but fell forward on his face. Lying on the wet pavement now inches from the cellular, he realized he was paralyzed.

Two words came to mind. Two words that he said aloud for the emergency operator. "Nerve gas."

An hour had passed by the time Andros turned his rental car up the street. He could see a dozen flashing red lights ahead as squad cars and EMT crews lined Euclid Avenue. God, he hoped he wasn't too late.

Andros eased on his brakes as he came to a small line of cars waiting at the roadblock. All were turned back. Finally it was his turn. A deputy came to the driver's door wearing a yellow raincoat, a pair of latex gloves and a gas mask. They were standard county issue, but worthless for what they were up against.

Andros rolled down the driver's window. "Evening, Officer. What happened?"

"Chemical accident. Toxic fumes. You'll have to turn around."

"But I need to get to Demong Drive. Is there another route?"

"No, sir, it's at the top of the hill," the deputy answered. "We'll have it cleared by morning."

"But I can't—" Andros countered.

"You got no choice here," the deputy answered, tapping the hood. "Turn your vehicle around." The deputy motioned to the next car to move up.

Andros rolled up his window and began his turn. "I see. Thank you," he said aloud, though he was the only one listening. He glanced in his rearview mirror as he headed back.

He had come too far to give up now. Seeing his chance, he swerved into a wooded driveway. In the dark of the pines, he opened the trunk and pulled out his own bio-suit. He locked on the helmet and pressurized the oxygen. Then on foot, he headed back up the hill. From the thick brush of a neighbor's yard he could now see he had passed the barricade. Up ahead were three Fire Rescue units.

Andros moved closer. He had to see if it was a chemical accident or the bio-weapon. So far, he had not seen any overturned chemical trucks, trains or cars. Or for that matter, any casualties.

Andros had crossed a lawn a few doors down from his target when he saw two medics in oxygen pressurized bio-hazard suits wheeling a man, his arms and legs flailing in apnea tremors. The medics held him down on the gurney. A third trailed the cart, filling the victim's lungs with an Ambu-bag, a football-shaped bladder that sent air to the mask covering the man's mouth and nose. Andros moved closer and heard the sound of a baby crying from a neighboring home.

What had Fire done? How many had been affected?

There was a frantic knocking across the street. He turned and saw two more medics waking neighbors, warning them not to come out, then placing the yellow quarantine seals over their doors.

Andros was in the maze of squad cars and EMT ambulance trucks when he saw the first body bag.

Who was it? He had to know.

He had started toward the dark blue bag, when two medics stepped out from around a truck. Suddenly behind him, voices.

"Oily sheen on the epidermis," a medic said, coming quickly up the sidewalk with a gurney. Andros dived behind a squad car and watched as a teenage girl moved past, followed by more medics holding her crying baby.

"Blood pressure dropping."

"Hurry, get the defib ready, truck three," the first said, changing the course of the gurney toward a closer truck.

"We're losing her," the first medic called.

It had to be the same virus. Fire had tested it at Dreamland, only to use it here. He needed to find Max. He had to get up the hill. But as he started back through the maze of rescue vehicles toward the shadows of trees, he came face to face with several medics. Andros turned to retreat, but was blocked by two deputies. "You're under quarantine arrest," said one, training his gun dead on Andros's heart.

Andros said nothing. He knew it looked bad to be found in a level-four bio-suit. Surely he would be a suspect, but he was surprised when the deputy announced on his radio, "We have him, Sheriff. We got the terrorist."

211 DEMONG DRIVE, SYRACUSE, NEW YORK. 9:15 P.M.

The only light in the room was not from emergency vehicles but from a single romantic candle flickering on the side of the bathtub. Stan held Annie's foot up out of the water and ran his hands over her smooth legs, modeling them as if they were clay. He brought one to the side and kissed it. Then he slid his hand under the warm water toward her. Annie closed her eyes and did not stop him as he lifted her, so that she sat upon him. Her back arched, so that her wet breasts fell in his face; his hands slid from her butt up her back, caressing her. He heard her breath catch.

The rhythm of their lovemaking became faster. He could feel himself climaxing and Annie seemed to melt into his moves as if they were one. Her fingers grabbed his shoulders and dug into his skin. Stan suckled her breasts hard and Annie cried out. And then together, they wept as the act ended.

"God, Annie, I love you so much."

She held him close. The years she had rejected him were finally over. They had made love, beautiful love. Stan held her close, breathing in the freshness of her wet skin. And when they finally left the bathtub, it was as if they were young lovers again, afraid to let go. Holding hands in bed. Dreaming of each other as they slept.

EUCLID AVENUE, SYRACUSE, NEW YORK. 10:05 P.M.

Andros stared in disbelief at the handcuffs over his bio-suit. It surprised him that he had been stupid enough to be caught. But no amount of talking was going to change the overweight, middle-aged sheriff's mind.

"That militia shit is not going to fly up here," the Sheriff said from under his gas mask. "You'll get the death penalty."

"Officer, I am not trying to be Timothy McVeigh, I assure you."

"Let me tell you something—when they strap you into that big chair and flip the switch, I'll be there."

"I'm sure you will be," Andros agreed. It was no use arguing without ID. Why not a militia? It made more sense than a rogue military group out to destroy visiting aliens.

In time, he knew he could clear it up, but time was what he didn't have. The flashing blue lights of the squad car reflected off his helmet.

"Get in," he heard as a wiry deputy pushed him into the back seat of the sheriff's car. Andros fell against the heavy-gauge grille separating the front seat from the back. It took him a second to pull himself up. By that time, the sheriff had gotten behind the wheel. He was personally driving him down to the SUNY Health and Science Center for decontamination and questioning.

They had just headed down the street when the radio crackled in the front. "We have two deputies down at 412 Euclid. Repeat, two deputies down at 412 Euclid. Immediate medical assistance needed—"

Andros watched the sheriff grab the radio's mike and give him a telling glance in the rearview mirror. "What's the problem, Deputy?"

"Sheriff, everybody's sick up here. Something's wrong—"

"What the hell do you mean?" the sheriff demanded, but as he asked, his thick stubby fingers suddenly knotted up in muscle spasms. "Ahhhhh!" he wailed, then stared in horror as his legs began to shake and his foot mashed the gas pedal. With a lurch the car took off. Andros watched the speedometer rise from 30 to 45 to 60 to 70. The lights, the houses blurred at this speed.

The sheriff could barely control the steering, his arms were trembling so badly. They sideswiped a couple of parked cars, ran over a lawn, through a picket fence and down a busy cross street.

"Stop! You've got to stop the car!" Andros yelled. The poor bastard was infected. He figured the gas mask had protected his eyes and throat, but enough skin had been exposed to absorb the airborne poison.

The car bounced off the curb and the sheriff abruptly slumped to one side. In the mirror Andros could see only the whites of his eyes. The sheriff had lost consciousness.

There was a loud deep horn blast and Andros looked up. The car had crossed into oncoming traffic. A gas tanker was ahead and closing fast, no way to avoid it. Its loud horn blew again and again until they hit. The driver swerved, avoiding a head-on, but clipped the front bumper off the car and spun it around.

"Shit," Andros screamed as he was slammed hard to the seat.

He watched the red letters of Texaco blur past. A second later, glass blew in as the tanker erupted in a huge fireball and a wave of heat whooshed by.

Andros pulled himself up and saw they were still moving fast. He pounded on the grille separation, but it was obvious the sheriff was dead. His head was pushed at a strange angle against the wheel and his foot was jammed on the gas. If the poison had not killed him, his broken neck would have. Of all the ways for the lawman to die, Andros thought, he had to pick one that would kill his prisoner too.

There was a jarring bang, followed by a sick feeling of being airborne. The car had jumped the curb, then landed with a heavy thud. Grass and trees blurred as Andros looked out. The car raced through woods with branches smacking the windows and scraping the sides. Then finally, a clearing ahead, a moment to take a breath.

As he got closer, Andros realized it wasn't a clearing at all, but a rain-filled ravine. Andros clawed at the door, but it was locked and without handles. He was trapped.

He turned just in time to see the big pine. WHAM! The car hit it full on, then spun 360 degrees and landed in the ravine. There was another flash of bright light, as if a second tanker truck had exploded, then darkness.

When Andros came to, the car was sitting on its side against a boulder. The roof had been smashed in and he could hear the sound of water splashing. He looked up and saw muddy streams of water flowing in from the broken rear window. The car was filling quickly. In minutes it would be completely filled. He peered into the dark. The water outside roared past, like a dangerous river. If he wanted to live, he had to get out fast.

He pushed his hands through the broken glass of the rear window. The handcuffs were making a difficult job nearly impossible. With them on, he could not grab hold. All he had to work with were his feet.

Andros twisted himself halfway out the window. The muddy cold water slapped him. He gave a kick, then shoved a knee through. Sharp pain rippled through his thigh where a large shard of glass impaled it. But before he could think about it, the car suddenly shifted, fell off the rock, and began moving downstream.

Andros pulled his bleeding leg the rest of the way through the broken window and jumped. He hooked his handcuffs around the edge of the big rock to keep from going with the car. His legs flew out from under him, and he swayed in the current like bait dragged behind a boat. In minutes his wrists were numb from the twisting of the cuffs.

He looked up the bank of the ravine. Here it was about two feet high, but it was higher downstream. If he was going to get out, this would have to be the place.

He pogoed on his good leg to get behind the rock where the water was shallower and there was no current. He caught his breath and reviewed his situation.

First, he had to pull the glass from his leg. The pain had become a throbbing deep bone ache. At the surface he saw the five-inch shard that had ripped through the bio-suit to stab into his thigh. He was not losing a tremendous amount of blood, but enough to make him dizzy. Especially when he looked at it.

Andros probed the wound and tried to get a solid grip on the shard of glass without ripping his fingertips. He looked away, took a deep breath, and pulled, as rapidly and smoothly as he could. "Ahhhh—shit," he said. But the shard was out. He looked at it, shuddered, and dropped it to the ground. He took a deep breath and, as a thought hit him, held the breath.

Had the bio-weapon infected him?

There was no way to know until it was too late. He could hope that the running water in the ravine had served as a natural decontamination force. It was a slim chance, but possible.

For now, he had to proceed as if he were not contaminated. There was no point in waiting to die; either he was infected or he was not. If he was, he would know shortly. If not, he had a job to do.

First, he had to get rid of the handcuffs. Holding his hands up he slammed them down on the side of the rock. After ten hard minutes of whacking it, he realized that although there is only one link in American-made handcuffs, it is far from weak. But after another twenty minutes he finally broke them.

Wounded and exhausted, Andros closed his eyes for just a moment to catch his breath and then thought, *Breath. I'm not infected.* With a ragged grin he stood and dragged himself out of the ravine, up into the woods. At the top he rested. He could see two streams of lights on the hill. One came from cars on the street, the other from homes that backed the ravine. Together, they flowed like lava down the hillside. All he had to do was follow the ravine. He could bypass the deputies and their road blocks and finally reach the Katzes' home.

Andros unzipped his bio-suit and ripped the sleeve off his T-shirt. He bit his lip with the pain as he tied off the bloody gash on his leg. Then he limped through the woods up the hill.

CHAPTER 25

211 DEMONG DRIVE, SYRACUSE, NEW YORK.
11:20 P.M.

Annie awoke with Stan's warm arms holding her close. They had fallen asleep on the bed, like two spoons fitted together. She remembered making love, enjoying a warm bath and before sleep, his taking her again. His hands had caressed the sleekness of her hips and fullness of her breasts as if for the first time. His mouth had explored her and, when orgasm came, it had convulsed her whole body. Thinking about it renewed the tingling and made her smile. She squeezed Stan's hand and then moved to climb out of bed.

She had not checked on Max since Stan had put him to bed at eight. She crept downstairs and entered Max's room. There he was, surrounded with all Stan's security—video camera, light sensors, movement lasers and a battery-operated Gerber baby monitor.

Max had pushed off his *Men in Black* comforter in his sleep, so that it sat in a pile beside his race car bed. The moonlight coming in through the window reflected off his white hair and gave him the appearance of an angel. But he wasn't, Annie reminded herself. He was just a boy. A little boy. Her boy. And his room, filled with books and toys, served as a reminder that all she wanted was a regular boy, one who would put together his train set and beg his father to play conductor. That day would come. He was almost there.

Annie leaned over Max and kissed him on the forehead. She brushed his bangs from his eyes and was startled to see him awake, staring at her.

"Oh, I didn't mean to wake you."

"Mother," he said, reaching up to touch her face.

"Yes," she answered, but felt a chill as his fingers touched her cheek. They didn't feel like his fingers; they were soft, rubbery and cold. She took his hand in hers and watched as five human fingers melted into three. They were long and thin, below them a strange double-jointed thumb.

"Oh God," she said and stared in horror as his eyes dissolved into solid black. Her beautiful blue-eyed child was an alien, his pale skin darkening to gray, his hair falling out, his lips receding to a slitlike mouth.

"No!" she screamed. "Don't do this." And in her mind she heard, *It is already done.*

Annie grabbed Max by the shoulders and cried, "Please, not this!"

Just then, Annie felt a stronger hand grab her shoulder. Her body shook—and suddenly she awoke in bed next to Stan.

"Honey, honey, it's okay," he said. "It's just a bad dream."

Annie rubbed her eyes and sat up. "I'll say. What time is it?"

Stan rolled over and looked at the clock. "A couple minutes after two. But everything is okay." He reached for Annie and stroked her back.

"Max?" she asked.

"I just checked him. In fact, I was just coming up the stairs when I heard you yelling."

"You're sure he's okay?"

"He's fine. Honest. But check on him yourself."

Annie tossed back the heavy comforter but as she did, a bright blue light shot down outside their window.

"Max!" Annie screamed.

Both she and Stan felt the strange numbness strike their bodies. It started at their feet and worked its way up.

"No!" Before them, on their 27-inch television, was a grainy picture of Max's bedroom.

"It's activated by the light sensors. This is real, Annie."

They struggled against their paralysis, but it was a fight they could not win.

The strange blue light streamed through into Max's bedroom. There was a whirl of electronic noise as various small motors were activated.

Max awoke, rubbing his eyes. He turned toward the sound, the servo-motor on the camera's focus. As the camera panned the room from left to right, he watched with interest. For a moment he wondered what was happening. Then he saw them.

They appeared first as shadows on the glass, then as real figures, passing through the glass and into the room.

Annie watched horrified as the four small gray creatures approached her son. "We've got to help him," she said and saw Stan struggling to do just that.

He had forced himself to the side of the bed but without control of his legs he had fallen to the floor.

His eyes seemed glazed over as if he were in a trance. He was lying there on the floor staring up at the TV. Annie realized she couldn't move either. She could not turn her head, move her hand or even open her mouth. The only thing she could do was move her eyes and when she did, she saw the TV. It was like watching a horror film, only she couldn't turn it off or make it go away. These aliens were real and they were approaching her son. The taller one reached out his thin arm to touch Max's head. There was a moment of stillness, anticipation, and then her boy screamed.

He screamed as only a small child can, in that high-pitched, nauseatingly long shriek, the kind that bypasses logic and digs straight into raw nerves. It was the shriek of a child saying, "I'm hurt." And while Annie knew Max was not hurt, at least not yet, she knew he was scared. Scared in a way she had never seen before.

Max stared into the black liquid eyes of the taller being. He knew they wanted him to calm down. But his fear was not really his own. Fear until that day had been a foreign emotion, but he had made it his own when he shared Stan's feelings. Now, he was overpowered by fear. his body stiffened and shook, like a baby in mid-tantrum. He felt the air scream out from his lungs in a noise that hurt his ears and left him gasping.

In his head he heard their comforting words. *Do not be afraid. We will not hurt you.* He turned to the video camera and screamed, "Mother!" At that moment, the taller alien seemed to recognize the camera for what it was. In that same moment, all the electricity in the house suddenly went dead. In the dark there was only quiet, quiet ripped by the shrieks of the child.

This was the hardest moment Stan could remember. He lay on the floor unable to move. He knew they were there. He could see the light from the ship filtering through the window blinds. He could hear his son's cries on the battery-powered baby monitor. The aliens were inside his house. Everything he had done to protect his family had failed. He felt the pit of his stomach rise up as if some invisible force had reached down, yanked it up and watched as he lay choking on it.

Rolling his eyes to glance at Annie, he saw the tears on her cheek. *Damn them,* he thought. *Leave us alone.* And then, the shrieks clipped off into abrupt silence. The light of the ship moved off and he knew they were gone.

Stan closed his eyes and wept.

A quarter of a mile from the house, in the thick of the woods, Andros rested his bad leg on top of a fallen tree. He was slowly making his way up the hill when he saw it. At first, he thought it was a full moon.

Then it moved.

It was coming closer, closer, and then it passed silently above the tall pines, a huge triangular craft glowing white. Slowly it changed course to the west.

Andros wanted to signal it, to make contact. But short of throwing stones, he had nothing. He watched as the craft turned away and without a sound shot up into the stars.

INSIDE ALIEN SHIP; SPACE.

Max wanted to run, but his legs were too heavy. Instead he continued a slow, almost mechanical, pace down the long gray, fog-filled hall. The small beings next to him held his hands and tried to comfort him. *Don't be afraid. We won't hurt you. Don't be afraid.*

But Max was afraid.

He now felt the human emotions within him. He could see with human eyes and felt repulsion toward the strange little doctors. He could smell the alien chemicals in the fog and he could feel his heart race, his hands shake, while sweat formed on his brow.

You are one of us, the small being insisted with no movement of his lipless mouth. *We won't hurt you.* Max felt the alien's cool rubbery touch on his arm. They turned and entered a room filled with hundreds of humans on examining tables. Max was surprised to see how enormous the room was. From where he stood it seemed to go on forever. And the only sounds in the room were the shuffling of feet, the chitter of medical equipment and a few weak moans from humans.

"I am not one of you. You're ugly," he said. But the creature showed no emotion, leading him in a procession past dozens of humans being examined or operated on.

They stopped at an empty table beside an overweight man. The man was on his back, naked, and four small doctors stood around his abdomen. A steady hum pulsed from a central machine with a hose running from the ceiling to a metallic funnel over his groin.

Max could hear the thoughts of the taller being bending over the man. *Calm down,* she said and put her hand on his forehead. She leaned in close, very close, to the man's face. *You're okay.* But the man argued, "You have no right. No right to do this." Max felt her mild amusement as she assured him, *We have the right.*

The smaller doctors poking at the man's privates suddenly seemed pleased and removed the funnel. Max could sense their thoughts and knew the man had done well for them.

Heat came from a light above Max and he saw his table had its own set of bright lights and tools hanging from the ceiling. A shiver ran down his spine.

Hearing a moan, he turned. The man was being helped down from his table. A small doctor on each side seemed to control him. Such a large, powerfully built man could easily have beaten away these small beings, but they had taken his will. His face was contorted in a fearful grimace.

Cold rubbery fingers wrapped around Max's arm. *Come up on the table,* the being said. Max found himself unable to resist. Two more small doctors joined them, grabbing Max's shirt and pulling until it slid up over his head.

Don't be afraid, he heard in his mind. *You're one of us. Part of the plan.*

"What plan!" Max demanded, not certain if he had said it aloud or only in his mind. "Where is Father?"

The being did not reply. Max felt his underwear tugged down his legs. Only after he was cold, naked and thoroughly frightened did the doctor answer him.

It is time. Come with me.

Max was led to another room across the hall. In it was a large oval pool filled with blue liquid. *Renew yourself, enter.*

"No. I don't want to," Max said, but the little doctor urged him again. *Come, it's not bad.*

Max stared into the being's hypnotic black eyes, for how long he did not know. His mind no longer seemed his own. He wanted to get into the pool. He wanted to do whatever this being told him to do. He watched as the little doctor eased himself in and stood chest deep. *Come in,* he ordered, and Max obeyed.

As he stepped into the pool, he felt the warm liquid slide up his legs. It was thick like pudding and gave his skin a bluish cast. With each step, he sank deeper until he was under. He kept his eyes open and saw the thin legs of the being across from him. He felt the little doctor in his mind again. *Breathe,* he said.

Max opened his mouth and took in the liquid. It had no taste, but filled him. His chest felt heavy and, to his surprise, he had no pain. Air burst from his lungs and rose to the surface in a cloud of bubbles. He gave in to the choking and inhaled even more of the fluid. Everything seemed to slow down. His heart beat in rhythm to his breathing. The last air bubbles rose from his body and he suddenly felt a part of a bubble. He was aware of its movement through the liquid, could feel its motion, its struggle to reach the surface, its connection with the fluid. He was the bubble. He was fluid. He was connected to everything in the pool.

And as the bubble reached the surface, his eyes closed and his world went black.

THE ANTHILL, DULCE, NEW MEXICO

Max did not remember leaving the pool. He did not remember getting dressed in a white smock. His first memories were of a huge dark triangle below a starry sky. This time it was not from the familiarity of his own backyard. The alien ship was one of dozens lit by thousands of artificial lights hung from a cavern ceiling. Max was underground.

Bustling activity surrounded him. People were being led in slow lines off ships. Groups of gray beings moved glass containers of floating fetuses. But what caught his attention were the strange animals, unlike any Max had ever seen. They were held behind energy bars that formed crates. A set of three crates were being moved on a tram. Max held his hand out toward one of the creatures. It had the legs of a kangaroo, large batlike wings and a face not unlike that of a human. Its eyes stared at him with intelligence, seeming to plead for escape. He eased toward it and the creature smiled. Its teeth were fangs and its hands were sharp claws.

Do not touch, a small being warned. But Max still stepped forward, wanting to help the animal. He suddenly felt dizzy and his inner ear hurt.

It will pass, the doctor said. Max turned and saw that the being from the ship was with him. He was glad. In the pool, the being had entered his mind and given him a sense of peace, even though he had been terrified.

"Why have you brought me here?" Max asked.

You will understand soon, he heard in his mind. They continued toward what appeared to be a series of elevators. There was an alien symbol on the wall above the elevator. *Level two,* Max read.

"Where are you taking me?"

Do not be afraid, the being answered. Soon they stood before the elevator. The door did not open like most doors, but more like the iris of the eye enlarging in the light. Max felt a tug at his arm and entered. There were other small doctors with them, but no other humans.

"Where are the people going?" Max asked, noticing they were leaving on another bank of elevators across from them.

They go to level seven.

"What happens then?"

Do not be afraid.

"Why won't you answer me?"

We are not going to hurt you.

Max tried to probe the being's mind. It had been so easy with humans, picking up thoughts and feelings. But if he sensed anything now, it was only slight amusement. Max turned and stared into the eyes of these doctors—nothing. Cold as marble.

"What's going on? Who are you?" He tried to demand answers, but picked up only what they wanted him to know.

He watched the four long fingers work the control panel.

Suddenly the elevator took off. Down at first, then a quick turn to the right, followed by a 45-degree angle to the left. Max envisioned himself sinking deeper and deeper into the ground. It would have been impossible for a standard elevator working with cables to make such moves, but nothing about this place was standard. The elevator continued to float, twisting and turning in its descent.

Abruptly they stopped. *Level five,* the alien-sign said. Several of the small doctors stepped out into an enormous chamber. Max could see hundreds of yellow honeycomb-shaped hexagonal pods lining the walls. He knew these were their living quarters. But before he could ask questions the door closed and the elevator dropped.

Max felt his ears pop twice more before the door opened again. Their stop, level six. The doctor led Max into a hub that connected three hallways, each lit by a strangely glowing ceiling, as if it was painted with purple phosphorus.

They walked down one of the halls toward a large room. As Max entered he heard clearly, *Welcome, my son.*

"Father?" he answered. The tall reptilian creature turned to him and held out his long, thin arms. Max wept as he saw him. "Father," he said again and moved to embrace him. He was not frightened. The being looked at Max with its immense dark eyes. The mouth did not move as he spoke. *You know what we are doing.*

"No, no I don't," Max answered, looking at Father.

But you do.

It was then that Max noticed something else about the room. Built into the walls were small cells holding more strange animals. Exotic snakes, endangered panthers, colorful birds.

"Is this a zoo?" Max asked.

The being did not answer. He turned his attention to the center of the room and continued his work. On a table was a small, rare bat. Father used his strange alien tools to take from the animal what he needed. The genetic sample was then placed in a clear slide. He turned and loaded it into an elaborate filing system. A conveyor belt of sorts held millions of these samples.

It is a record of every creature on this planet. Come, Father said and took Max's hand. He led him through an adjoining door to another room. Here were a dozen children. Children Max's age. All had his white hair, thin lips, and large blue eyes. Some were dressed in white smocks, others in black jumpsuits. They stood in silence as Max entered.

Max could sense their curiosity about him. Slowly they moved in. A few daring ones reached out to touch him. The touch energized them. Suddenly one wiped tears from his face, another felt the fear, another simply smiled. It was as if they were living moments from Max's life by simply touching him.

Now you will know what we are doing, he heard Father say. And the being looked deep into Max's eyes and the boy felt himself accept the images. A vision of catastrophic destruction: huge icecaps breaking off, volcanoes exploding, storms ripping through buildings, tidal waves crashing over shorelines, cities and towns flooding.

"Nooo!" Max begged. "Don't do this." The human in him was terrified.

It is necessary for the planet's survival. Father's statement was strong and clear.

"But we must stop it," Max protested.

The gentle being put a hand on Max's temple. *We are your future, we are your past.*

"So it cannot be stopped?" Max asked.

He stared at Father, but received no further message. A second later, an icy feeling enveloped Max and he felt his whole body vibrate. He stared up at Father and saw the gray skin turn a brilliant white and then, as he watched, the being became pure light.

CHAPTER 26

211 DEMONG DRIVE, SYRACUSE, NEW YORK. 6:20 A.M.

The early golden rays of the rising sun cut through the window and shone on Max's face. He awoke with his fists clenched and his body aching. Was it just a bad dream, he wondered? How had he gotten back to his bed?

"Max! Max honey. Thank God you're safe!" his mother said, running into his room. Stan followed right behind her. Max curled into his mother's embrace and inhaled her sweet, soapy scent.

"Mother!" he whispered. "I'm okay."

"Max—I'm so sorry," Stan said, running his fingers through his boy's hair. "Did they hurt you?"

"No, I'm okay," he assured them and leaned back against his feather pillow. A patch of sunlight shone on his face.

"Wait," Annie muttered. "Your eyes." She tipped his chin back. "They're very red."

"Yeah, the lids look a little swollen," Stan added.

"Did they do anything to your eyes?" his mother asked.

"I saw the future."

"You what?" Stan asked, sitting on the foot of the bed.

"I saw"—Max looked between his mother and Stan and thought how best to put it—"what will happen."

"Lies," Annie answered. "These are creatures you don't understand. They want you to believe."

"But I do," Max answered and looked at his mother oddly. He wondered, *How could she forget Father's love?*

"What did they show you?" Stan asked.

"Storms. Big storms. Cities going under water. Big ice melting, lands flooded, lots of people dead."

"Max, you remember the maps at the office? Could you show me what areas were flooded?"

There was a sparkle in Max's eyes. "Yes." Even if he could not stop these terrible things from happening as Father said, he could still help.

"Annie, this is incredible." Stan's voice rose with excitement. "This information could save lives."

"But don't you understand, they're using him, like they used us? We're just pawns in some bigger game."

"Annie, we know global warming is having an effect on the weather. All our studies prove it." Stan moved toward the door, "Put in its perspective—all the war and disease mankind has ever known never threatened to wipe out the human species—weather can."

"You're serious?"

"Very. Droughts produce famines, floods give rise to disease, storms produce mass destruction. Since the birth of this planet there have been only two major extinctions of life—both credited to meteorites. It wasn't the meteorites themselves, but their influence on our weather that caused the extinctions. Our pollution has triggered the same kind of effect. Whatever Max has learned will only help us." He looked at Annie, pleading.

"All right."

Stan grinned. "Great, I'll call Alexis and have her meet us at the office."

"Stan!" Annie protested, but it was too late. Stan had stepped out to the hall phone.

Max watched his mother and felt her jealousy toward Alexis. He sensed her silent outrage that Stan would even consider talking to the "other woman." It was a shame his mother still worried about such things. Stan was right. They needed to get this information out.

The phone rang five times before someone picked up. Alexis had never let her cellular ring more than twice in the few months Stan had known her. "Alex," he said, "we've got to talk."

"Fine," a man's voice said, "but Alexis can't come to the phone right now."

"Who's this? Where's Alexis?" Stan asked, pacing the floor. He could think of a lot of reasons why Alex had not answered her phone, but he was not prepared for the answer.

"She's dead."

"What? Who is this?" Stan asked again.

"Who are you?" The man sounded irritated.

Stan said he was a professor who worked with Alexis.

"Good. What's your name?"

"Why?" Now suspicious, Stan demanded, "Who is this?"

"Detective Wiezman, Syracuse police. Now, full name and address?"

Something ran past the window. Stan caught just the shadow passing. He moved toward the window and whispered into the receiver, "Stan."

"Full name?"

"Stanley Katz," he answered, pulling the curtain back. "As I said, I work with Alexis"—he looked to the left—"at the university." He glanced to the right. Nothing. There was nothing out there that might have made the shadow.

"Good. Now we're getting somewhere. Mr. Katz, we need to talk. What's your address?"

"Why? What happened?" Stan moved to another window and glanced out.

"I'll tell you when we get there."

"No!" Stan mentally flashed on Wesley's assassins entering

Carol's home. Scarcely able to breathe now, Stan remembered the way Carol's body shook when the shots hit her body. The strange calm of the Black Berets. The hairs on Stan's neck stood up and his gut told him—*trust no one.* "You're part of that group, aren't you?"

"What group?" The man sounded angry.

"I'm not stupid. You can't have Max. Leave him alone. Leave us all alone!"

"Mr. Katz."

Stan slammed down the receiver. What should he do? Who could he call? Who could he trust? Again, the shadow passed another window in the next room. He ran to the window and peered out.

Nothing. Was he losing his mind? Okay, get a grip. Think, damn it. Think. Friend—Jerry. Sure—Jerry would help. Stan ran back to the phone, flipped through the Rolodex and dialed.

No answer. After fifteen rings Stan gave up.

Okay, don't panic. *I'm not panicking,* he told himself, and wiped the sweat from his brow. Ahhhh—where could Jerry be? Eva's. That's it. Stan found Eva's number and dialed.

No answer again. Okay—*Now panic!*

The odds that both of his co-workers were out at 6:30 A.M. after a long trip were nil. The odds that they might be dead? Stan thought for a moment. Pretty good. Damn Wesley. Damn his past. It was obvious the government wanted Max back. The aliens were in contact with the boy.

But why murder his university colleagues? Stan paced the floor and pondered, but all he came up with seemed completely crazy. The only possible tie-in—*weather. Their study on the weather and the aliens' predictions about the weather.*

Annie called out, "So what did Alexis say?"

"She didn't—" He stopped, unready to tell her anything. He needed something more logical before he frightened Annie and Max.

"Okay—would you bring in the paper? Maybe someone reported unusual lights or something."

"Right." Stan started toward the door, then stopped. What about the shadow? They could be waiting. Stan took a deep breath. How do you explain this kind of neurosis? For all he knew, Alex's death was accidental and Jerry and Eva had merely un-plugged their phones. They might do that so jerks like him couldn't wake them at such an ungodly hour.

"Paper, Stan?" Annie asked.

"Right." He started for the door, then turned to the old hall closet and took a small black 9mm down from the top shelf. After what had happened to Carol in New Mexico, he had decided he must be able to protect his family, though he had never supposed he would own a gun before. Now the cold steel felt good in his hand. It gave him a sense of security and power. He headed for the front door and swung it wide.

A gentle rain fell. The paper sat wrapped in soggy plastic on the sidewalk twenty yards away. He glanced around the yard. Nothing out of the ordinary. *I can make it,* he decided, and bolted down the slippery porch steps. Grabbing the paper, he turned back.

Had he turned two seconds earlier, he might have seen the figure jump from the bushes and enter the house ahead of him. As it was, he had set himself up for a surprise.

"Are you okay?" Annie asked, studying Stan, who stood in Max's bedroom doorway. He was soaking wet, holding the paper, face pale, eyes wide and stunned.

"Stan?"

"Yeah." He nodded. "It's just that—well, I didn't expect to be right."

"What?" She had not seen Stan act this way in a long time. Not since— "What's going on?"

Stan stumbled as he was pushed forward. Andros stepped from behind him, holding Stan's 9mm. "Hi Annie," he said with a sheepish smile.

"Andros," she whispered, both shocked and terrified. This was the man who had been there when the aliens took her baby.

The same man who promised her the baby would be *all right*. The man who said the government would never bother them or Max again. "Why?" Her voice cracked. "Why are you here?"

Andros, still in his bio-suit, looked much the worse for wear. His leg streaked with blood, his suit muddy and ripped, he took a deep breath before he answered. "I came for Max—"

"Well, you can forget it!" Annie snapped. She felt Max push from behind her and peer at the stranger.

"Thank God you're safe!" Andros seemed genuinely relieved.

"Why wouldn't he be?" Annie asked. "Why the gun?"

Andros stepped forward but Stan put an arm out to stop him.

"I can't let you do this. You'll have to kill me too."

"Kill? Who's been killed?" Annie demanded. She put a protective arm around Max and watched as Stan stared at Andros with absolute hatred.

Stan answered, "Alexis—Jerry—Eva."

"I assure you, I had nothing to do with their deaths."

"Oh, that helps," Stan countered. "Why don't I believe you?"

Andros lowered the gun. "It doesn't matter what you believe. I—"

Stan saw his chance and gave a powerful kick to Andros's bad leg. Andros dropped the gun and fell to the ground. Stan lunged for the weapon, but met a punch. It was not pretty, but it sent him hard against the wall.

Annie was yelling, "Stop, stop, stop!" But neither man listened. Trading a few more blows, Stan landed only inches from the gun and grabbed it. He pulled the slide back, and took aim. Andros froze.

"Sit down," Stan whispered through gritted teeth. Annie kicked one of Max's small child-size chairs toward Andros.

"Please, I'm not your enemy here."

"Good imitation," Stan said, rubbing his jaw.

"I came in the way I did, because I didn't know if you were alive or dead. I didn't know if the Berets were waiting."

"Why would they be?" Annie demanded.

"Because they want Max as much as I do," Andros answered.

"Can't happen," Stan countered.

"Annie, Stan." Andros looked at both before continuing. "Your son is the key. He can communicate with them."

"Them?" Stan asked. "You mean the aliens?"

"Exactly."

"What happened to the happy little family in the desert? Why don't you communicate with them yourselves?" Annie asked.

"We've tried. But since their return, we have failed to understand them, to find their agenda. Until now."

"What do you mean?" Stan asked.

"We've uncovered a library of ancient alien texts. Before this, the only communication has been—well, one-sided. What we heard in our minds."

"What did you expect?" Annie asked.

"I'm only human. I guess, I expected other species to communicate on our level. Wrong as it may be, we expect no less from any other species on this planet. Like—a dog, call him, he comes. Tell him to sit, he sits. Roll over, he rolls over." Andros paused and smiled bitterly. "It's a case of the dog doing all the understanding. He has learned our language. But do we understand his? Have we even tried?"

"No," Annie answered and started to relax. Stan leaned against the wall and listened.

"After thirty years of really studying dolphins, all we can do is identify different whistles for different pods. That's it. The dolphin, on the other hand, understands human language, both verbal and sign. You can argue that he's doing tricks for food. But if mankind's food supply were suddenly based on our understanding another species, we'd starve."

"But the aliens do communicate," Annie argued. "They communicate telepathically."

"Exactly. In hundreds of human languages. Everything that is said is on their terms. How do they think? What do they feel? What do they want? We don't know. But if we could read their writing—for the first time we might learn the answers to these questions and more. Like, where they come from. Who they are. Why have they returned? *What's their agenda?*"

"And Max? Where does he fit in?" Annie asked again.

"You know he's a hybrid. If anyone has a chance at understanding their language, it's him," Andros answered. Unzipping his bio-suit, he reached for his shirt pocket.

"Slowly," Stan said, holding his aim.

"It's just paper." Andros took the fax from his pocket and handed it to Annie. On the page was a strip with a series of strange symbols, several of which were repeated. Annie looked at it for a moment then glanced at Andros. "This is ridiculous," she said, "Max doesn't even read."

Stan interrupted. "But he does. He's read to me. In fact, he read Japanese."

"You mean the translation?" Andros asked.

"No. I mean—I know this sounds crazy, but considering everything that's been going on—I didn't even think about it. But he read. He said the paper spoke to him."

"Maybe this page will too," Andros said.

Puzzling over this, Annie passed the paper to Max, sitting on his bed.

"Max, honey—can you read this?"

Max looked hard at symbols on the page. *What did they mean?* he asked himself. Then, for a moment he connected somehow to something larger. It was a part of his human identity, a part of his alien identity, it was as much Father on the ship as mother at home. A part within him, that was not him, but a communal, collective consciousness. Something so great it brought a tear to his eyes. It had hundreds of millions of individuals living and dying separately, while sharing a common understanding. A bond that crossed time and space and connected all who reached out.

"This line here—" Max pointed to the strange little symbol. "It means circle. These others—'what is, has been.'" He moved his finger along as he read. " 'What will be, already is.' " He looked up at his mother and handed back the paper.

"That's it?" Annie asked, looking again at the page.

Max nodded. "Uh-huh."

"There are a lot of ways to take that," Stan said.

"Yeah, time travel," Andros pointed out. "Some say the visitors come from our past, some say from our future. I lean toward the future."

"But I thought they were from deep in the Vega region. I mean, that's where I found their signal."

"It could have been an explorer ship or base. We're talking about a race light-years ahead of us," Andros pointed out.

"What makes you think they're from our future?" Stan asked.

"You remember the Chernobyl disaster in Russia? It released twice as much radiation as Hiroshima."

"Of course."

"Well, a decade later, our researchers found the area was far from lifeless. Trees grew, plant life survived and animals thrived. Only everything was different. A field mouse whose DNA had been breaking down with the radiation for generations, mutated. In fact, it evolved. In the ten years since the meltdown the rats evolved more than they had during the previous eight million."

"The effect on humans?" Annie questioned.

"Humans take longer to procreate. We won't know for a dozen generations. But there was speculation that like the rats, we would become smaller, hairless, smarter. Different, but the same."

Annie looked at the paper again, the strange alien symbols. " 'What is, has been. What will be, already is.' "

"Weather," Stan answered as if it were a riddle. "Sure, it has to be."

"Weather?" questioned Andros, looking puzzled.

Stan nodded. "Max said that during his abduction he saw

great disasters in the future. Huge storms and flooding, like the great flood. It's from our past and our future."

The small voice of Max piped up from the bedside. "Is there more?"

Andros smiled. "Yes, back at the base. There's a whole library of these strips. Would you like to come—"

"Hold on. Just a minute," Stan interrupted. "I already told you, he's not leaving us."

"But he would be safe."

"Safe from what? You can't protect him from abductions any more than we can."

"True. But it's not the aliens you should be worried about."

"Who then?"

Andros looked away. They could see his jaw work. He looked back and his eyes had changed. They seemed darker, harder. "Within MJ-12, there is a traitor. They've designed a biological weapon to kill the aliens."

"Great," Stan laughed.

"No. They intend to use your son to deliver this poison."

"I don't believe you," Annie said.

"They've already tried once. Open the paper, Stan."

Stan raised the paper and read the headline: "Toxic Gas Kills Three, Injures 12." He read on a moment before passing the paper to Annie. "It happened a mile from here."

"I know," Andros said. "I was there."

"Then how do we know you aren't the traitor?" Annie asked looking up from the paper.

"Because—" Andros began, but was interrupted by a loud cracking smash of the door breaking open. "Hide him, quick!"

Annie looked down the hallway. Four large figures stood in her living room. All wore white bio-suits. They had a surreal look, like Apollo astronauts walking into your living room. She found it hard not to march out and demand answers. But she could see that two of the men were armed.

And they saw her.

CHAPTER 27

"It's okay, honey," Annie whispered, grabbing Max off the bed and holding him close. "We're not going to let anything happen to you."

"Who's here, Mother?" Max asked, looking up at her.

"We don't know," she answered and backed into his closet, closing the door. "But you need to be very quiet. Can you be quiet for me?" She tried to smile, as a way of reassuring him that everything would be okay. She could see him nod in the light that shone through the slats of the door.

"Good boy," she whispered, then poked the door open a crack. Stan waved at her to close it. Andros was beside him and both were kneeling behind the child's bed. On the wall the mirror reflected the two intruders who guarded the front and back doors. The others must have begun a room-to-room search.

The house was silent, except for the sounds of breathing coming from the four oxygen respirators worn by the intruders. This was more than a waiting game. The longer they waited, the less chance for escape. "Stan," she hissed, "We have got to get out of here."

* * *

Stan nodded. He stared at the boy's bedroom window. *Damn,* he thought; he had nailed it shut to install the monitoring devices. Unlike the aliens, they could not pass silently through. *Okay, plan B. Not pretty, plenty of risk.* But it was a matter of logistics. With both front and back doors blocked, their only escape would be through the hall to the stairway, then up to the master bedroom. Stan motioned for Annie and Max to join him.

"Andros and I will lead," he whispered. "You get Max out. Use our bedroom window to the porch roof, from there to the big tree. No matter what happens—I mean it—don't look back, don't hesitate." Stan looked at Annie, hoping she understood, and found her staring back with admiration. She said nothing, but her look was perfect, pure, angelic. She leaned in and kissed him. Her soft lips pushed against his and all he wanted to do was hold her, but there was no time. "Just get out safe," he whispered. "Both of you."

Andros was at his side. "Come on, surprise is our only advantage."

Stan nodded. He looked at Max in Annie's arms and rubbed his boy's head, as if it might bring him luck. "I love you, son," he whispered. He did not wait for a response. "I take the closer one, and you rush the other," he told Andros. "On the count of three," Stan said. "One . . ." He felt his heart race . . . "Two . . ." A bead of sweat rolled down his forehead and his hand felt clammy against the cold steel of his gun . . . "Three!" He sprang from the doorway squeezing the trigger as he charged.

But his aim was wild, both from movement and lack of skill. Of the four shots he got off, only one hit Getz, and only because the poor bastard turned into the line of fire.

Unfortunately, Getz got off a return shot as he went down. It surprised Stan that such a small thing as a bullet could knock him back so hard, an invisible punch socking the wind out of him. He slammed against the wall, given just time enough to grab at his gut and feel his knees buckle. He slid down, leaving a red stain on the wall.

Stan saw the wet sticky mess leaking out onto his shirt. In a moment of self-awareness, he thought, *I've been shot. Damn, I've really been shot.*

"Stan!" Annie screamed. He turned and saw her halfway up the stairs, Max still in her arms. The boy looked down at him, his face contorted as if he could feel Stan's pain.

"Go!" Stan yelled, but it came out in a soft gurgle of blood.

Annie turned and started up the stairs. Stan saw a red laser dot flicker on her back as the second Beret took aim at his wife.

"No," he screamed. He saw Andros leap forward as the Beret fired. His body jerked in midair as he took the hit. Then McKenzie and Andros fell together against the back door.

"Are you crazy?!" Fire screamed, kicking Andros's body off the Beret. "I want that boy *alive!*" McKenzie nodded and hurtled up the stairs.

Stan had no feeling from his chest down and his arms had become remarkably heavy. A pool of blood formed around him. He was surprised he could bleed this much and still be alive. He looked over at Andros and the two jumpsuited killers leaning over him. They appeared to be women. How ugly, he thought, for a woman to be a killer. God's creators, turned to destroyers. His mind drifted for a moment, and then he thought of Annie. That beautiful look on her face when she last kissed him. How proud she made him feel.

That's how he wanted to remember her.

"Run, Max! For God's sake run!" Annie screamed, tears in her eyes as she pushed Max out onto the roof. But the boy just stood there watching his mother struggle to pull herself through the window.

I won't leave you, Mother. She heard him clearly in her mind. She tried to contain her shock—he was doing things *they* did. He really was a hybrid. But she shook the thought off. "No, please, they'll kill you. You must run! Hide!"

No, Mother, he said to her again. She heard heavy footsteps running across the old wood floor. "Max. Go, damn it!" Suddenly the bedroom door splintered open. "Max!" she screamed one last time. But the boy just stood there, worried and silent.

Annie pushed again in a final effort to pull her leg clear of the window. But as she leaned forward to jump, she felt a karate kick smack her back. Her whole body slammed against the wall with such force that she felt the air leave her lungs and she fell like a sack onto the wooden floor.

"Max," she croaked, opening her eyes. *Yes, Mother, I'm here* he answered. *I'm with you.* She heard him and saw his tiny body lifted back through the window by the beast in the white suit. *I'm sorry.*

"He's not infected," Valerie said through the helmet intercom. Fire stared at the boy. No doubt her examination was correct. He did not appear to be sick.

"Damn it," she screamed and pulled off her golden helmet. There was a hiss of oxygen. "My plan was foolproof." She kicked Andros in his bloody wound and ignored his pained grunt. "What did you do to him?"

"Nothing," Andros moaned and spit blood.

"Leave him alone," cried Annie.

Fire turned her attention to the mother handcuffed on the couch beside Andros. "It's not too late, you know. Your boy will infect these creatures."

"No. He's just a child. Use me, you know they abducted me."

"I have a better idea." She turned to Valerie. "We have enough for two doses?"

Valerie nodded yes, though she seemed hesitant.

She turned back to Annie. "Okay, you'll join your son."

"Wait," Annie said. "You don't want to kill a little boy."

"You're right. We're not monsters. But hell—" She glanced from Annie to Max. "He's not a little boy." She added with real hatred, "He's just an unlucky hybrid, in the wrong place at the wrong time. Just know that his death will ensure the survival of our species." She paused and then added, "Kind of funny, a couple of lesbians saving mankind's ass from the aliens."

Annie stared at her with shock. How dare anyone harm Max? Every fiber of her being wanted to stand and fight, but she was unable to break free of the handcuffs.

"The aliens?" Andros groaned. "How do you know what they—"

"I know," Fire took pleasure in telling him, while he winced in pain. "When I was young and naïve"—she smiled and inched closer to his end of the couch—"Wesley found me. I went from being a clinical psychiatrist, who on occasion worked for OSI, to the silent director of Project Grudge. Publicly we were to give psychological answers to the UFO phenomenon. Privately, I worked with one live creature. For two years I studied him in a nine-by-twelve cell."

"What did you learn?" Andros asked.

"It was quite clear, really. They're here because mankind is about to make the next evolutionary step, to extinction—but you knew that." She kicked Andros's wound again and watched him contract in pain.

"You knew the hybrids were being grown to repopulate this planet. Why else bother to have abductees interact with them?"

"Is this true?" Annie asked.

Andros turned to the mother, but did not answer her.

"No matter. Ultimately they'll fail. Just like that first little explorer." She turned to Annie and casually explained, "One day, he just died. No reason, no harm came to him. At least not the kind they're planning for us. That's why we have to stop them." She nodded to her lover. "Ms. Ross has seen to it." She snapped her hand out, palm up. Valerie placed in it two vials of the K1397.

"This woman is one of the finest minds in biological weapon designs. But like so many, she was overlooked and underpaid. Until I gave her her greatest challenge. Saving mankind."

"Please," Annie begged, "don't kill my son." There was a stirring against the wall. Fire could see the father was still alive, but just barely.

"Seems Daddy-o has hung around for your demise."

"Stan? Honey?" She watched him struggle to sit up. "He's alive. You have to get him to a doctor."

"Sorry, that's not in the plan. You see, I'm about to break a vial of poison on you and Max and leave."

"What makes you think the aliens will return for them?" Andros asked.

She smiled at her former boss. "We both know that their bio-implants will transmit distress. If we've learned anything in forty-five years, these creatures hate to lose their lab rats."

She pulled Max in front of her and looked into his deep blue eyes. Then without remorse she shoved him down to a kneeling position by his mother.

"Wait." Andros tried to yell, but it came out as a gurgle. He spat blood. "If you're really doing this for mankind's survival"—more blood dribbled from the corner of his mouth—"have the boy read their texts. He can translate them."

"You son-of-a-bitch!" Annie snarled, "Is that all you care about?"

Andros paid no attention to the mother, but stared hard at Fire. "You don't have a chance, if you don't understand them."

"He might have a point," Valerie agreed.

"Shut up," Fire growled and stood to think. She paced the floor twice before returning to Max. "All right. It won't matter where we do this." She held the boy's face in her hands and talked to him. "They'll come for you—and you'll infect them."

She pushed a button on a homing beacon on her belt. "The chopper will be here in three minutes. Move it."

The Black Beret picked up Annie and hefted her over his shoulder. Fire reached down and grabbed the boy. It surprised her how light he was.

It would have surprised her more if she had heard his thoughts.

Max looked down at Stan from over Fire's shoulder. He could see a big puddle of blood around him. His breathing was slow and labored. Death was moments away. He could feel the emotional hurt. The feeling that he had failed to protect his son and wife. The freedom from his pain would come swiftly if he believed in their love. He needed to hear it. He needed it to come from Max and Max knew it.

Daddy, he whispered in his mind, *I love you.*

As the front door swung closed, Max saw a gentle smile cross Stan's lips. Then his body went limp. The light passed from within and Stan was free.

Everything seemed in slow motion for Annie—the rotor blades of the huge black helicopter descending, the movement of the men pushing and pulling to get her and Max on board. And it seemed so strangely quiet. Instead of the heavy thud, thud, thud, there was only a whoosh of air.

In seconds, with a rush of speed similar to a jet takeoff, they rose until they cleared the rain clouds and the sun's rays shone down, turning the clouds a brilliant silver.

Mother, Max said.

She glanced at Max, who had spoken in her mind as clearly as the aliens. The boy had their gift. He could feel her thoughts and send his own.

Stan has passed on, she heard him say.

No. He's alive, she told him. *He was alive when we left. Someone must have seen the helicopter, one of the neighbors, someone will help.*

No, Stan is with Him now.

Who? Annie asked.

He who wills us to rediscover our union with Him.

God? she questioned. This was ridiculous. How could a five-year-old know such things? Was Stan really dead?

I do not lie, Mother.

Annie closed her eyes and felt her hands shake. Stan was dead. Her mate, the man who had seen her through so much, and, yes, put her through so much—was gone.

Tears streaked her cheeks and she could not control her grief. She had never felt so alone, so vulnerable. After ten years of marriage, knowing he would be there when she awoke, that he cared what she felt, what she thought, the phrase "missing him" seemed hugely inadequate. They were a team, up against whatever the world could throw at them. Which was more than anyone could have imagined. How could she survive without Stan?

Annie cried.

For several hours they headed west, fleeing the rising sun. The ground below changed from the silver white of clouds to the reddish browns of the southwest desert.

Annie glanced over to her son. Max had not moved or even blinked since he had told her of Stan's death. He had gone deep within himself. She had seen this behavior when he was very young. She used to try to imagine what he was thinking. Reliving the moment of birth? Thoughts of heaven? Events from past lives? Or—maybe nothing at all. The dark side she feared was his connection with aliens and this might be merely down time.

McKenzie noticed Max's faraway stare. He took a long drag on his cigarette and smiled. He glanced at Valerie and leaned closer to the boy.

"What are you doing?" Annie asked.

"They say the buggers don't feel pain," McKenzie smirked.

"What?" Valerie inquired.

"I'm sure they're wrong," he grinned and took another long drag till the tip glowed a fiery orange, then stubbed it out across Max's forehead. There was a hiss of skin burning and the stink of flesh and ash mixing.

"No!" Annie screamed. She struggled against the handcuffs and seat belts holding her down. "Max. Oh God, Max?"

Max did not cry, wince, or even acknowledge this action. Instead he continued to stare ahead, wide-eyed.

"You sick bastard," Valerie sneered and turned away from the Beret to stare out the window.

"I was just having fun," McKenzie laughed. He leaned forward like an awkward teenager trying to gain the attention of a pretty girl and put a hand on Valerie's leg. "Look, they aren't really human." He gave a little squeeze on her thigh and tried to work his caress higher.

Valerie smiled and slammed her hand down on his, as if she were squishing a bug. "No thanks."

Annie turned away and looked at her son. Dark red burns crossed his forehead, like so many jewels on a crown. She tried to reach him, using her mind.

Max, honey, are you okay? Where are you?

Max was flying, though that was not really the right word. Gentler, more like the bubble rising in the pool, he had floated up and up. He had heard his mother and he had looked down at his body strapped in the seat. A silver cord connected him, but it seemed to stretch without snapping. He was in control.

The landscape below the helicopter was visible, as was the sky above. He rose higher still. The stars were out, set against the black velvet of space.

He was now high above the earth. The brilliant blue greens of the oceans below, the tan reds of the land, the clouds swirling with the wind. He felt conscious of everything.

When the Beret had burned his forehead, the pain was like a distant memory. He hurt more for his mother. He wished she would follow him up, leave the pain of the body behind and soar free. He must help her. He must find Father.

Father, he cried out. A moment later, he felt a wave of energy, a soothing, gentle wave. He was connected to this wave and directed himself downward, down far ahead of the helicopter.

Father, he called, *I need your help.*

CHAPTER 28

**211 DEMONG DRIVE, SYRACUSE, NEW YORK.
11:23 A.M.**

Lying on the hard wood floor, Andros thought he hadn't heard any movement from Stan for a very long time. How much time he was not sure, because he had drifted off. But through the window, he could see that the sun was up. It seemed fairly high in the sky. Close to noon, he guessed. The light tapping of the rain on the roof had stopped. The whole house was quiet, too quiet.

He strained to sit up. The muscles from his neck to his groin were a solid block of pain. He screamed as this simple move ended with him face down in a warm sticky pool. Inhaling deeply, he could taste and smell the rich metallic iron flavor.

He struggled again, but failed to move. God, he was tired. Pure exhaustion. From eye level, his blood seemed to pool out across the wood like a majestic great lake. His mind played tricks, giving the darker colors depth and the lighter colors the appearance of a shoreline.

I'm dying, he thought, *and I'm losing my mind.*

He had heard that at the last minute before death, the brain hallucinates. Oxygen deprivation creates visions of dead loved ones, golden white light, and visitations of angels. He hoped he could stay awake long enough to enjoy it.

And it happened. The light outside became incredibly bright and he heard the sounds of small feet padding across the floor toward him. Andros smiled. Who would it be? His mother? His grandfather?

"I'm in hell," he said as he looked up into the cold killer eyes of Colonel John Wesley. This can't be happening, he thought. He's dead. But I'm dead. *No, I don't deserve to die with him,* he protested. But Wesley said nothing, just stood, towering, looking down.

"I don't deserve this," Andros spoke again. Yet in his heart he feared he did. While he had not pulled the trigger that had killed Wesley, he had set it up. He had betrayed him. *Do something already,* he thought, *get it over with.* If this was karma, he was ready to work it out.

But Wesley did not move. As Andros watched, the figure of Wesley transformed. First the eyes. From Wesley's bright blue they turned an oily black. Then his face melted so that the cheeks became higher, his nose and lips shrank, and his chin disappeared to a point. Now his body seemed to be a mirage and the waves that made up the appearance of the man dissolved to that of an alien. He was shorter, thinner than Wesley and his skin had a gray reptilian texture.

Don't be afraid, Andros heard the alien say in his mind. He would have laughed out loud, but felt the exertion would kill him. After twenty years of working with abductees, it was now his turn to be taken—and unlike so many before him, Andros was grateful.

DREAMLAND BASE, GROOM LAKE, NEVADA. 7:32 A.M.

As the sun rose over the Badger mountain range, a large black helicopter swooped down. Dr. Katherine Fire looked to the dry Groom Lake bed below. Billions of cracks rippling across the smooth flat surface gave it a texture unlike anything else in the world. Ahead was the six-mile-long airstrip, flanked by three large steel hangars and a dozen smaller buildings.

She was home. Dreamland was hers.

"This is Dr. Fire," she told the radio. The small voice on the other end continued. "Operation Lockup is complete, Doctor. You are cleared for landing, bay four."

"Thank you," she answered. She had left two other members of MJ-12 in charge of her loyal Black Berets. They were NSA and CIA officers who, like her, believed Wesley had been right. The aliens had to be destroyed.

She really didn't expect much of a fight from the remaining MJ-12 personnel. They were all scientists and engineers who lacked the ability as well as the courage to rebel against the lethal Black Berets. The safest thing for the base was Operation Lockup. Take those who remained loyal to Andros and secure them until they could be reasoned with. If she failed to persuade them, she would return to Wesley's old policy of shake and bake.

She had seen it used only once. The shake occurred during the interrogation. The bake lasted five hours. The traitor had been tied to a large Joshua tree in 129-degree heat. A video camera was set up, so Wesley and his men could watch. This was Nevada desert; the Berets had bets going on time and cause of death. Sunstroke paid the shortest odds. Seven hours seemed most likely. Wesley, however, played a long shot and, as it turned out, won. Suicide.

The vultures had begun to work over the man, pecking at his flesh, when a rattlesnake passed by. The man had kicked at the snake and caused it to coil. The defensive posture caused the birds to back off. He could have left it alone, but he didn't. With the good eye the vultures had left him, he took aim and kicked again. The rattler struck and held on, pumping enough venom into the man to kill two horses.

While Fire could not then imagine giving out such a painful death sentence, base security rose tenfold with only a slight decline in morale after Wesley's little display.

"Everybody all buckled up?" she asked and gave a thumbs-up to her team. The mother and son were handcuffed, and the Beret and Valerie still harnessed. The boy was leaning forward toward Valerie. Whatever he said, Fire could not hear. But from the young woman's face, she could tell the hybrid had upset her.

Fire was angry. How could Valerie let a five-year-old get to her? Perhaps she had expected too much from this young woman. As a psychologist she should have calculated Valerie's maternal needs. That's it, she decided. Valerie has made the mistake of thinking of the boy as human. It was a vulnerability Fire had not foreseen. The aliens were so damn clever. If they could get to her lover, perhaps they thought they could get to her. Unlike Wesley she would not allow an insider to betray her. Until this was over, she planned to distance herself from Valerie.

The chopper passed low over the brick building. A line of Black Berets ran single file out to the tarmac to greet them. Fire watched their descent to the red dot marked FOUR. There was a soft thud as the Black Hawk helicopter settled to the ground. Fire reached for the door latch and opened it.

The parched desert air hit her, frizzing her hair and drying her sinuses instantly. "Ah, desert life," she whispered and stepped to the ground. There was handshaking involved in all successful coups and Fire knew it. Had this not been a supersecret black project, she might have been met by federal marshals, but in the world of clandestine operations, her actions, no matter how severe, could be justified. It was merely a matter of lining up the right supporters.

"Congratulations again, Doctor," the NSA officer, J. D. Baker, announced.

"No, please. Could not have done it without all of you," she maintained, and shook hands with several other officers. Head of CIA, Naval Intelligence, Department of Defense.

The cries of a child were heard and the group turned back to watch the mother and son being unloaded from the chopper.

"Now that's a surprise," Baker said. "I thought he was the bait."

"Yes, but it seems the little bugger can read their writing. I thought it prudent to learn what we can."

"You're not going soft on us, are you?" Baker teased.

"Don't you wish," Fire laughed.

Valerie joined the group as they headed into the main building. The Black Berets were the last to leave, again forming a single-file double-time march into the hangar.

"We need to talk," Valerie whispered to Fire.

"Not now," Fire muttered though gritted teeth. She did not want any hint of weakness associated with her. It would be all the good ol' boys needed to turn against her.

"But Max—" Valerie protested.

Fire glanced at her. In a hushed tone she asked, "What?"

"He's refusing to read the texts," Valerie answered.

"The hell he won't," Fire said loudly enough for several in the group to glance at her.

Baker hung back to walk with them. "What's wrong? The hybrid won't cooperate?" he asked.

"He'll cooperate. He just doesn't know who he's dealing with." She signaled McKenzie. "Bring them to the lab."

Dr. Keller puffed on his meerschaum pipe. The rich warm smoke stung the gash around his lip. The bastards had worked him over pretty thoroughly. He had expected it. He had even expected the Black Beret to hold a gun to his head during the interrogation. But he was surprised when J. D. Baker ordered it shoved in his mouth. Before that moment, Keller could never have imagined the feeling of cold hard steel against his teeth or the burning taste of the gun oil on his lips.

"Now, you answer with nods," Baker had told him.

He had tried to do just that. He had always hated the greasy-haired NSA bastard. But he had to admire his plan to interrogate everyone. Baker used the new security camera. With only minor recalibration, it not only identified internal heat patterns, but continuously read pulse, heart rate and blood pressure. The damn thing was more accurate than a top-of-the-line polygraph.

And that was where he had failed. "Are you loyal to Colonel Michael Andros?" Baker had asked.

What's loyalty? A damn stupid word. If he had not taken time to think about it, his pulse might have kept steady. But as it was, he had been loyal, even faithful and dependable. Shit, he even liked the guy. But since Baker had shocked him with news of the Colonel's death, *was he still loyal?*

"No, I am not," he answered.

"He's lying," a Beret shouted from the control room. The gun was yanked from his mouth, loosening some teeth and ripping the inside of his lip. He supposed he should have been grateful that the Beret didn't just squeeze the trigger, but all gratitude was off when the butt slammed hard against his right temple. The room faded into a thousand black dots and when he came to, he was in the base cafeteria.

Three other MJ-12 members lay on the floor. One suffered a minor concussion, another a broken arm, the third a lacerated ear and cheek. The Berets had not been so hard on the handful of lesser employees—secretaries, cleaning crew, the base chef. But they, too, had failed Baker's little test.

Now, Keller took a long puff on his pipe and exhaled. The smoke formed a series of little gray ringlets. This was not an attempt to show off, but a ritual to help him meditate. He focused on the swirling smoke. The ringlets entered larger bands, and those rose and dissolved into gray puffs.

The events that had led up to this were no surprise. Andros had warned him about Fire. He had even taken precautions to place certain items that could help in an escape at various places throughout the base.

One of his first choices was the cafeteria. But the items had been placed out of sight and at the moment were impossible to reach, at least without alarming the Berets guarding them.

How could he get the Berets to order him into the freezer? If he made any overt move, they would kill him. That's it, he thought. *If I were dead they would place my body in the deep* freeze. No, that's stupid. These guys are professionals. If they think you are dead, they will make sure of it by shooting the corpse a dozen times. Time to rethink.

Whatever the next move, it would be for keeps.

"Helmets on," Fire said to Valerie and the other officers. There was a hiss of oxygen in the hall as the group sealed the air locks to their bio-suits. "Okay, let's go," she said and slid her ID card into the slot on the wall. The scanner recognized her and the lab door whooshed open.

Inside the cold room, mother and child were both strapped to medical gurneys. Around them were several lab tables with the gold strips laid out. Fire glanced at the strange alien script then turned her attention to the boy.

She stood over Max, staring down at him. The glass on the helmet was clear so she knew he was looking into her eyes, and wondered if he had the same alien abilities to hypnotize humans with eye contact. "The eyes are the windows to the soul, Max." He looked back at her blankly and she smiled. "You know I'm serious. You know what I'll do. Tell me what I want to know."

"No," came his small voice. Max blinked the wetness from his eyes and fought not to cry.

"Come on, now. You know you will. Because if you do—I promise, your mother will live."

"No, Max," Annie whispered. "She's lying."

"I keep my promises. I assure you. In fact"—Fire turned to Valerie—"the poison, please."

Valerie handed over a vial of K1397. Fire broke it open and dripped it on Annie. The strange amber liquid sprinkled on her face and almost immediately Annie began gasping.

"Mother!" Max cried.

"Now," Fire said, and her smile did not change, "I mean what I say."

"No! Mother!" he cried out again.

Fire leaned close to Max's face. "Listen, boy. Listen good. Do as I tell you and she lives. Fail me—she dies. It's really that simple. You understand?"

Max tore his eyes off his mother and studied Fire.

Then he nodded yes.

"You bitch! Max—don't listen," Annie gasped as she struggled against the straps holding her to the gurney. But in seconds, the thought of freeing herself and her son was replaced with a frantic desire to wipe the blistering liquid from her face. The sharp pinpoints of pain moved to her eyes and nostrils, burning . . . itching. It was as if ammonia had been mixed with garlic, leaving a chemical vegetable smell. The sides of her head ached.

It's working into my sinuses, she thought. The ache grew into a stabbing pain. "Oh God," she screamed out.

"Stop it. Stop it," Max begged. "You're killing her."

"And you, hybrid. It will affect you too. Just a little slower."

Annie knew he was already suffering, he could feel her pain. *Damn them,* she thought. "Max," she whispered. Her throat burned like hot lava. The pain had increased tenfold. Her throat became so swollen she could no longer speak, not even a whisper.

Fire stood again over the boy. She smiled horribly. "Now you know I mean what I say."

Max nodded.

"Would you like to save your mommy?"

From the corner of her eye, Annie saw a man whisper to the young blonde, "Oh she's good."

Who are these people? Annie screamed in her head. But there was no answer. Not from the faces in the helmets.

And not from Max.

CHAPTER 29

Anything worth doing is always a bitch kitty, Keller reminded himself. He had come up with a plan, but first he needed to talk with the chef. He had taken three steps toward the hulking bearded man when the blaring horn alarm over the cafeteria doors sounded.

Keller glanced toward the lights. The color combination disclosed the cause of warning. "Red and yellow, shit!" a voice in the crowd cried.

Everyone knew this meant a biological toxin had been detected by the air filtering system. They had two minutes to evacuate before it would spread throughout the base. They'd had practice drills for this emergency and every other imaginable wartime scenario. Only now, there was no set routine. No escape plans. Without biological hazard suits, everyone would die.

"We have to leave!" shrieked a woman. The Black Berets stood their ground and guarded the doors.

"But you'll die too," reasoned the chef.

"Everyone stay back. We have our orders," the Beret answered.

"This is crazy!" one of the cleaning crew hollered and marched up to the Berets. "We're leaving!"

The Beret leveled his Glock at the man and clicked on the laser sight. A red dot of light flashed on the man's chest. "I said—stay back."

The man looked down at the light and growled, "You don't scare me. What difference does it make if I die now or two minutes from now? Our only chance is to evacuate." He took two steps closer and with a coughing sound the little red dot turned into a wet leaking cavity.

The sound of the gunshot shocked everyone. Keller's voice broke the silence. "Look, no one wants to die here." He raised his hands as he stepped forward. A laser dot appeared on his shirt. At least he had their attention. He glanced at his watch.

"In a little less than a minute, what I have to say won't matter. However, right now, there is an alternative to dying, for all of us."

"What's that?" the younger of the two Berets asked.

"In the back is a deep freeze. It's the only room on the base not hooked up to the central air system."

"That's true!" the chef agreed.

"We'd have a couple hours more of air. It may be all they need to flush the system." He watched the Berets exchange glances before adding, "You will have done your duty. Technically, no one will have left the cafeteria."

The plan was brilliant. It was completely improvised. Life had a funny way of throwing him those curves. But when it did, he always managed to run with them.

His luck was holding. The older Beret answered, "Okay, everyone to the freezer."

Valerie stared in disbelief. What she had feared most had become reality. It was too real. Instead of using her bio-weapon on some hidious alien, she was watching a mother and child die. What had she done? There would be a special place in hell for her. Her and her lover.

"Read," Fire demanded and shoved the boy's face closer to the gold strips on the table. "Read, damn it."

The boy rubbed his watering eyes and Valerie knew the poison had reached him. He looked up at her with his big blue eyes and she felt her stomach drop. She swallowed hard to keep from retching. It was the same sick feeling that had almost overwhelmed her when she had poisoned the old woman. But unlike the old woman, the boy did not give in to the pain. He fought back the tears and turned to his mother.

"Read and I will save your mommy," Fire hissed. A moment later, the boy nodded.

No, he heard his mother cry out to him, but he could not let them kill her. He felt her pain, her body weakening, her heart racing. He had to help.

He picked up three strips and laid them next to each other. Two men pointed video cameras and audio mikes at him. He took a deep breath and exhaled to clear his mind. Suddenly he heard the voice. As it had earlier, the writing was talking to him.

"This says"—he held the strip in his hand and felt the symbols like Braille—" 'Many worlds, many universes, are greater than this, but the soul of man is greater still. It is creation. A part of Him whom you call God.' "

"Cut the religious crap," the older woman jeered. "I heard that forty-five years ago."

"Perhaps he's reading your mind?" a man questioned.

"No," Max answered. "I read what is here."

"Bullshit," the older woman said and grabbed a few strips from another table. "Here! Read these."

Max took them and breathed again. But now he felt the pain of the poison fill his lungs. It was harder to hear the voice.

" 'All that is big can be examined small.' "

"Like what? The atom?" the officer questioned.

Max continued. " 'Each has three parts, held together with the highest form of energy.' "

"Sure," the man agreed. "We all know the atom has neutrons, protons and electrons. Nuclear power comes from smashing 'em."

"Where's he going with this?" the younger woman asked.

Max continued. " 'The spark at the smallest level is still a reflection of the Source.' "

The mean man laughed. "I thought you said they were an advanced culture."

Max listened as others in the room raised more important questions. "What's the source?"

"Energy that fills the inner atomic space?"

"The subatomic energy that holds the atom together?"

"What if this isn't about atoms?" the younger woman asked.

Max looked at her, then laid the gold strip on the table. "The Source is energy that makes up the soul. Without it, what is—dies."

"That's rich," the man howled. "Tell me again why you brought him here?"

"Knock it off," the older woman said and reached for him. She pulled him so close his face touched the plastic of the helmet. "You're not here to explain God," she said. "I want to know their plans for taking over. Their vulnerabilities. No more space brother-love crap."

Max glanced at his mother. He could feel her breaths becoming even more shallow. Then suddenly, her fear. She was staring so oddly at him.

What is it, Mother? Why do you fear me? He closed his eyes and saw from her his own image. It was as if he were looking through her eyes, but more than that, he was feeling her thoughts. *The skin's not right. My God, my baby's skin is changing.* As Max watched, his pale white skin turned a warty, bumpy, grayish green. His hair thinned and his forehead became more pronounced. *What are they doing to my son?* He looked at her and his eyes dissolved into large black, elliptical eyes. *No this isn't right, Mother's dreaming.*

I'm not changing! he screamed in his mind. But it did not stop the hallucination. In seconds his human body had become fully alien, with a triangular face, narrow chin, black eyes and gray skin, and the strip of writing in his hand changed too. It was now a needle, about a foot long with a glowing tip. As he stared at the strange instrument he could feel his mother's heart racing. *Keep that away. Please, Max, don't!* she begged. He tried to reach her again, to calm her.

Mother, I'm here. I'm not going to hurt you.

It was no use. The dream had a life of its own. He watched the figure push the needle into his mother's neck just below the ear. Pain shot throughout her body.

Max opened his eyes. It had been only a few seconds but it seemed forever. "Help my mother," he demanded of the older woman.

"When you're done." She smiled.

"No." This could not wait. "Now," he said.

"What a little pisser," the man laughed.

The older woman glared at him. He knew she acted this way because she worried about her authority. If he had time, he could have gone deeper and found the moment in her life when it all began. But he didn't have time. He had to save his mother. He took a step back and hurled the gold strip down on the floor. "Then I stop now."

The older woman raised her hand to slap him, but the younger stopped her. "You did promise him," she said.

"Stay out of it, Val."

"No," the younger one protested. "You want this information. He's got it. You've always kept your word."

"I said, shut up."

"I'll shut up. But there's a chance these strips are nothing but religious insights. You'd be better served to have him look at the scout ships. If you want to understand alien technology, start there."

"Not a bad idea," the man said.

"All right," the older woman agreed.

"No. I'm not going anywhere. Not until you help Mother," Max insisted.

The man spoke softly to the older woman. They seemed to agree on several things. The woman even smiled and that made Max feel uneasy.

"All right. Give her the injection," she said and the younger woman moved to do so. But before Max could follow, he felt a hand on his shoulder. The older woman bent close to him and whispered, "You haven't won, hybrid."

But he had. He could feel his mother getting better with each passing moment. The antitoxin pulsed in her blood. The virus was dying. Her heart rate returned to normal, her breathing became deeper. The bad dream was over.

"Max honey." His mother spoke aloud, her eyes now open. He reached out and placed a hand on hers. "Max, you should have saved yourself."

"He can't," the older woman said. "We have a deal." And with that she pulled him away.

Fire fell back from the group leading the child down the hall. She leaned next on McKenzie's shoulder as they walked. "On my order," she whispered, "you are to kill the mother." The Beret nodded and turned back to Annie.

Fire quickened her pace to catch up with Max. "Come, dear boy," she said and slid her card through to open the heavy steel doors. The boy squinted at the bright morning sun. She placed her hand at the nape of his neck and hurried him out. The group continued past the tarmac to the first hangar.

Inside the three-story hangar were nine very different alien scout ships, a variety pack. One was shaped rather like a top hat; another was cigar-shaped; the third was a Jell-O mold, shaped with a hole at its center; the fourth egg-shaped; the fifth delta-winged; the sixth like an upside-down acorn; the seventh a boomerang; the eighth was a simple flat thirty-foot disc, a scaled-down version of the ninth. Fire led the group to the smaller disc.

Baker laughed. "Oh, the sports model. Good choice."

"Did Keller have any luck loading the power source?" Valerie asked.

Baker nodded. "Yes. A series of tests determined it stable and nonradioactive. He cut it into small triangular wedges and loaded it into the ships' reactors. But he hadn't found the correct sequence to get it up and flying."

"The hybrid will solve that."

Fire helped the boy into the craft's irislike portal.

Keller lifted a lid off the silver container in the back and ran his hands over this stash: a folded level-three bio-suit, a Glock .45 and a 200,000-volt police stun gun.

As everyone filed into the freezer, he checked to see where the Berets were. They were still up toward the front. The people around him were gathered in groups for body warmth. No one noticed him or his actions. He didn't really want to kill anyone, least of all a couple of cooperative Black Berets. On the other hand, he was not about to wait around. The fact that the air system had detected a biological virus meant Fire had already decided their fate. They were as good as dead, all of them. If there was to be any help, he had to get out.

He grabbed the stunner, one of two that was base-issued along with the Glock. But unlike the Glock, he liked this tool. It reminded him of the family hog farm in Iowa. Working with cattle prods they used to herd thousand-pound hogs. He had seen a raging boar turn into a wet noodle with a snap of that blue arc. The downside to this weapon was that you had to be close enough to touch the victim.

He pulled the arms of his jacket down, like a man trying to keep his hands warm. Had anyone in the group known what he was about to do there would have been anarchy. But no one seemed to notice as he worked his way up toward the front.

He was just closing in on the older Beret when he felt a hand on his shoulder. "Good thinking," the chef said. Jesus God, he thought, and felt his heart skip a beat.

"I thought we were goners out there," the chef continued.

"Yeah," Keller whispered. "Thanks." He smiled and pushed his way still closer now to the Beret. He looked for the younger one, then spotted him outside the freezer helping a woman with a twisted ankle. As he turned back, he found the older Beret beside him staring coldly. There was an almost catlike sense of curiosity about the man.

Keller told himself this was not the time, but his body did not listen. The adrenaline rush was already pulsing through his veins. His arm suddenly snapped out with his finger squeezing the trigger. The crackle of the blue plasma snapped against the Beret's hand—the same hand that held a drawn gun with a perfect bead on Keller.

There was a sudden hush in the group and the crowd parted, leaving Keller hunched over the stunned Beret. In seconds the younger Beret was pushing his way in, screaming "What happened? What happened?"

"We don't know," someone in the group said. Keller thought it sounded like the chef.

"Heart attack," Keller answered. The older Beret stared up at his partner, unable to warn him otherwise. The younger Beret knelt down.

"He's breathing. Keep him calm," Keller said.

The younger Beret nodded, but then noticed his partner's gun drawn. Keller struck before the young man could unclip his holster. The plasma strike, to the horror of many, made the young man's body convulse. But what had taken only seconds would last but a few minutes.

"Out of my way," Keller ordered the crowd and made his way back to the bio-suit. He paused only when the chef asked, "Why?"

"Ask them," he answered. "They'll be up in about seven minutes." There was no time to explain the rationale behind his decision. He suited up and closed the freezer door, before the final horn sounded, indicating that the toxin had entered the room.

He waited for the horn to stop before entering the main hall. The air system worked in a series of blocks. If one room was contaminated, the whole section was contaminated. This was no test. He found an unsuited Beret beside a water fountain in an adjoining hall, clawing at his eyes. Keller hurried past and continued toward the building exit.

Max looked at the small gray seats clustered around a clear cylinder in the center of the craft. There were four-finger handprints set inside the control panel. Max, like any child, immediately placed his hand in one. To his surprise and everyone else's, the panel lit up.

Baker grabbed his hand off the imprint. "Easy, son," he said, looking around warily. "We're not in any hurry to go airborne."

"Where's the weapons system?" Fire demanded. She stared hard at the boy and watched him finger the controls. He seemed to be reading the alien symbols above each control. He then hopped up on one of the chairs and spun it around. "Stop it. This is not a game," Fire glared.

The boy looked at her and said nothing.

"You know it's funny how the damn thing is so perfectly sized for children." Baker laughed but quickly stopped when Fire shot him a glance. "Sorry, my first time in one of these."

"Weapons?" Fire asked again.

The boy gave a big innocent smile. "It doesn't have any."

"Then what's its purpose?" Baker asked.

Max shrugged and spun around to face the controls. He placed a hand in both imprints before Fire or Baker could stop him. Suddenly before them, six holographs glowed, hovering about a foot above the main console. They were identical to the plates Jerry and Eva had found in Peru.

Valerie spoke up. "I've seen those. They were down in that cave in Peru." She stood by the door where the video crew were filming.

"What do they mean?" Fire asked.

"They're maps. From the past and future."

"Why do I feel I'm not getting this?" Baker asked.

"They can help."

"My God, that's North America," Fire said as she recognized it. "The West is gone."

"California is just a series of islands. Washington and Oregon are gone," Baker agreed.

"The Pacific has flooded the whole region," Fire said, pointing. "Nevada, Utah, Arizona."

Baker took a step closer, squinting at the map. "The whole Southwest, and lookit." He pointed to the Northeast. "My God, New York City." His finger slid along the Southeast. "The Carolinas, Georgia, Florida, all the coastal areas—"

"Gone," Fire finished.

"Goodbye sweet Texas."

"When's this going to happen?"

"It's begun," Max answered.

"Well, gentlemen, if you ever doubted me"—Fire turned to the group, her gloved finger pointing back to the holographs—"there are the battle plans. Recolonization! Our population is dead."

Max stood up and faced the group. "No. Use these maps to save lives."

"How?" Valerie asked from the back. She seemed to be the only one listening to the boy.

"Warn everyone," Max said innocently.

"Right, absolute panic. Two-thirds of the world's land mass underwater. Alien arrival. Chaos," Baker answered.

Fire glanced around and thought, *My God, they're all looking at me. Waiting for me to decide. She took a deep breath.*

"If we stop the aliens," she said, "we stop their control of our future."

CHAPTER 30

Max stared at the young woman in the back. How could he communicate with her? His mind was becoming clouded with pain. His only escape would be to rise from his body as he had done before, but if he did this, he might not be able to help these people. They were about to make the biggest mistake ever, because of fear. He fought to control the tightening in his chest. Each breath had become a struggle. He could feel his heart beating faster. Time was running out.

Do you hear me? he asked, staring right at her. The young woman jerked around as if someone had snuck up and whispered in her ear.

Do not be afraid, he said. This time the woman turned and looked right at him. *I need your help*. He could not hear her thoughts back. Perhaps she was afraid.

He suddenly felt a heavy hand on his shoulder. "Show us how this works," the older woman said and pushed him back toward the ship's controls.

"How does it work, son?" the man said, repeating the older woman.

He placed his fingers in the hand impressions on the control board. The clear cylinder in the center of the craft suddenly came to life, glowing a bright orange.

"How'd he do that?" one of the men in the group asked.

Max felt a voice in the ship, and spoke what he heard. "You cannot control this."

"Nonsense," the man standing closest to him answered. "Keller's already determined the damn thing runs on amplified gravity waves." He turned to the young woman. "That stuff you brought back from Peru produces a gravitational field. He figures the ship distorts time and space for long travels."

Max felt his breath slowing. The pain throughout his body grew. Soon he would not be able to answer them. His body began to shake. Tears flowed from his eyes as the pain reached its peak. He tried again to reach the young woman. *I need your help. You must help.*

She was looking at him, her eyes wide. But she did not answer, and he was out of time. He felt the energy of life slipping away.

He was dying.

A young Black Beret grabbing a smoke just outside the hangar was the first to see it. It appeared so quickly, he thought it had materialized in the clear desert sky. The undercarriage glowed bright orange. Waves of green and blue seemed to pulse through its underside as it settled down on the tarmac.

The size was what impressed this warrior. It was well over two football fields long, shaped like an Indian arrowhead. It made the ships in the hangar look like children's toys.

The Beret stared—just a second too long. By the time he got his radio out, a blue light had engulfed him. He felt his body rise slightly and then his world blacked out.

Annie did not know why the Black Beret was staring at her or for that matter squatting down. He had the look of a golf pro trying to decide the best angle for his putt on a difficult green. He moved first to the left, then to the right. She tried to turn, but her arms and legs were still strapped to the gurney. In her peripheral vision she followed him.

"Please, could you cut me loose?" she asked.

The Beret did not answer. Instead he glanced at the walls and ceiling again.

"What the hell are you up to?" she questioned again.

"You don't want to know," he answered.

McKenzie pulled his gun and flipped on the laser sight. The beam bounced up off the steel back wall of the lab sink, ricocheted down off the tiled ceiling and landed in the middle of Annie's forehead. Antitoxin or not, she suddenly felt very sick.

"You can't be serious—they made a deal."

"I do what I'm ordered to," he answered with a smile. The smile told her he felt pride in being a sick son-of-a-bitch.

The sound of static came from his radio. McKenzie answered it. "This is McKenzie, over."

More static, then a couple of recognizable words from Fire. ". . . under attack . . ." The Beret suddenly stood up and turned toward the open hall door. He came face to face with Keller. Before the Beret could raise his gun, Keller zapped him in the neck with the blue plasma charge. The Beret fell to his knees and his body jerked before he finally keeled over. Keller grabbed the keys and uncuffed Annie.

"Who are you?" she asked.

"More important, who are you? Why aren't you dead?" Keller asked, releasing the gurney straps and helping her up.

"It's a long story." A wave of nausea hit her and she began retching—dry heaves since she had not eaten since the night before. Keller held her hand and smoothed her hair back.

"Come on," he said, "I want to live long enough to hear it."

As they left the room, she squeezed his hand. "My name is Annie," she finally answered him.

"Well, Annie—" he began, and stopped as the hallway lights flickered off and on.

He squeezed her hand and hurried his pace. "You can tell me all about it after we get off the base."

As they came to the steel double door, Keller fished out his security card. "Don't move," he whispered, leaving her against the wall. "As soon as the door buzzes open, run."

He slid his ID card through the recognition buffer. The security camera came on and scanned his heat pattern. But instead of the door buzzing open, an alarm sounded and the light above flashed red.

"Damn, access denied. They've erased me off the central control bank."

"You mean we're stuck?" Annie asked.

"No." Keller was not about to give up. He ran back toward the lab where he had paralyzed the Black Beret. He found him in the same position on the ground. The effect of the stunner was still in force.

He grabbed the man and dragged him by the shoulders back down the hall to the scanner.

"Okay, we won't have long," he called to Annie. "The moment that door buzzes, run for it."

He straightened McKenzie so his head lined up for the scanner and ran the Beret's ID card through the buffer. The camera flashed on and read his heat pattern.

But the moment the light blipped green and the door buzzed open, Keller felt a hand grab his throat. He reached for his stunner and found it gone. The Beret had him.

Annie pushed open the door and glanced back. Keller wasn't behind her. Instead the Beret had him pinned against the video scanner. This was the bastard who had killed Stan and hurt Max. She could see the blue plasma charge snapping in the reflection of Keller's helmet. The man who had helped her was about to die.

"No," she screamed and charged the Beret. Her hand caught the air hose on his helmet and as the Beret shoved her back, it ripped loose. Within seconds McKenzie was on the ground gasping, the virus eating at his eyes.

Annie watched the man flop on the ground, clawing at his face through the faceplate. She knew she should feel horror, guilt, but all she felt was a weary sense of justice. "Bastard," she whispered.

A hand fell on her forearm. She turned. Keller tugged at her. "Come on," he said.

She turned and went through the door with him.

Fire could see the huge alien ship just outside the hangar doors. There were dozens of Black Berets lying lifeless on the tarmac. Some held their weapons drawn, others were frozen in midstride.

"Tell me you planned this, Katherine," Baker demanded. The glow of the ship glared on the metallic skins of the scout ships.

"Of course," she lied. "Nothing is ever valued without a fight. If we turned the boy over, they'd treat him with caution. Deliver him as the spoils of war and he's in."

As a trained psychologist she prided herself on her ability to think on her feet. Reason out all actions and reactions. Besides, it sounded good. Maybe it would even work. She had intended to return the boy to his residence. But hell, seize the day and all that. Here they were. She felt a surge of triumph. By God, it would work even better than her original plan.

"Val, bring the hybrid," she called on the radio mike. A few moments passed and there was no sign of Valerie or the boy. She looked toward the small saucer. "Val?" she called again, making sure her headset was working. "Answer me."

But Valerie could not bring herself to answer. Tears flowed as she knelt over Max, who lay on the floor of the ship. She checked his eyes. The pupils had turned up and his breathing was shallow. *Goodbye*, she heard him say in her head. "No!" she said.

"No what?" Fire asked, now standing inside the ship. "I called. But you didn't answer!"

Valerie held a hand on the child's chest. She felt his last breath and then no more. "He's dead," she said. "God forgive me."

"Forgive you? You stupid bitch. We're this close to finishing a project that took half my life and you blow it." Fire put a hand on the hybrid's neck to check for a pulse.

"How can you say that? You made me do it. I didn't want to do it. He's just a boy. Look at him."

"Stop it!" Fire screamed and smacked Valerie's helmet. Her neck snapped back and hit the control console.

"The hell I will," Valerie whispered and stood to fight.

"Val, we don't have time for this," Fire said, taking a step back. "The mothership is out there. Forty-five years I've waited."

"I don't care if it's an eternity," she answered and delivered a swift kick to Fire's stomach. Fire slid across the ship's floor and smacked against one of the child-size chairs. Valerie stepped forward as Fire climbed to her feet. "It's all been a big lie."

"What are you talking about?"

Valerie took another step. "Us. You used me."

"Of course I did. But you're a big girl. You knew the stakes."

Valerie charged Fire again. Only this time, Fire pulled her pistol and shot.

Valerie felt a burning pain in her abdomen and her legs twisted. She fell in a heap at Fire's feet. Looking up she whispered, "You shot me."

Fire bent over her. "I did. I could say I'm sorry. But it doesn't matter, does it?"

Valerie's face contorted with pain. She tried to answer, but her throat was too dry. She watched Fire leave and heard her ex-lover mumble, "I can still use the boy."

She could, too, Valerie thought. Even the body would deliver enough toxin to infect and kill those on the ship. *To hell with her,* Valerie thought. *I can inject the antidote into the boy and neutralize the poison.*

She screamed as she turned over, spitting up more blood. Only her arms moved. She had no feeling below her wound and far too much above. As she inched forward, she glanced ahead. Max's body lay only ten feet away, but it seemed like a mile.

Two Black Berets took strike positions behind the strange top hat–shaped scout ship. They flipped open the targeting system for the weapons tube and locked on the surface-to-air missile.

Fire and her group were still gathered behind another saucer, looking on. Baker turned to her. "What if it works?"

Fire smiled. "Not a chance." She lifted her radio and whispered, "Go, Beta team."

The rocket took off in a screaming trail of white smoke. Only a few feet from impact there was a flash of blue light. When it stopped, Fire glimpsed the rocket skipping along an energy field under the ship, then rising into the air.

She turned and saw the Berets. Both were on the ground paralyzed. "Good. The Bug Eyes will gain confidence, then come for the boy. Nothing can stop us."

CHAPTER 31

"Do you know where they took him?" Keller asked as they hurried down the sidewalk between two hangars.

Annie nodded. "They said they were going to the scout ships."

"Damn. Then it's impossible. There are two platoons of Berets guarding the S4 hangar. We'd never get in."

They turned the corner to the intersecting walk between buildings. Keller saw several Berets lying on the ground, their bodies toppled like so many bowling pins. He sneaked up to one and checked his pulse, then waved to Annie to join him.

"It must be the poison gas," he whispered.

"I don't think so," she replied.

"Why not?" he asked, then answered himself. "Because he's still alive."

"No," Annie said, looking up to the sky. "I've seen it before." She glanced at him. "Here. About six years ago."

"Oh—" Then as if it suddenly made sense, "You're the one. The mother of the hybrid."

"He's just a little boy, damn it."

Keller ignored her outburst, shook his head. "There were

those of us who doubted if you existed. I mean, Andros explained everything, but aside from him and Wesley, no other member of MJ-12 ever saw you, or any abductees."

"Well, we're real."

"Indeed." Keller nodded and checked the Beret's eyes. They were focused on some faraway point. "What was he looking at?"

Annie had moved to the corner of the building. "Oh my," she said. It wasn't what she said, but her tone. Keller turned and he too saw it—the enormous alien ship hovering over the tarmac.

"They're here for my son," she whispered, then with determination she started toward the ship, adding, "I've got to stop them."

"But, but—" He didn't finish. In all the years Keller had worked back-engineering alien technology, he had never had the desire to come face to face with the beings that created it. Perhaps it was easier from a distance, like an anthropologist studying some ancient society. Nothing connected his work to his world. Nothing until now. "Wait," he called, but she was already on the tarmac running toward the ship.

All was silent except for the whirlwind pushing down. Annie stared up at the ship. It looked even bigger up close. It seemed to fill the entire sky. The hairs on the back of her arms and neck stood on end. She passed the last of the Black Berets and stood alone beneath the center of the glowing ship.

The small voice of common sense reared its ugly head. *What now?* it bellowed. If Max was on board, she had no way of gaining access. If not, where was he?

And then a bright light shot down before her. It did not hit her or engulf her, but made the ground ahead as hot as the sun, if just for an instant. She covered her eyes and when it stopped, she looked. There stood a figure. A man.

"Annie," he said, and stepped toward her, holding out his hand. "I'm so glad you're okay."

"Andros?"

"Yes."

With great relief, she gave him a hug. For a brief moment she felt that everything might be okay. Then terrible hope hit her and she could not stop herself from asking, "Stanley?"

Andros was still for a moment. It seemed an impossibly long moment, and she knew her son had been right, and she wept.

"You said Andros was dead!" An angry Baker turned on Fire.

She took a step back and raised her gun. "He was—and will be. Now spread out. Wait for your shot. Remember you've turned your back on him and he knows it."

Her plan was going to work. She was sure of it. Still she had to admire their cleverness. Patching up the human and sending him in first. If it had been anybody else, she might have let them take the boy. But it was Andros, the man who had betrayed Wesley, their group and all mankind. She chambered a new round and climbed up on a forklift to get a better angle. This time, the bastard would stay dead.

"Where's Max?" Annie asked as they entered the hangar.

"They're not sure. But they're looking. They think he's in one of the scout ships."

Andros left Annie by a worktable and climbed aboard the closest saucer, a cigar-shaped one. Inside, he heard Annie's warning.

"But he's been infected."

Andros stuck his head back out. "What?"

Just then a bullet whizzed by Andros and ricocheted off the skin of the hull. "Get down," he yelled.

Annie ducked behind the table and Andros jumped to the ground. Two more shots rang out. The echo made it impossible to determine where the shots came from. Andros ran to Annie.

"Are you hurt?"

"No, but what do we do? We don't have any weapons."

Shots spanged into the table shielding them. Three neat

holes punched through the metal. "Well, we can't stay here." He looked around. The room seemed unusually still. Then out of the corner of his eye he saw a small gray figure. By the time he turned, it had disappeared into the sports model at the far end of the hangar. "Okay," he said. "On three, follow me."

"Wait. The last time we did three—" Annie began.

"You're right. We won't do that."

He edged to the end of the table and peeked out. There was not a breath of movement. "Ready . . . Go!" He grabbed Annie's hand and they sprinted across the hangar floor. More gunfire from several locations. Shots hit in front and beside them. Annie was terrified but she kept running.

They ducked behind several wooden crates and paused to catch their breath. "There, that wasn't so bad," Andros said, peeking over the box.

"Oh? What's your definition of good?"

"Come on." He took her hand. They ducked behind crates, avoiding the next volley of shots. And then the roof of the hangar wobbled in waves of energy and disappeared. Annie looked up and her breath whooshed out involuntarily as the sky disappeared.

The mothership hovered overhead.

Everyone in the room looked up. There was a brief second of awe, and then all hell broke loose. A flurry of blue lasers to rival a major rock concert shot down on many parts of the hangar.

"Don't look, Annie," Andros yelled and grabbed her, holding her close. One of a dozen beams hit only a couple of yards away. They heard a man scream and smelled the stink of burnt flesh.

A moment later, absolute silence. Annie looked up at the ship and asked, "How did you know?"

"They're protecting him," he answered.

"Max?"

"No," Andros said and took a few steps.

"Who?" Annie asked.

They found a very crispy J. D. Baker perched behind a wooden crate, gun drawn, his arm raised to shoot.

"Come on,'"Andros said, gagging. They continued toward the small sports-model scout ship just ahead.

"You still haven't answered me," Annie said. "Who are they protecting?"

"Your son's father," Andros said finally.

Annie was stunned. Stanley was Max's father. All the nightmares she'd had meant nothing. Tricks of the mind. After all, she might have believed they had manipulated the DNA, but not the father of the child.

"Grab hold," Andros said, reaching out his hand. She grabbed it and pulled herself up into the small saucer. Its dull silver interior and domed ceiling reminded her of her own abduction. *My God*, she thought, staring straight ahead. "It's Mr. Boojum," she whispered, using the childhood name she had made up.

But when the creature slowly turned, his face was slightly wrong, his eyes larger, forehead more wrinkled. It was a different being, not Mr. Boojum. As it stood, she could see Max lying on the floor. Next to him lay the young woman in her deflated biosuit. There was blood everywhere, most of it pooled around her son. Annie ran to Max.

He is alive, she heard in her head. But that did little to calm her fears. She grabbed Max and held him close, rocking his body slowly. "Max, honey," she whispered, "wake up." But her son did not wake. She looked at the alien being. "Help him, please."

Do not cry, Mother. I am here, she heard. She stared into the creature's dark unworldly eyes and watched as he changed. His skin became human, his face transformed into a familiar image.

Max.

He was finally the butterfly free from his cocoon. He was beautiful. "Max?" she asked.

"Yes, Mother," he answered with his human voice.

"How can this be?" She stared in disbelief.

"It just is."

Annie shook her head. Was this another dream? Would she wake up?

"Believe." And he pointed down at her lap.

She glanced to where she had held her son and found him gone.

Father and I are one, she heard in her mind. *The transformation is complete. As a man I'll live to help those chosen to survive. As a boy I will serve as a warning.*

"But the poison?" his mother objected.

"I live," he answered.

Andros rolled Valerie's body over and found a hypodermic in her hand. "She gave him the antitoxin."

"Why?" Annie asked.

"Because she was a cowardly, double-crossing bitch," Fire said, standing behind them. Annie stood and Max clung to her as a child might. "Mother," he cried.

"That's right, you should be scared," Fire hissed.

Annie looked down at her son and saw the Max she knew. A vulnerable, innocent child. There was nothing she would not do in that moment to save his life.

Fire stepped closer. "You know, you ruined a perfectly great strategy. Everything should have worked. Only I didn't really expect your alien identity to touch so many lives. I mean, Valerie for Christ's sake. You got to her." She raised her gun and took aim at the boy.

Max hid behind his mother.

"Come on, hybrid," Fire snarled. "Afraid you don't really have nine lives?"

"Enough!" Andros commanded and stepped in the way.

"Ahh, Andros. Can't keep a good man down. Well, humor me and let me try again." She veered her aim and squeezed the trigger. The blast rattled the ship. But Andros did not fall.

Instead Fire collapsed. The glass on her helmet splattered red. As she fell forward, Annie saw the hole blown in the back.

Standing in the doorway was Dr. Keller. "I—I—" He dropped the Glock and turned away, sick.

"It's over, Annie," Andros said. "It's finally over." He put an arm around her and Max and led them out.

On the floor of the hangar, surrounded by the alien ships, Annie finally answered. "I wish it were over," she said and looked down at Max. "But it's just begun, hasn't it?"

Epilogue: Three Years Later

The house smelled of potato chips and cake. Hanging across the dining table was a colorful HAPPY BIRTHDAY banner. A half-eaten cake sat in the center of the table.

"Max," Annie called. There was no answer. She moved around the table with a large trash bag and picked up the mess. She made a face at the fingerprints in a half-eaten slice of cake.

"Kids—"

She stopped and looked at the toys gathered in the corner. All had been ignored, but not because Max didn't like them. It was just that one in the pile had caught his eye—a gift from his father. At least she told him it was from Stan. He never questioned how a dead father could give him such a gift. Instead he answered with a simple "Cool."

"Max," Annie called again. She heard the model train set still running in his bedroom. She had saved it all these years, rewrapped it and added a few extras from the local hobby shop.

She had gotten her job back at the Syracuse planetarium and though it did not pay well, it did meet the bills. On occasion Max would help. At one point her boss found him logging in star systems and she explained he had a natural gift for such things. He did.

In the last year, Max had won the state fair science prize with a project on proactive ecology. He called it New Genesis. A project, Annie mused, that would have filled both of his fathers with pride.

Stan would have been truly pleased that Max had celebrated his eighth birthday playing only with the HO Gauge train set. The dozen kids who had come had been put to work laying track, building clay mountains, setting up miniature towns. By the end of the party, the train was up and running.

Annie picked up a few more plates and cups. The dining room windows let in the summer storm's breeze. The smell of rain filled the room. That smell more than any other reminded her of Stan. How she missed him.

"Max, honey, I could really use your help," she called out, and moved to close the windows.

Again no answer. That's strange, she thought and started down the hall to her son's bedroom. Just as she got to the door, lightning struck. *Crack.* The bolt struck in the backyard. "Max!" she screamed and threw open his door.

Max stood staring out the open window at the huge old oak tree behind the house, its core burning, split open, hissing in the rain. "Mom?" he said, not turning around.

"Yes," she answered, moving toward him.

"Are you afraid of the rain?"

"No," she said and closed the window. They could see the embers from the fire die in the downpour.

"You should be," he said. He turned to look down at his train set. Annie tried to smile, but didn't. Instead she followed his gaze and saw why he was so serious.

He had created the perfect disaster. His train tracks were washed out, the small trees splintered. Water flooded the miniature town and the train had flipped onto its side. A herd of small plastic cows lay on their backs, feet in the air as though dead, and the tiny farmer's wife figure lay next to them.

Max looked up at his mother, up from his small, flooded world, and whispered again, "You should be."